Family for sure

A Big Brah cozy mystery

by Ishwar Chandra Sen

Publisher: Sen Fiction, Hawaii (www.senfiction.com)

Sen Fiction, Hawaii

ISBN-13: 9781957022017

Learn more about the author at:
https://www.senfiction.com

Cover art: "My family by Umi Waialeale"
Cover artist: Rita Sen

Editor: Mele Sen
Editorial and Publishing Assistant: Rita Sen

Published in the United States of America

For my island family:
Thanks for all the love.

Contents

Chapter 1: Striking Hibiscus Tattoo

Where there is love, there is family. Big Brah and I sat at the kitchen table, talking story over lunch. Tall windows let in the warmth and light of a late winter afternoon, along with a refreshing ocean breeze. The comforting sweet, smoky aroma of cooking lingered in the kitchen.

For lunch, Big Brah had served crispy salmon and soft-boiled eggs over perfectly-cooked rice. All slathered with gravy and bursting with flavor. The wholesome goodness of the fish, egg and rice tasted just right. He was a big man, my big brother, sinewy and strong.

He hid a sharp mind behind a kind face and an easy smile. I called him Big Brah fondly. Everyone did. We called him Big Brah mostly for his big heart. His name was Koa Waialeale. He ran the Waialeale Detective Agency. I was his assistant. I forked a bite. I savored it.

I waved my fork in the air to emphasize. "This is an upgrade!"

"You taste the ginger in the gravy?" Big Brah said.

"Yes, great touch," I said.

The doorbell chimed. It had to be one of our cousins. They worked for the agency sometimes and had an open invitation to breakfast, lunch or dinner here. They were all capable of fending for themselves, but Big Brah's delicious cooking tempted them often. They knew to come right into our home's roomy kitchen. We ate on in silence. No one entered.

Big Brah looked up from his food. "There's someone waiting at the door, Umi," he said.

I knew his rules. No interruptions during a meal. And no rules if someone needed our immediate help. I reached for the remote and turned on the wall-mounted screen. The screen displayed whatever the front door camera saw. A woman stood outside.

She looked familiar. When you lived on a small island in the middle of the vast Pacific Ocean all your life, you got to see your fellow islanders sometime or the other, but you didn't always know them. Our visitor had her graying hair done in a tight top knot. In local island fashion, she wore a blue and white floral-patterned shirt, long blue shorts and flats.

I didn't know her. She had a round face and no makeup. She took out a phone from a large handbag. She got busy answering a text. Clearly, she needed private time.

A visitor. Maybe even a new case. Things had been quiet for a while. I set the remote down. "Should I go get her?" I asked, eagerly.

Big Brah was interested in cases we could be of genuine service. The rest he helped by advice and support. Rarely did he take on anything off island.

"Any observations?" he said.

Observations. A Big Brah favorite. He was asking for observations. He was interested. I didn't want to miss any of the action or the food. I started to speed eat, my eyes on her. She had impressive tattoos.

Impressive tattoos were common on the island. "Nothing outstanding," I said.

"What about the striking hibiscus tattoo on her right forearm?" he said.

"The hibiscus is a symbol of summer, of lightheartedness."

"Right on. She had it done to mark a colorful occasion in her youth. How about the turtle inked in black on her right leg?" he said.

"The turtle is a symbol of fertility, maturity and wisdom."

"You're good with your facts, Umi. She must aspire to be like the turtle. Fertile, she's a mother. Mature, her kid's an adult. And wise, she loves her kid." Big Brah nodded, approvingly.

Spurred by his approval, I said, "The tattoo's inked using the traditional Hawaiian method of kakau, hand-tapping."

"A way preferred by the older families. She belongs to one."

Amazing. The way he figured things out. I liked to think of his immense reasoning powers as his sixth sense. "Why do you think she's here?" I asked.

For a moment he didn't say anything, thinking. Our visitor finished with her phone. She looked worried. Nervously, she slipped the phone back into her brown handbag. She looked expectantly at the front door.

Big Brah realized something. He set his fork down. His handsome face grew animated. "Her kid must be in trouble! Maybe we can help. Umi, go get her."

I jumped up. "I'm on it."

"Hurry!" He called after me.

I exited the kitchen fast and ran to the foyer. Briskly I opened the front door. On seeing me, our visitor relaxed her shoulders.

She let out a soft sigh of relief. "You're Umi, I recognize you from the news," she said.

Not too long ago, with his customary discreetness, Big Brah had handled a case involving three celebrities. Afterward all three celebrities thanked Big Brah publicly. The news went viral. As Big Brah's assistant, I featured in the news prominently. I wasn't on my way to celebrity, only a social media presence. But it was good to be recognized.

Pleased, I used the island-standard way to address her warmly. "Aunty...how can I help you?" I asked.

Her round face contorted apologetically. She pointed to the signboard on the lanai wall showing the agency's office hours. "I'm terribly sorry, I know you're closed for lunch, but this can't wait. I need Big Brah's help, I want to see him immediately."

I invited her in. She followed me across the foyer to the main office. The office had soothing overhead lights and teak-paneled walls. I pulled back the blackout curtains.

Daylight flooded in through the big windows, making the room brighter. The teak-paneled walls were decorated with a series of my sketches of Big Brah fire dancing, Big Brah's spectacular photographs of island flora and fauna, my family sketch from years ago and my award-winning poem, "Spread aloha." All keepsakes from our pursuits: canoeing, fire dance, cooking, art, poetry, entomology and more.

The walls were also a wonderland for awards collected over the years. Top investigator of the year, best security professional, meritorious service and outstanding achievement. And framed copies of our private investigator certificates. The large office had a formal conference table, our desks, chairs, refrigerator and cabinet. The clean top of Big Brah's desk gleamed.

Big Brah kept his desk clutter free. All his tools were organized neatly in the desk's ample drawers. He allowed only a swing-arm lamp on his desk. When necessary, he used the lamp to inspect things closely. My desk was several feet away, facing his. The desk had lots more of my things on top of it.

Books, notepads, sketch pads, pencils, pens, markers, paintbrushes, magnifying glasses, boxes of tissue paper and a basket full of rolled canvases. Organized clutter. The refrigerator hummed, breaking the silence. Big Brah was going to enter through the inside door at the far end. I made sure the door was unlocked and turned back to find our visitor still standing. She looked distressed.

I hastened to settle her into a chair. She sat clutching the brown, leather handbag on her lap. Big Brah entered the office from the inside door. Quietly, he sat down at his desk. He faced her, as she sat across the gleaming desk from him. I took my place. I had a clear view of her and Big Brah. A sympathetic smile played on his kind face.

I had seen the smile before. Whether he accepted the case or not, he was willing to listen to see how he could help.

"How can I help you, ma'am?" he said.

"I'm Lei Bomino, I'm here to...this morning, just hours ago, Izor...my husband, he was found murdered...." She had difficulty continuing.

Murdered. The word was a body blow. Big Brah's head jerked back a full inch. He was moved.

But he kept his composure. "I'm sorry," he said.

She could use a cool drink. I got up. I got a can of chilled coconut water from the refrigerator, emptied the can into a glass from the cabinet and took the drink to her. She gave me a grateful look. I resumed my seat. Sipping the coconut water slowly, she gathered herself.

She set the glass down. "A tourist called 9-1-1. Police found my husband by the coastal trail, where the Waikahe River meets the ocean. They-they had our son, Ohia, identify the body...."

Big Brah nodded, gravely.

She said, "If that wasn't bad enough, the police have taken Ohia in for questioning, they are treating him like a suspect! He doesn't deserve this, my boy, first to see his father dead then to be suspected of murder...."

Big Brah had been right. Her kid was in trouble.

"Terrible, terrible," Big Brah murmured.

Her lips trembled. She was going to cry. She rummaged her large handbag. Had to be for tissues. I kept a box handy for guests. I took her the tissues. She took the box and mutely patted my arm to say thanks. I got back in place.

Her voice shook. "I love Ohia, Izor loves Ohia, we love our boy." She cried.

She spoke between sobs. "I know this, Izor loved Ohia, as much as I do, he wouldn't wish any harm on our son. He'd want me to save Ohia from this ordeal, Ohia's innocent!"

Big Brah and I exchanged glances. Clearly, she loved her son.

Lei Bomino extracted tissues from the box and wiped her tears, recovering. "Besides, to have something like this happen in our family? Izor would want me to restore the Bomino family honor, I know it. My poor Izor!"

Big Brah sat frozen in his chair, thinking.

She spoke in a steady voice. "Until the murderer is

found, Izor's soul won't rest in peace. So, I'm here to ask you, can you please, find the real murderer?"

I leaned back, curious. What would Big Brah figure out from all this? Save an innocent son from being accused of murder. Bring the real murderer of the father to justice. Restore the family honor. Whether she knew it or not, she had given Big Brah a perfect trifecta of reasons to take on the case. As he decided what to do, those reasons would weigh most on his mind.

Coming out of his trance, Big Brah took in a deep breath and then exhaled slowly. "I'll find the murderer," he said.

Chapter 2: High School Sweetheart Kali

Justice, here we go again, I thought, with a rush of excitement.

Unburdened of a great weight, Lei Bomino closed her eyes. Then she opened her eyes and looked at Big Brah. "Before you start your investigation, I want you to make me a promise," she said.

A promise. My excitement got a shot of surprise boosted by curiosity. Big Brah's broad brow creased with puzzlement. He waited, always patient.

She said, "Promise me, you'll protect the Bomino family honor!"

Big Brah was big on family honor. "I promise," he said.

She rummaged her handbag again and took out a check book. "I don't know what your rates are, whatever it is, I'll pay," she said.

Politely Big Brah raised a hand. "Right now, you've many things to worry about, ma'am. Let me help first, we'll talk about the money later," he said.

We didn't call him Big Brah for nothing. Lei Bomino left. Big Brah and I returned to the kitchen. He was calm. I was excited. My head swirled with possibilities about the investigation. But Big Brah had his methods.

We followed his methods. First thing would be to talk with the island's lone medical examiner, Kali. Big Brah's girlfriend. Smart and beautiful, Kali missed nothing, an incredible ally in any investigation. She shared Big Brah's passion for justice. For years, she had helped Big Brah crack tough cases. The two of them could be twins.

Actually, Big Brah and Kali were high school sweethearts. Like him, she loved to cook. They shared a softer side too. They were both nurturing individuals. I knew. I was his little brother. She made me feel I was her little brother too.

I got their constant love and attention. I fervently wanted them to get married and have babies, so I could be uncle. While I cleared the round kitchen table of our lunch plates, Big Brah used his phone to call Kali.

Kali was at work, busy. He left her a message asking her to come over in the evening. She never turned down an invitation to our place. Then again, Big Brah always began an investigation with a trip to our family temple or heiau. To pray.

He said he needed the goddess behind him in his work. A trip to the heiau always boosted my spirit, my life energy, my mana. *When were we gonna go there?* Big Brah had me sit at the clean table. I was super curious to know why he had accepted the case. It had to be the perfect trifecta, but Big Brah had his wisdoms, and I liked to verify details.

He said, "I know you have questions, Umi, but first let me make us a smoothie, our lunch was interrupted. Then we go to the heiau!"

Big Brah believed in thinking things through before he acted. He liked to think, while he worked in the kitchen. He moved about putting together each ingredient of the smoothie. His big mind no doubt meditated on the case. He had soaked almonds earlier.

Patiently he peeled each of the almonds.

From his caringly tended garden, he had picked oranges, pineapples and bananas. He juiced the fragrant oranges. To the juice he added milk to make the smoothie base he liked. There would be no bananas, even though they grew plentiful. He had special recipes for bananas.

For the flavor du jour, he emptied a pack of frozen blueberries and expertly chopped up a pineapple. Making no mess at all, he slid some of the pineapple chunks into the blender. On the island, it was common sense not to waste anything. Meticulously, Big Brah set away the rest of the pineapple in the refrigerator for use later.

Now, things were moving along. I was happy to wait for the answer to my one burning question. *Why had he taken on the case?* To pass the time, I reached for my phone. I was tempted to look for news about the murder.

On the island, even feral roosters scrapping over a hen made the news. The murder wouldn't just be on the news. It would be the only news. The murder was sure to have attracted strong and unique opinions with each viewpoint interesting and compelling.

The comments on the news would be endless, all pure wisdom. Talk story, a staple of the island scene. It made our culture thrive. Big Brah had a rule about the news and comments about an investigation.

While working on an investigation, he didn't read or watch the news and comments related to it. He investigated, relying solely on his five senses. He was so good at it, I believed he had a sixth sense. What Big Brah did, I did.

I was curious, but I wasn't going to read the local news. To stimulate the imagination, Big Brah encouraged me to read good fiction. Perfect time to get back to the novel of my favorite mystery series. I used my phone to read, until the smoothie arrived.

With the aftertaste of the divine smoothie still fresh, I headed out to the heiau with Big Brah. It was a couple of weeks to spring. Already the garden was green and colorful with the first blooms and starts.

The birds, the anoles and the butterflies were busy. From the front of the house, we strolled down the sloping garden path to the beach. The sun was mild. The ocean shimmered blue. White-capped waves rolled in smoothly. I'd have enjoyed it all.

But it was impossible to forget the murder. We stepped onto the soft sand of the beach, turned right and walked the short distance to the heiau. The heiau was a simple affair. It was a collection of small and large black lava rocks arranged in whimsical patterns. Put together, years ago, by the hands of two kids. Big Brah and me.

Big Brah was seventeen and I was five, when our family ship sank killing all the grown-ups--parents, tutus, uncles, aunts. Big Brah and I came here, every day. Brothers, no means to express a grief so big to each other or others.

Together we built the heiau to be close to the ocean, close to our family. It was a temple to the Island Goddess. We had no one and so we had the goddess. We stood head bowed in front of the heiau, our eyes closed. Strangely I forgot the murder. For a moment I was one with the island. Then I felt Big Brah's firm hand on my shoulder. I opened my eyes. Big Brah was done.

He looked at me intensely. "You had questions," he said.

"Yes, just one, why did you take on the case?" I asked.

"Think, Umi. Ms. Bomino gave us three good reasons,

save her innocent son, find the real murderer, restore the family honor," he said.

"I know, but why did you do it?" I asked.

He shook his head, smiling. "Your curiosity, a definite virtue," he said.

I smiled big. Then his smile faded away and mine too.

His eyes shone with unshed tears. "You know how you've been a blessing, Umi? Watching you grow made my growing up easier. I realized what a gift it is to have someone to care for."

A gentle breeze swirled around us. The ocean murmured aloha.

Big Brah blinked his tears away. "Lei Bomino cares for her son."

I nodded, agreeing.

"I want to help her continue caring for her son," he said.

The Bomino ohana was in trouble, ours had to help. *For your ohana from ours,* I thought.

Big Brah said, "This time it's for ohana, family!"

Go, Big Brah! His answer satisfied. His words motivated. Back home I waited for Kali with renewed energy. She would have important information about the victim. Evening arrived.

The birds quietened down. The night was still. Kali drove her late grand-aunt's old, blue truck. I heard the familiar sound of her truck approaching on our driveway. I ran to greet her. I swung the front door open.

Kali was smaller than Big Brah, but looking at her, you wouldn't know. She walked tall. She had taken time to change out of her boring work clothes. She had on an attractive sarong-dress and high heels. Dressed for a party.

I flashed her my bright smile. "He's in the kitchen," I said.

She strode in just as usual, confident and energetic. She hugged me, warm, firm and reassuring as always.

She drew back and studied me. "What's the trouble, Umi?" she asked.

"Trouble is, I want to be an uncle, and I'm still waiting," I said.

She laughed, pleased. Affectionately she squeezed my cheeks and patted my head. "Give it time, Umi." She breezed past me. "Will you tell me why I'm here, or do I have to find everything out myself?"

I fell in step behind her. "He's taken on the Bomino murder case," I said.

She turned back, so I could see her roll her eyes theatrically. "He's in worse trouble than I thought." Then she swirled into the brightly-lit kitchen, a dance in her steps.

Our house cats lived upstairs. Poli`ahu was the girl. She was snowy-white and green-eyed. Wiliwili was the boy. He was gray-and-white and golden-eyed. They must also have heard Kali. They pranced down the stairs. I followed them into the kitchen. Big Brah and Kali hadn't seen each other for two days. She flew into Big Brah's waiting arms.

He clasped her tight. Poli`ahu and Wiliwili fussed at her feet, giving her furry kisses, until she couldn't resist. Slowly she disengaged herself from Big Brah's arms. She petted Poli`ahu and Wiliwili. They returned the aloha with loud purrs. Then she went to the wall and slipped on her apron. She joined Big Brah. They cooked.

I sat at the table, watching them fondly. "There, the whole family is here," I said, happy.

The five of us. We were an ohana. When Big Brah and I had lost our ohana in the ocean tragedy, Big Brah and Kali had been high school seniors then. In love. They had plans to go to college, study and party. But Big Brah had to take care of me. So they studied, worked, took care of me and we partied together.

"Why don't you two have kids?" I asked, wishing it.

"We already have you, Umi," she said.

Both of them laughed.

True, I was their kid. Even though they were just twelve years older. "But I'm ready to be uncle!" I said.

Always kind, Kali said, "Oh, Umi, you'll make such a good uncle!"

I couldn't wait to be uncle. We gathered around the table. We worked our way furiously through delicious pork adobo, stir-fried okra with shallots and rice. Conversation about the investigation broke out naturally.

In her cheerful, optimistic way, Kali said, "I'm ready to help with the investigation."

Both Big Brah and I knew how much she helped us. Big Brah nodded, sagely.

I asked, "What can you tell us about the murder?"

"The Bomino family has been on the island for a long time, very quiet, well respected, it's an important case for the Police Department and the chief," she said.

The island's police chief was a good man. He did a great job of interacting with people. And, he never missed a chance to serenade the community with his karaoke skills. For homicide cases, the chief relied on the man who ran the PD's small homicide unit. Big Brah and Kali's friend from high school. Loni.

Kali said, "So Loni's handling the investigation himself. The victim's father, he's ninety-three, in good

14

health, but this afternoon, after he was told the news of his son's murder, he naturally took it hard. Family took him to the Island Hospital."

Big Brah sat up. "I have to see the father."

"He'll be at the hospital for a while, I hear," she said.

Big Brah frowned. "About the victim, how did the man die?"

Kali said, "A stone dagger. Struck from behind. Not much blood. The dagger found the heart, stopped it."

A cold, calculated stab in the back. "What kind of stone dagger?" I asked.

"Traditional, handmade, the kind you can buy on island from anyone who still practices the art," she said.

I said, "Gift shops sell those to everybody, tourists and locals, how are we to trace a stone dagger?"

Big Brah said, "Precisely why the murderer used a stone dagger. And it can't be an accident the dagger found the heart, shows the murderer must have practiced or have some sort of prior experience."

She said, "That fits, Loni told me the murderer was careful, left no fingerprints, no evidence, nothing at all on the dagger's blade or handle."

"What about the time of death?" Big Brah asked.

Kali was an expert at determining time of death. Big Brah absolutely trusted her opinion.

Thoughtfully, she said, "The 9-1-1 call was at 8:19 a.m. presumably within minutes of the murder."

"Do you agree that's when the murder happened?" he said.

"Yes, earlier, I'd say 7:45 a.m."

"Does Loni have anything else?" Big Brah said.

She shook her head. "Nothing, but he has a suspect, the son, Ohia."

"Why does Loni suspect Ohia?" Big Brah said.

"He was tight-lipped about it, you'll just have to ask him yourself," she said.

Big Brah fell silent, thinking.

To Kali I said, "What do you do next?"

She said, "It's a definite homicide. Tomorrow, I start the mandatory autopsy."

Autopsy. A chill passed through me. Looking at her, pert and alert by Big Brah's side, her sarong-dress colorful, her pretty face animated, you never suspected she opened up dead bodies at her work. Years ago, she had explained to me the compassion and service required for the job. She provided closure to the loved ones left behind. It was her way to help. I was always in awe of Kali. We would know more after the autopsy.

"Can't wait for the results," I said.

Kali left. Now that Big Brah had talked with Kali, I was charged for action.

Chapter 3: Cold, Calculating Killer

To my satisfaction, Big Brah called Loni and arranged we meet at the crime scene in the morning. The murder had occurred at the northern end of the coastal trail's bridge over the Waikahe River. Of the three eastside rivers, the Waikahe River was the one in the middle. We had to get there. The following morning, Big Brah drove the big, black truck.

Big Brah had a stoic air about him, as he did, when he was on the job. I rode in the passenger seat, ready for anything. We had the windows down to take in the fresh air. No matter where you went, you almost always had to take the coastal highway to get there.

The coastal highway looped around the entire island. Distances were short. We left our home behind, and we were on the highway. The grass next to the highway had dew on it. The breeze was in my face. It was cool this early in the morning.

I shivered in my t-shirt and board shorts. Big Brah couldn't be doing any better in his shirt and cargo shorts. To stay warm, he sipped hot coffee from a travel mug. The highway curved closer to the coast.

From the ocean, a fishing boat sped back, its night's work done. The waves rolled in steadily, stopping short of the coastal trail. Early risers had already made their way to the trail. They strolled, jogged, skated and biked. The island was awake. The bridge over the first eastside river came up.

For a brief time, the rhythmic sound of the truck's wheels rolling over the bridge replaced the muffled roar of the nearby ocean. After the bridge, the highway curved inland. No land on the island was really flat. An expanse of rolling plains now separated the trail from the highway. The coastal trail continued on hugging the coast. The trail was lost to sight.

Soon, the bridge over the Waikahe River came up. The crime scene was close. After the bridge, Big Brah slowed the truck down. To our right was a dirt road. If you were driving, the dirt road was the only way to get to the coastal trail's pedestrian bridge over the river.

We took the dirt road. We bounced along for a while, until the land evened. In front of us, the trail was a concrete snake hugging the coast. Past the trail, Waikahe Beach was a heavenly patch of golden sand.

Beyond the beach, the ocean stretched pink and blue. The dirt road ended. Big Brah pulled the big truck over to the side and parked. To my right, in the middle of innocent nature, yellow police tape secured the crime scene.

Past the crime scene, the steel structure of the pedestrian bridge glinted in the early light of the rising sun. We were early. Big Brah had planned it this way. He was going to study the crime scene undisturbed. It was the second part of his method. The way he studied a crime scene was unique.

The crime scene was the place the victim was last alive. Big Brah liked to breathe the same air, walk on the same ground, feel the same breeze on his skin, see the same sights, hear the same sounds and smell the same smells, as the victim had done.

He said it helped him begin a connection with the victim. What got the victim here? Why here? Numerous questions played on his mind, as he tried to figure out what happened. Never failed to blow my mind. Lost in thought, Big Brah took his time getting out of the truck.

He opened the door. He squinted at the yellow tape of the crime scene. He slid out of his seat and stepped onto the sand in fluid motion. Absent-mindedly, he shut the door behind him, while he continued to appraise the crime scene. He was in the zone, focused sharply.

The rule here was not to disturb him in any way. I followed him without asking any questions. He neared the yellow tape of the secured crime scene and stopped. The murder happened here. I got chicken skin, as we call goose bumps on the island. Inside the secured area, a vehicle was parked, presumably the victim's truck.

The white truck was clean and full-sized with regular island plates. The rising sun cast an eerie red glow on the white surface of the truck. The empty truck still waited for its owner. Big Brah closed his eyes and bowed his head, communing with the surroundings.

Closer to normal, a tourist bike group approached from the direction of the bridge. As they swished by in their bikes, they waved. I waved back. A few of them glanced curiously at Big Brah. He would commune for a while. I strolled away to the trail. I walked toward the bridge. The ocean stretched smoothly to my left, the rising sun on the horizon.

Frothy, white pillars of water sprayed up from the ocean's smooth surface at random, the blows of a cavorting humpback whale family. Closer to shore, an inquisitive monk seal floated, head bobbing above the waves. The bridge had a viewing area. I lingered on it.

The rising sun's light and warmth stirred life all around. The calls of shore birds filled the air. On the rocky riverbank, crabs proliferated. Fish teemed in the waters below. Life erupted everywhere. I looked back at the crime scene. There, life had been snuffed out by a heartless killer. I shook my head. *It shouldn't have happened.* Big Brah stirred, his meditation over.

Big Brah circled the crime scene several times, pausing to look at it from different angles. Three times he dropped down on his knees to peer inside, once even going flat on his stomach. He was only getting started. I watched him for a while, willing him on to catch the killer. In the distance, Loni's unmarked green sedan backed up next to our big, black truck.

The sedan's door flung all the way open. Loni got out, turned back and slammed the door shut. Deliberately, he turned around and surveyed the scene in front of him. Then, with measured steps, Loni walked to Big Brah. I joined them. Loni was a brooding man stuck in his ways.

He had a dark, overgrown mustache. Whenever he thought hard, he pulled at the ends of his mustache. He had two daughters in elementary school. His lively daughters didn't give him much time to brood at home. He did all his brooding during work time. His lovely wife made yummy cupcakes and musubis. As a result, Loni packed just a few extra pounds around his belly.

Loni hugged us both. "I'm on my way to the PD, had to drop off the girls, their school. Sorry I'm a few minutes late, they took longer than usual to get ready. Children."

I nodded.

"Children," Big Brah murmured.

Loni was very warm. He put a friendly hand on Big Brah's shoulder. "Come on, now. Big Brah, you know all about children," he said.

Big Brah smiled.

Loni's hand lingered on Big Brah's big shoulder. "You've been a parent to Umi," Loni said.

Loni was in a good mood. He wasn't brooding. Why?

Loni took his hand off Big Brah's shoulder. He rubbed his hands together. He spoke with unusual gusto. "I'm glad you on the case, Big Brah, together we'll nail the killer faster!"

Big Brah agreed. "I hear you have a suspect already."

Slowly, Loni said, "Yes, true, I questioned the victim's son, Ohia, he's the last person to see the dead man alive. He lives with his mother. He says he came out here to meet with his father. Prior appointment. Apparently, he and his father were fighting over something.

"Ohia won't say over what. He met his father. They had a good meeting. A reconciliation, Ohia claims. His story doesn't ring true, then again, I don't have any evidence...yet. I let him go, after questioning. If any evidence shows up, I won't hesitate to arrest Ohia Bomino."

Arrest Ohia Bomino? I shivered. Life in police lockup or worse in prison was scary. Especially if you were innocent. Big Brah's goal was to save Ohia from such an ordeal. Surely, he didn't want Ohia arrested.

But Big Brah was patient. "Show us what you got so far," he said.

Loni looked pleased. Often Big Brah showed him things. This time Loni was ahead. Grandly he took us inside the secured area.

Loni stopped near the back of the victim's white truck. "The lab folks are done here, won't hurt if you guys get closer to the action. Here's what I think happened. The two of them, father and son, arrive in their vehicles. This is the area Ohia also parked his car. Ohia brings a stone dagger. The dagger, he hides."

I glanced at Big Brah. This couldn't be going down well with him. But he displayed no reaction. Loni, on the other hand, brooded on.

Loni gestured with his hands as he talked. "Note again, the father's truck is parked facing the trail. So likely Ohia's vehicle had to be parked the same way. He gets out, meets his father, he lures his father here, behind the vehicle. Say he tells his father, you don't want others to see us, let's get some privacy.

"Father agrees, seeing no wrong in what his son says. They're father and son, they know each other really well. They talk. Father suspects nothing, trusts, even turns away from Ohia. Ohia takes out dagger he has hidden and stabs his father, kills him. Boom!" Dramatically Loni pointed to the ground.

I stared down at the sandy ground. Had it really been as Loni had described? Loni made it sound plausible.

I had to speak up for Ohia. "What does Ohia have to say about this?" I asked.

Behind us, our big, black truck and Loni's green sedan were parked at the end of the dirt road. Loni snuck a thumb over his shoulder at the vehicles parked far away. "Ohia says, he parked over there. His father was waiting for him. They strolled down to the beach. Had their talk. When they returned, Ohia got back in his vehicle.

"He saw his father walking back to this white truck here. It was the last time he saw his father alive. Bugger denies being at the crime scene, says he didn't even come near."

Ohia denied being at the crime scene. Why did Loni

think Ohia had been there?

"Is there any evidence tying Ohia to the crime scene?" Big Brah asked.

Loni pulled at the ends of his thick, black mustache, thinking. "Evidence...can you keep a secret? The Chief's asked me not to tell anyone, but Chief instructed me yesterday, when he didn't know you were interested."

Big Brah waited, always patient.

Loni took a deep breath and came to a decision. "Okay, Big Brah, I'm going to tell you this. When we found the victim, he had a hat, you know, the kind that's strapped at the chin?"

"A boonie hat," Big Brah said.

"Yes, the boonie hat, it was still there. But, next to the body, we found a baseball cap. It didn't belong to the victim. No, the baseball cap has to belong to the killer, dropped there by accident. How's that for evidence!"

Big Brah and I stared at Loni.

Loni concluded. "In the killer's scheme, the cap is the flaw."

Big time flaw, if Loni could prove the cap was indeed Ohia's. There was a silence. Big Brah took advantage of the silence. He opened the tailgate of the white truck and examined the empty cargo bed. I got there beside him. Loni followed our movements.

Annoyed Big Brah and I weren't paying him our fullest attention, Loni raised his voice. "I showed Ohia the baseball cap. Again, denial. He says, the cap is not his. Now, I believe the cap belongs to Ohia."

The cargo bed of the truck was sandy. Big Brah reached inside, took a handful of the sand and slowly poured the sand back onto the bed. We exchanged glances.

Big Brah turned back to Loni. "Do you know how the sand got here?" he asked.

Loni sounded even more annoyed. "Look around you, Big Brah, it's a beach, there's sand everywhere!"

Big Brah said, "But the cargo bed, how did the sand get on the cargo bed of the victim's truck?"

Loni snorted. "The sand is unimportant! The baseball cap is important. To prove the cap belongs to Ohia, I'm going all out."

Loni going all out sounded sinister. We forgot the sand on the cargo bed. "What are you planning to do?" Big Brah said.

Loni drew closer. "DNA evidence! The lab folks will be examining the cap for DNA, you bet they will. Whether they get a viable sample or not, I'll know tomorrow. You know what a viable sample means?"

Big Brah and I shook our heads.

"I'll be a step closer to arresting Ohia," Loni said.

After delivering the chilling news about Ohia, Loni left to start his day at the PD. Like Loni, most investigators of a murder focused on suspects. Big Brah focused on the victim.

He found out everything he could about the victim from family, friends, coworkers and acquaintances. From the research, he built a profile. He said he walked in the shoes of the victim. By being one with the victim, Big Brah figured out the killer. It was Big Brah's method. It worked. Our client was the murdered man's wife.

She probably knew him best. Surely Big Brah would want to start with her. Loni's green sedan disappeared from view down the dirt road.

Sure enough, Big Brah leaped into our big, black truck. "Get in, Umi, we have to see our client…and find Ohia," he

said.

Distances being short on the island, it took us just fifteen minutes to get to Lei Bomino's home. She lived with her son in a big house on a large lot. It was still early morning. The grounds were neat, the grass mowed. The large carport had a single SUV parked in it and familiar clutter.

Old TV, used bookcase, scruffy recliner and storage boxes. Still left room enough to park a couple more cars. And there was ample parking space next to the carport for visitors. We parked there. Sunlight slanted onto the front lanai.

The wide lanai had signs of Ohia's childhood. A kid's bike, a big basket full of well-loved footballs and a pile of rubber slippers. Lei Bomino must have heard our truck. She opened the glass-and-wood front door. She had aged a decade overnight.

Her shoulders sagged. Her hair was uncombed, grayer. Her round face had shrunk with sorrow. Her sad eyes were tired and weary. Her grief was for real.

She looked at us, concerned. "I heard your truck, is everything all right, Big Brah?"

Big Brah nodded, reassuring. "I just spoke with Lieutenant Loni," he said.

"Oh. Come in," she said.

The comfortable living room had big windows and solid furniture. Framed family photographs decorated the walls. The wall clock had a bamboo frame handcrafted in the shape of a rooster. The clock displayed the time, a few minutes past nine. Lei Bomino asked for a minute to tidy up.

She quickly rearranged the cushions on the couch, slipped a couple of books from the top to the bottom of the coffee table and opened the windows. She had the ease of someone who knew her home well. She invited us to sit down. We sat on the couch. She sat in an accent chair across the coffee table and looked expectantly at Big Brah.

Investigators in the mystery novels I read liked to fire questions at their client and suspects. But not Big Brah. Big Brah didn't always conduct an interrogation, especially at the beginning of an investigation. By nature, he kept an open mind and listened with all his six senses. He talked story and helped in any way he could.

Caringly he said, "I heard old Mr. Bomino had to be taken to the hospital, hope he's all right."

Sadly she shook her head. "Papa Bomino is still in intensive care, I just got a call from the hospital, it was big brother Romo."

"Big brother Romo?" Big Brah said, politely.

Lei Bomino looked from Big Brah to me, then back at Big Brah. "Romo Bomino. My husband's big brother. Romo and Izor were brothers, like the two of you. For Izor, big brother Romo was his angel."

Big Brah was certainly my angel too. I couldn't imagine a big brother otherwise.

Following his method of gathering information about the deceased from family members, Big Brah promptly said, "I must meet big brother Romo."

Lei Bomino nodded. "You must meet big brother Romo, you will. Without him, don't know how I'd handle all this. He's taking care of us, doing everything for the family."

Big Brah was moved by the circumstances. I knew I was.

Concern lined Big Brah's handsome face. "If Umi and I can be of any assistance, please, tell us."

I joined in. I nodded fervently.

She almost smiled. "By finding the murderer, you're helping already." Then her face clouded up. "Tell me, do the police still suspect poor Ohia?"

"Unfortunately, yes," Big Brah said.

She sighed. "Is he in trouble?"

"I'd like to see him, find out for myself," Big Brah said.

"Oh. Ohia's not home right now, I can have him home in ten minutes, can you wait?"

"Sure, I can wait," Big Brah said, polite as ever.

She went and got her phone. As she texted Ohia, she laughed, nervously. "Ohia's with his girlfriend, sweet girl named Kela, lives in the neighborhood."

Girlfriend. My ears perked up. Anything about Ohia could be important.

She said, "It's Kela's birthday, she cancelled the party, of course. The news, TV, internet, The Island Times, it's awful, they're all calling Ohia a suspect. I told him, go to her, tell her the truth."

She finished texting and looked up from her phone. "There. He'll be home in no time, he knows this is important."

"It's also important we know where he was yesterday, in the morning," Big Brah said.

She said, "I can tell you where he was. I remember it well. I've been going over it in my head, again and again. Lieutenant Loni, he was here in the evening, he asked me about it for more than an hour. I'll tell you what I told the lieutenant. Ohia left home before 7, he told me he'd be back for breakfast.

"I don't question Ohia when he goes in and out, he's a big boy. He came back at 8:30. I'm sure it was 8:30 because I told him he had just 30 minutes to shower and eat. He leaves for work at 9, and he did. He was in his office, working, when the PD contacted him."

Kali had set the time of death at 7:45 a.m. If Ohia had left home before 7 and returned at 8:30, he could have killed his father. But what about a motive? We'd find out, from Ohia. Meanwhile Big Brah wasted no time in finding out more about Ohia.

Big Brah said, "How did Ohia describe the encounter with the PD?"

Lei Bomino said, "He was upset. He says soon as the lieutenant identified himself, he got a bad feeling. He doesn't know why, but he knew it was about his dad, something bad had happened. So he asked the lieutenant, is it about my dad...." Her voice died out. She covered her mouth with a hand.

Loni. He always suspected someone close to the victim, in this case, the son. Loni called Ohia to inform son of father's murder, and son already knew it was about dad. Mm-hmm. *No wonder Loni suspects Ohia,* I thought. Next to me, Big Brah stirred.

Family was his all-time favorite thing in the world. "Ohia was naturally feeling protective for someone in his ohana, someone he loves, his father," he said.

Lei Bomino moved her hand away from her mouth. "You're so right, my Ohia, he's protective of his ohana. He was devastated by the news, but he kept his cool, he acted responsibly, he went to the morgue to identify... answered their questions, did everything."

Everything. *Help us, Goddess Pele!* I imagined Ohia acting responsibly, his emotions firmly in check, as he coolly identified the body and answered questions. By then, to Loni, Ohia was not just a murderer but a cold, calculating killer. Big Brah lived by responsibility and advised me to stay cool no matter the adversity.

He nodded approvingly. "Good boy, Ohia did good," he said.

Lei Bomino said, "Yes, Ohia is a good boy, Izor and I, we're proud of him. Izor loved Ohia. We both did. Back then, Izor's new business had started to thrive. To be nearer his work, we moved to this house, away from the Bomino estate. We were all so happy. Then, Izor was hit by a setback in his business.

"Izor was devastated, Papa Bomino and big brother Romo rescued him. Throughout the ups and the downs, Ohia grew up, knowing his father loved him. But the setback left its mark on poor Izor. He grew withdrawn and depressed.

"He wanted to live alone, be left alone. Our old house in the Bomino estate was empty. Izor started to live there, from time to time, whenever he wasn't feeling so good. I didn't mind, he wasn't all alone, he was nearer his father and big brother, it helped him.

"Ohia was still in school, he and I continued here. Izor visited us, and we could always call him anytime. There was still love, aloha. We were still an ohana, but he lived there, so we could all be happy."

Big Brah nodded. "Understandable, happiness is paramount, every ohana must figure out how to keep the aloha," he said.

Wise, very wise, but Loni will focus only on the dysfunctional aspect of their living arrangement, I thought. A shuffling noise and the front door opened. Was it Ohia, the major suspect?

Chapter 4: Typical Island Hospitality

A man entered. He didn't knock. He didn't say a word. He strode over to a side table. The side table was under the rooster wall clock. On the table, there was a wicker bowl. The wicker bowl had keys and key chains. The man dropped his keys into the bowl. He had done this routine a thousand times. He lived here.

It had to be Ohia. Ohia wasn't much older than me. He was taller and bigger. He had curly hair, a sharp nose and a jutting chin. He was dressed casually in shirt and trousers. We were all on our feet.

We greeted each other in hushed tones. Big Brah and I murmured our condolences over his loss. Ohia accepted our words quietly. He had a dreamy look and an overall softness some island girls swooned over.

His eyes on us, he hugged his mother protectively. "Don't worry, Mom, I'm here," he said.

She hugged him back fiercely, closing her eyes in silent prayer. She didn't say anything. Her love for him was there for all of us to feel. She opened her eyes and separated from him. Solemnly she gestured for him to sit down in the accent chair she had just vacated and for us to resume our seats.

She looked at Big Brah. "I trust you'll keep him out of trouble," she said.

Big Brah nodded, reassuringly. "I will," he said.

The facts were against Ohia. The only thing he lacked was a clear motive. If a motive surfaced, Big Brah's task would get tougher. I didn't know how he would keep Ohia out of trouble. No doubt, he would. After all he had the sixth sense.

Lei Bomino said, "And the Bomino name...you'll protect all of us, right?"

"Right," Big Brah said.

I knew he would.

"Please, carry on." She left.

We sat down.

Ohia said, "I can't thank you enough, Big Brah, for helping us out. I told Lieutenant Loni, I didn't do it. I love my father, he was a good man, I wouldn't dream of hurting him."

Big Brah nodded, sympathetic. "Of course, of course."

Ohia said, "It's true Dad and I'd been fighting, but we reconciled, everything was cool between us. It wasn't really a fight, just a conversation any son can have with his dad."

"Still, you refused to tell Loni about it," Big Brah said.

"Loni! Why should I tell him? This is my private business, he has no right to intrude."

This was a murder investigation, a matter of life and death. Loni had no right to intrude, but it was his job to find the killer.

Big Brah sat up and scrutinized Ohia. "Now, you're being childish!" he said.

Ohia turned defensive. He crossed his arms. "Loni made it clear he suspects me. He suspected me before he asked me what the fight was about. Why would I tell him anything?"

"Because this is serious business," Big Brah said.

Ohia thawed. "Of course. I can tell you what it was all about."

Big Brah nodded, approvingly.

Ohia spoke in a soft voice. "You don't think I killed my dad, do you?"

Without hesitation, Big Brah reassured Ohia. "No," he said.

I shook my head, in total agreement.

Ohia got a shot of confidence. He uncrossed his arms. "Good. Well, here's what happened. Kela and I want to marry, I'd asked Dad if he'd give me my inheritance early, I wanted to start my own business.

"At first, Dad refused, he wanted me to save my inheritance. We went back and forth, we talked, father and son, you know. I knew he'd come around. He met Kela, he saw we loved each other, aloha melted his heart. Yesterday, we had agreed to meet at the beach, so we did. We talked it over in peace.

"To my surprise, he had a compromise ready. If I started the business with a loan, he'd pay the down payment. Keep my inheritance intact. I was stoked. We met at 7 in the morning, talked for about 40 minutes.

"I left walking on air. Everything had been put right. Perfect. I was working in my office, all happy. Loni barged in with the dreadful news. Devastating."

There was a silence, as Ohia relived the devastating scene. Big Brah sat immobile, obviously commiserating with Ohia. I sat back. Ohia and his father had been fighting over money.

I glanced at Big Brah. He had his eyes closed. He was in a deep trance. Money was so often a motive for murder. Good, then, Ohia had not told Loni about the fight over money. If Loni knew the money angle, he wouldn't need the evidence of the baseball cap. He would have arrested Ohia already. The silence intensified.

With a shiver, Big Brah snapped out of the trance. He had seen a disturbing vision.

Big Brah opened his eyes. "A baseball cap was found at the crime scene."

Ohia threw up his hands. "I didn't even go near the crime scene. Dad always parks near the bridge, but he had walked down to the end of the dirt road, he was waiting for me. I parked there, went to the beach. The last I saw of Dad, he was walking toward the bridge, toward his white truck, I drove away. I was happy, I never thought I'd never see him again."

At least Ohia's story was consistent. He had told Loni the same thing.

Ohia wrung his hands. "Unfortunately, Loni thinks the baseball cap is mine."

"Is it?" Big Brah said, softly.

"I told Loni it wasn't."

Big Brah looked inquiringly at Ohia, as if to say, "What are you going to tell me?"

Ohia said, "Okay, I'll be honest with you, I don't know. I'd certainly remember if I wore it, when I went out to meet Dad. I didn't. I did have a cap like the one Loni showed me.

"I came home and looked for the cap, but I can't find it. I haven't seen the cap or used it in a while, it's lost."

Big Brah and I looked at each other. Ohia was in trouble. How bad the trouble was we'd find out. It made the task of finding the real killer urgent. Outside in the sun, as we drove home, I asked Big Brah what he thought of Ohia.

Big Brah said, "I think Ohia's hiding something, his story is incomplete."

"What makes you say that?" I asked.

"His mother says Ohia left home before seven to meet his father. Ohia claims he met his father at 7, talked with him for 40 minutes. So, he last saw his father alive at 7:40. Kali is sure death occurred at 7:45. So far, no problem. But then, Ohia claims, after seeing his father, he drove home.

"His mother says Ohia returned home at 8:30. Now, it took us 15 minutes to drive from the crime scene to his home. What took Ohia 50 minutes?"

Typical. Big Brah never missed anything. It couldn't have taken Ohia that long to drive home after seeing his father. A tiny arrow of disappointment pierced my heart.

Why hadn't Ohia told us everything? The big truck took the familiar exit from the coastal highway to our home. Oh, well, Big Brah would find out, soon.

Looked like Ohia needed more saving. On our driveway, the big truck drove past the readerboard marquee sign proudly displaying "Waialeale Detective Agency" and turned the corner. Our two-story home with its sprawling second floor lanai and fantastic views of the beach and ocean appeared before us. My heart warmed at the sight of our cozy home.

I got a shot of enthusiasm. "What do we do next?" I asked.

"The method, Umi, we follow the method," Big Brah said.

That afternoon, following Big Brah's method, we headed to the victim's neighborhood. After a lunch of tempura and musubi washed down by coconut water, we were energized. You could call this part of his method familiarize, learn or absorb. But there was no one word to describe what Big Brah did. Let me just say Big Brah liked to soak in the neighborhood. In the big, black truck we drove down the coastal highway.

Dark storm clouds shrouded the island sky. Early gusts of wind but no rain yet. After the bridge over the Waikahe River, the dirt road to the crime scene came up on our right.

Big Brah slowed the truck down. "The victim also took this dirt road," he said.

"But he was coming from the other direction, the direction we're headed," I said.

Big Brah sped the truck up. "This was his familiar route," he said.

Soon we exited the coastal highway and headed for Waikahe Hills. The road climbed the hilly island terrain. Past ridges and ravines, the big truck made a roundabout way inland. With time and a little human help, the Waikahe River had patiently found and created a linear path.

Without meandering, the river hurried to pour its waters into the ocean. Once in a while, the foliage of wild bushes and trees parted. The river was visible. The darkened river waters matched the cloudy sky. We drove past rural homes and farms. The Bomino estate was spread over a large acreage. The estate was large enough to have its own cul-de-sac. Big Brah turned the truck into Bomino Court.

I sat up, alert. Anything here could be important. Big Brah drove the big truck slowly. We looked around. There were no homes to our right. Rolling plains stretched all the way to distant cloud-topped mountains. The view was breathtaking nature.

To our left, the view was as remarkable but man

made. A row of big homes in sprawling lots. Bomino Court. The first home had a low hedge, no gate, just a welcoming open entrance. The home number matched the victim's address. A familiar play structure was the centerpiece of the huge front yard.

The much-loved metal slide was shiny and smooth from enthusiastic use in the past. Rust crept on it now. The ample, two-story home was painted dark green. The shine of the paint had dulled with time. The home looked like it could be warm and lived in. But it had all its windows dark and doors closed. The home was silent and empty. The truck rolled forward.

The next lot had a clear fence and an open gate. The home was brighter, freshly painted. The golf course like front yard had many flower beds all precisely organized. A woman in a straw hat, shirt, jeans and gardening boots tended to a bed of island lilies. She looked up at us and waved. We waved back. Big Brah drove the truck forward. We looked at each other. A neighbor.

Big Brah had to talk story with her. The method. A tall, thick hedge started on our left. The third lot. The thick hedge had no gaps and a barred wrought iron gate had a no trespassing sign. Beyond the gate, a concrete driveway, manicured lawn, sparkling swimming pool and perfectly upgraded home and garage. But the last home was the best.

The home's wide, concrete driveway started at the end of the court. The driveway led all the way up to the front of the big, sprawling home. Built on a mound, the old-style home rose royal and majestic. An established garden of fragrant perennials and big, beautiful ancient trees adorned the lot. No hedge, no gate. The trees provided enough privacy. Big Brah turned the truck around.

The homes now were nearer and on my side. The truck trundled back down the court. I strained to see if I had missed anything. The tall hedge still had no gaps. The hedge ended. The clear fence started. I had a view of the terrain behind the homes. There, the ground sloped to meet the deep waters of the Waikahe River. Closer, I looked for the woman in the straw hat.

She had walked up to the gate. She was curious. Big Brah saw her too. At once he pulled the truck over to the side of the road and parked. Promptly we joined her at the gate. She had high cheekbones and an angular chin. Her skin was roughened and toughened by many hours spent in the sun. Avid gardener? At least she spent a whole lot of time outdoors. At the sight of Big Brah, all big and solemn, her eyes narrowed.

A puzzled frown came over her suntanned face. "You look familiar, do I know you?" she said.

Big Brah introduced us, presenting her a business card.

"I'm going to keep this card, show it to my husband, so he'll believe me it was really you!" she said.

She introduced herself. Her name was Maria Gomez. She and her husband, Antonio, lived there. They had bought this part of the Bomino estate thirty years ago. This part of the estate used to belong to old Mr. Bomino's big brother who was now deceased.

Big Brah told her we were investigating the murder of her neighbor.

Her face fell. "Of course, I should've guessed."

With typical island hospitality, she invited us in. A stone pathway led to the lanai. The lanai had stylish patio furniture. The wall had Old Glory painted on it. Below the painted flag, a strange collection of hand tools was stacked up against the wall. Chisels, hammers, big, small, all sturdy. The sharp, pointy metal heads of the chisels looked sinister.

The tools looked oddly familiar, but I couldn't place them. Maria Gomez chattered. Antonio used to be a surgeon in the army. He was patriotic. She had painted Old Glory, Union to the left as required, on the lanai wall for his last birthday. Antonio worked.

He had a private practice downtown. He was a family physician now. But he was still attached to the army ways. Her painting Old Glory on the wall had made him quite emotional. After all, both of them loved Old Glory. And she had painted the flag with love.

She pointed to the collection of hand tools. "Antonio uses those for his hobby," she said.

I would have asked her what his hobby was, but she was talking so fast, I couldn't get a word in. And Big Brah never interrupted. The couple had raised three children. The kids had grown up, moved out to Boston, Austin and Seattle to pursue interests in medicine, business and engineering. She invited us to sit.

Big Brah and I sat down. We had a view of the garden with its lilies, the asphalt strip of the court, the stretch of rolling plains and the majestic, cloud-topped mountains in the distance. She insisted on snacks and drinks. Big Brah agreed to an arare platter and island-grown coffee.

Maria Gomez set the platter and the steaming mugs down on a table close by and sat down. "Terrible thing to happen, Antonio and I, we can't believe it, Izor's dead. I've been checking the Island Times for news, I've been thinking about it all day. I have no one to talk to.

"I used to talk with Papa Bomino all the time, his is

the big house at the end of the court. He was in good health and spirits, he took it hard, they had to take him to the hospital. And big brother Romo, he lives on the other side of us, you can't see the home from here, his hedge is too tall. His is the nice updated home with the swimming pool. He's busy looking after Papa Bomino and Izor's family. Suddenly I have no one to talk to, no one at all." She laughed, self-consciously.

Big Brah and I munched the crisp rice crackers, arare, a local favorite, and sipped the excellent coffee. Big Brah was a good listener, always, but this time, it was clear that Maria Gomez liked to talk. I had to listen.

She continued. "I suppose you'll want to know about the feud between my Antonio and Izor."

Big Brah stopped munching arare. I nearly choked on mine. A feud. A motive for murder. I leaned forward. I was listening.

She said, "Better you learn the truth from me, than someone else who doesn't know it as well as I do. My Antonio, he isn't violent, despite what you may hear. You see, the two of them, they've been feuding for years, it's true. But poor Antonio, last month, he slapped Izor. But my Antonio would never kill Izor." She paused overcome with feeling.

Her story was getting so interesting. Impatient, I felt my right foot start to tap on the lanai floor. Lest it distract her I stopped. Big Brah had a stoic expression on his face as if he was used to hearing such tales every day. He got up, picked up the arare platter and graciously offered it to both Maria Gomez and me, took some arare himself and sank back in his chair like everything was normal. A corner of Maria Gomez's mouth turned upward in a half smile. She was pleased she had captivated her listeners.

She said, "Antonio and Izor, if I think back to when we first moved into this house, it's not like they never got along. Antonio likes organization, order, he likes to keep his house, his land that way. Izor was a lot like Antonio. If Antonio liked the grass mowed, Izor liked that too. There was only one problem, you see those ohia trees—"

She pointed toward a grove of splendid tall ohias with perfect green leaves and bright red blossoms. "That grove is on the border of our two properties. Antonio likes to keep the trees pruned and trimmed. But Izor is overly sentimental about them. He says the trees are the first to sprout on the new land formed by the lava flow from Goddess Pele, they're sacred, he's loved them from the time he was a child, he's even named his son Ohia! He wanted to let them grow naturally. Antonio didn't like the trees growing wild, he tried to reason with Izor.

"Izor wouldn't listen, he was completely unreasonable about the trees. So, who helps my Antonio? Romo, the big brother. Now, let me tell you about Romo and Izor, the Bomino brothers."

Maria Gomez paused to sip coffee. Big Brah and I were taking in every word. He listened with an approving air. He totally believed every word she was saying. I listened, a lot more skeptical.

She said, "Two brothers, more different, you'll never get. Romo, the big brother is so responsible, look how he's taking care of his family in this trouble. He's always polite and ready to talk, very social, and he's successful. He followed his father into the furniture business, the family business is thriving, he's a bit older, but he's fit, you know, he's still an eligible bachelor! Izor, had troubles.

"Izor married early, too early, he wasn't ready for it, his marriage suffered. He needed support from his father and big brother to set up his lumber business, they were his only customers for months, before he got others. I don't think his business ever turned a profit."

Interesting. We had gotten conflicting accounts about the victim's business. His loving wife thought it had thrived. But his not-so-thrilled neighbor was telling us it never turned a profit. It had to be the viewpoint.

She said, "Izor had a wife, a son, he didn't even live with them. Lately, he'd been irritable and ill-tempered. Every year, me and a group of volunteers clean up the Waikahe Beach. Big brother Romo contributes generously to our charity, Izor never. So Antonio, frustrated over the ohia trees, didn't know what to do, he got talking with Romo, Romo offered to help. The three of them, the Bomino brothers and Antonio met over there, by the ohia trees. That's when it happened. Antonio, venting years of frustration, he slapped Izor!

"I saw the whole thing, sitting right here. I ran to the men. Izor would have struck right back, he wasn't scared of my Antonio, he was mad, I told you he was ill-tempered lately, but Romo threw his arms around his younger brother, wouldn't let Izor strike Antonio. And Antonio, remorse stricken by then, came to me. I held him, I comforted him, I know how sorry he was.

"Romo apologized, told us to go home, dragged his brother away. A few days later Romo had a tree cutting service come in and at least thin the trees as a compromise. Antonio and I are truly grateful to have him as our neighbor. The feud ended that day!" She took a deep breath and stopped.

Big Brah nodded solemnly, as if to say, he agreed the feud had indeed ended that day. I didn't know if he was also nodding to the implication that Antonio Gomez hadn't murdered Izor later. Maria Gomez seemed intent on convincing us her husband was innocent.

I'm sure it hadn't escaped Big Brah's attention Antonio Gomez was a surgeon turned physician. Someone intimately familiar with the human anatomy. Antonio Gomez knew where to strike a deadly blow. Just like the killer. And what were those sinister looking tools for? Somehow, I missed asking her about them. Now that the business of establishing her husband's innocence was over, she chatted on about this and that.

The weather. The returning whales. Monk seal habitats. The state of the world. The future of humanity. Together we consumed another arare platter and more hot, aromatic coffee at her insistence. The day was darkening early due to the clouds. Big Brah reclined in his chair, relaxed. I forgot the time. The growl of a car engine entering the court brought me back to reality.

Maria Gomez tilted her head to one side and listened for a moment. "It's my Antonio, he's back early," she said, unperturbed.

Lulled by her stories, Big Brah and I matched her unperturbed state. She had been so warm and welcoming. Her husband couldn't be otherwise. A silver sedan burst into view. I could see a man inside. Serenely she waved. The driver waved back.

"That's my Antonio, he'll be here in a minute, he's seen us," she said.

Antonio drove the silver sedan in through the open gate and parked. He got out. You could tell he was a physician from the white coat he wore over his regular clothes. He had a crew cut. He was buff. Strong enough to kill a man with a stone dagger? Yes. He strode down the stone pathway toward us. He had on a semi-formal smile to say, "Hello, I don't know who you are." He looked toward his wife for direction.

Maria Gomez continued to sit. "Join us, Antonio, let me introduce you."

Antonio Gomez came and stood by her chair. She smiled and took his hand.

Comfortably she gestured toward Big Brah and me. "This is Big Brah and Umi. They're here to investigate Izor's death. We've been talking story for what? All afternoon!"

Antonio Gomez's face froze. Hastily he lowered his head to gaze down at his wife.

She said, "They're nice, I told them all about you and Izor, they don't mind at all, I told them about your feud!"

"What feud?" Antonio Gomez snorted. He withdrew his hand from her grasp.

I sat up. So did Big Brah.

Maria Gomez frowned. "Your fight with Izor, when you slapped him!"

Antonio Gomez glared at us. Then he lowered his gaze down at his wife. "You talk too much! What've you been yakking about? You have no sense. I told you, I don't want to have anything to do with Izor!" he said.

She looked up at him, alarmed. "But, dear, better they get to know about it from me, than someone who doesn't know you as well as I do, they told me they're investigating the murder," she said.

Antonio Gomez straightened. His eyes blazed at us. "You've been bothering my wife, digging up dirt on me, behind my back," he said.

Big Brah tried to pacify the irate husband. He raised both his hands palms outward. "You're misunderstanding the situation, sir," he said, politely.

Maria Gomez said, "Antonio, you're making a big mistake!"

Antonio Gomez was adamant. He pointed toward the open gate. He raised his voice. "I want you to leave, right now!" he said.

Chapter 5: Deception So Close

Big Brah never stayed anywhere uninvited. He got up, calmly, and thanked Maria Gomez. "Mahalo, Mrs. Gomez, for your hospitality," he said.

I was shocked. Slowly I unglued myself from the chair and rose. Together Big Brah and I left without making a fuss, he still calm, me fuming. I fumed all the way home. After the events of the day, Big Brah had a lot of thinking to do. He took his time in the kitchen, cooking. My task was not to disturb him.

Since I wasn't going to read the news about the murder, I sat at the round kitchen table and used my phone to read the mystery novel. Gradually the aroma of cooking filled the kitchen. Both of us waited for Kali. She would have early results of the autopsy.

Kali was late. Her home was closer to her work. But while we were on a case, instead of going home, she drove here first. She lived in a little cottage hidden in a grove of big island pines. Quiet spot. Great place to meditate. Ever since she moved to the island, Kali had been living there. Kali used to live with her family on the mainland.

Her grand-aunt, Aunty Mahina lived on the island alone. She nursed the sick at the Island Hospital. She loved the island and lived with aloha. Aunty Mahina fell sick. She needed help from family urgently. No one in Kali's loveless family wanted to help.

Worse, the family had plans for Kali. Plans with no

aloha. Plans Kali didn't like. The family didn't want Kali to help. Despite their opposition, always compassionate, Kali arrived on the island to take care of Aunty Mahina. Wide-eyed and new to the island, Kali visited Aunty Mahina every day at the hospital.

Aunty Mahina returned home. With her customary poise and patience, Kali cared for her aunty. Aunty Mahina recovered fully.

Deeply moved by Kali's natural aloha, Aunty Mahina wanted Kali to stay on with her. So, Kali did. But her mainland family wasn't pleased. Nevertheless, Kali enrolled in the local high school, just a junior. Luckily, Big Brah was in her language arts class. He fell madly in love with her. After graduation, he asked her to marry him.

She agreed to marry him instantly, but she had to sort out issues with her mean-spirited family first. A few years ago, Aunty Mahina passed away. Kali decided to make the island her permanent home, happy to be away from her bad family. But, issues. Big Brah was still waiting for her to tell him when she'd marry him. Of course, she could be living with us.

Kali had rooms upstairs, alongside Big Brah's. He wanted this to be her home. He wanted her near him all the time. Big Brah would wait forever for Kali, if she wanted him to. Meanwhile Kali's forever love was Big Brah.

Kali spent as much time as she could with Big Brah. She kept her other home in loving memory of Aunty Mahina. It also gave her a place to deal with her belligerent family members. From time to time, they bullied her.

Their disapproval gnawed at Kali's self worth. She wasn't herself. They brought out the worst in her. Kali didn't want Big Brah to see her in this sorry state. This saddened Big Brah. But that evening, he didn't have to wait much longer for her.

Despite the grimness of the investigation, she breezed in cheerfully, same as usual. Lovingly, she hugged Big Brah and then patted the top of my head. We were her family now.

Kali grew solemn. "I worked late on the autopsy to get some answers for the grieving family. I feel so sorry for the Bominos. The little solace I could give them, death was swift, their loved one didn't suffer. I've put that in the preliminary report. It was a direct stab to the heart with a stone dagger. Such a cruel act."

I shivered. Cruel, indeed. *If the Bominos love and care for each other, their suffering may fade with time, but this tragedy will always be part of them,* I thought.

Kali said, "I'm sending lab samples for more tests, the autopsy isn't officially over, but the rest confirmed death occurred due to the stab trauma. I'll do what I can to help find closure for the Bominos. Thank you for taking on this case, Koa. Nothing new from the autopsy, really. I'm sorry."

Big Brah took the autopsy news, stoically. He smiled encouragingly at Kali.

He turned to the cooking range. "Umi and I made progress," he said.

Kali loved her new ohana. But Big Brah and I dealt with trouble constantly. Kali helped us fight trouble. Better, she made sure we stayed out of trouble. Like a goddess, Kali protected us. She had to know everything we did.

Energetically, she headed toward the stairs to go to her rooms upstairs. "After I freshen up, I want a complete report!" she said.

Soon she blew back into the kitchen spiritedly, face scrubbed shiny and black hair slicked back. She was dressed in regular home wear, a well-loved t-shirt, shorts and rubber slippers. Regular home wear or not, she looked absolutely stunning. Poli`ahu and Wiliwili scampered in behind her. They loved to follow her around.

Big Brah smiled at the sight of the three of them, beckoned Kali closer and couldn't resist kissing her. I thumped the table approvingly. Kali's big, brown eyes filled with fun and laughter. She joined me at the round table. The round table had five chairs, so we could all sit together.

Poli`ahu and Wiliwili didn't eat at the table, but they loved to sit on their chairs. For dinner, Big Brah put together a big salad, perfectly roasted red potatoes with caramelized onions and a juicy steak with mushrooms on top and creamy horseradish on the side. For a while there were only the sounds of us eating. No words in deference to the food. It was that good. Total steak-isfaction. After putting the plates away, I filled Kali in on the investigation.

She sat up straight, listening attentively, her strong, sure hands placed palms downward flat on the table. Big Brah sat mostly silent, nodding and making approving uh-huhs every now and then. I told her about the mysterious sand on the cargo bed of the victim's truck. How Loni had dismissed the evidence Big Brah had discovered. Worse, the antics of Antonio Gomez.

I finished, still fuming. "But Antonio Gomez...he's got no aloha!" I said.

"That's a lot of progress." Kali agreed.

Big Brah was listening, choosing to let the conversation develop on its own. Still calm, he looked at Kali.

Kali shrugged. "Koa, the autopsy didn't get us any new clues."

Big Brah smiled. "We'll find the clues."

Kali tried hard not to be surprised by anything he asked or did. "How?" she said.

"The murder weapon, the stone dagger, did you get a chance to examine it?" Big Brah said.

Kali frowned, thoughtfully. "I examined it, yes," she said.

"How good was the workmanship?" he asked.

I wondered where he was going with this.

Kali said, "It's handmade, chiseled and hammered. It has a smooth enough surface, the handle is adequately carved but not intricate, the blade obviously sharp enough to kill."

"Would you say the dagger was made by a professional or a hobbyist?" he said.

Kali thought for a moment. "Could be either."

"That makes it interesting." Big Brah closed his eyes, thinking hard.

Both of us knew better than to ask him what it was he found interesting, while he thought with his eyes closed.

He opened his eyes. "Umi, remember the chisels and hammers Maria Gomez showed us?"

I said, "Yeah, stacked against the lanai wall below the painted flag, so sinister, Kali. If the murder weapon hadn't been a stone dagger, I'd say, Antonio Gomez killed Izor Bomino with one of those sharp, pointy chisels! I wanted to ask Maria Gomez what it was her husband's hobby was, but I could never get around to it, she talked so much...."

Acknowledging Maria Gomez's chattiness, Big Brah nodded and smiled. "Those hammers and chisels are used to cut and shape stone."

"That's it! Antonio Gomez's hobby is to make things out of stone," I said.

Big Brah smiled, approvingly. "He could have made the stone dagger," he said.

Kali clapped. The corners of Big Brah's mouth tilted up. Pleased with the effect he'd just had on us, he got up to get us dessert.

But Maria Gomez had deliberately not told us what her husband's hobby was. Bothered me. *Deception, so close.* I shivered, again. Next to me, Wiliwili, draped on his chair, looked at me with his big, golden eyes.

He stretched out a reassuring white-mittened paw toward me to say, "It's cool, brah."

Poli`ahu jumped onto Kali's lap. Kali hugged Poli`ahu. Big Brah returned to the table with Kali's favorite dessert. Homemade lilikoi ice cream. He scooped out a dollop of the ice cream for Kali. The snow white Poli`ahu settled down on Kali's lap, purring. Kali ate a spoonful of ice cream.

She looked at Big Brah. Her big, brown eyes filled with adoration. "Yum," she said.

The aloha was mana for Big Brah. His thrill was like the thrill of surfing the perfect wave. He scooped me out an extra-large dollop of the ice cream. Lilikoi ice cream was also my favorite. I slurped up the cold, creamy delight fast.

Big Brah instructed Kali. "Tomorrow, Loni's going to find out if there's DNA evidence on the baseball cap found at the crime scene. Can you check in with him, find out the result?"

"Sure can," she said, cheerfully.

He ate some of the dessert. "What do you think we should do next, Umi?" he asked.

I was inspired by the dinner. "There's a definite connection between the murder, the hobby and the stone dagger. But we need more evidence. It's too early to confront Maria and Antonio Gomez. They'll know, we know. He's guilty, he'll run, make our job tougher.

"Better, we continue with the method. Talk story with others the victim knew. His father, his big brother, his church, his coworkers. We keep our senses open. We learn more about the connection."

Approvingly, Big Brah beamed at me. "Good thinking, you make us proud, Umi."

More Mana. I hung loose as I surfed the perfect aloha wave. It was my turn to be thrilled.

He said, "Tomorrow, we go see Papa Bomino at the hospital, then big brother Romo."

Things were warming up. More importantly, we now had a strong suspect who wasn't Ohia. Antonio Gomez. Good. The following morning, I was still feeling warm and fuzzy about the way the investigation was working out. Big Brah and I headed out to the Island Hospital in the big, black truck to see Papa Bomino.

The Island Hospital had provided hope and succor to our island ohana for over seventy-five years. The hospital was there for you, when you needed it the most. Our great grandpa Kahua Waialeale donated the land and the building for the hospital. The hospital still maintained the original quaint building painted yellow and white. Old-timers loved it. Great-gramps Waialeale was wise.

He was aware what we knew about health and healing must improve. To bring about those improvements and to pay for the day-to-day operations of the hospital, he had also set up the generous Island Hospital trust fund. Big Brah and I rode the big, black truck along the hospital's smooth driveway.

It was a misty morning. In the early sun, the expanded hospital building glinted in the distance. The building was an impressive, modern-day glass and steel structure. The garden around us was also tended to with aloha.

Neat lawn. Shade trees. Clean walkways. Convenient park benches. The shade trees caringly shaped to form leafy, protective canopies. A surge of family pride washed over me. I fisted my hand and landed a friendly punch on Big Brah's sinewy upper arm.

Big Brah understood my family pride. He shared it. Smiling, he flexed his biceps. Then he squinted, his eyes on the road. He was still on the job. We left the truck in the parking lot and made our way to the hospital's intensive care unit. We entered the somber waiting area.

The waiting area had recliners, couches and a row of leather-upholstered reception chairs. The walls got a touch of color from paintings of island scenery with monk seals, dolphins and whales. People had come for help. The efficient staff tended to them.

Loved ones, their faces full of concern, waited patiently for the latest update. At the nurses' desk, Big Brah inquired about Papa Bomino. A uniformed nurse with reading glasses perched on her nose answered his query. She naturally assumed we were friends or family. She looked at us over her reading glasses and made an apologetic face.

She spoke in a friendly way. "I'm sorry, Mr. Bomino had a bad night, he's sleeping now, he can't be disturbed.

His son, Romo Bomino was here all night, he just went home to sleep."

Double whammy. Papa Bomino couldn't be disturbed. After a sleepless night, big brother Romo had also gone home to sleep. We couldn't disturb him either. Big Brah thanked the nurse, politely. A little disappointed, I made my way out through the waiting area, Big Brah behind me. Suddenly, he gripped my arm. Wait.

I stopped. Near us, from a leather-upholstered reception chair, a silver-haired woman got up slowly but deliberately. It had to be Big Brah's sixth sense at work.

Sure enough, the silver-haired woman approached us purposefully. She was dressed modestly and in muted colors. A white long-sleeved shirt, gray ankle-length skirt and tan flat-soled sandals. She had something urgent to say. I examined her, curiously.

The wrinkles on her face had settled into the pattern of a permanent beatific smile. Her light brown eyes were sunken in, and there were dark patches under them. She looked tired and in need of sleep.

She came to a stop in front of us. "Aloha, I'm Sister Agatha, Brother Rex and I run the Pono Church."

I knew of her and Brother Rex. Big Brah did too. We had probably seen them around, but we had never met them before. Many island families attended the Pono Church.

Not surprisingly, she said, "The Bomino family belong to our church."

The victim's church. Big Brah would be interested, method and all.

Big Brah bowed his head. "Aloha, I'm Koa Waialeale, this is my brother Umi," he said.

She looked to the left and to the right. She lowered her

voice. "I know you, Big Brah! Lei Bomino told me you're investigating the murder, on behalf of the family. I've spent the night here praying for Papa Bomino, he sleeps now, may the mother goddess bless him. My work here's done."

Big Brah nodded, understanding.

Sister Agatha lowered her voice to a whisper. "About the murder. Brother Rex knows something important. He wants to share it with you himself," she said.

Something important? Well, Big Brah would also like to have a word with Brother Rex.

Swiftly, Big Brah said, "Sure we can talk story, where's Brother Rex?"

Sister Agatha spoke in her normal voice. "That's the problem. You see, Brother Rex, he meditates, he rarely leaves the church campus. But I can take you to him, we're up on Waikahe Hill," she said.

Sometimes the goddess just worked things out. My curiosity was all fired up. Sister Agatha's car was a hatchback. In the big, black truck, Big Brah and I followed the hatchback down the coastal highway.

The sky was gray. It had rained while we were inside the hospital. The air was cooler. The hatchback turned for Waikahe Hill. We followed. The enduring Waikahe River was to our left, its deep waters muddied by the rain.

Soon we drove past Bomino Court. After a while, the road turned steeper, as we drove up the hill. I kept thinking, what does Brother Rex know? The road leveled. A sign by the road placed to help visitors read "The Pono Church."

The campus started on our left. An assorted row of ancient banyans, monkey pods, kukui, royal poinciana and macademia marked the campus boundary. The trees formed a natural fence, blending with the tropical wilderness. We followed the hatchback another half mile, and then we entered a private driveway.

The driveway zigzagged through tall trees. Big campus. The truck's windows were down. The sound of the rushing waters of the Waikahe river here was clear and near. We passed a covered courtyard. Colorful streamers hung from the ceiling. Long tables and benches crowded the floor. No doubt the place for the Sunday potluck brunch. We reached a grassy slope.

To my right, there was a wide platform. The platform was made of black stone. The wide black stone platform had pillars reaching up toward the sky. The pillars made it easy to put the canopy up on a rainy day. The platform was the place to pray. Ahead, the Waikahe River fell in a frothy, white torrent, as the river roared down a steep part of the hillside. The driveway curved.

We drove alongside the river. Here the river flowed, undisturbed and pristine. The river bed was full of pebbles and rocks, small and big, white, black and gray, the water so clear. Pure nature. A lone home appeared in front of us.

The quaint home had a flower garden in the front. On the lanai, facing us, a man with a white beard sat in a wheelchair. He had a book open on his lap. It had to be Brother Rex. After we parked and got out of our cars, Sister Agatha joined us.

She must have seen me look wondrously at all the nature around us. "The river flows throughout the length of the campus, it disappears down a series of cascading waterfalls at the eastern end. The goddess has given us a beautiful island," she said.

"Indeed." Big Brah agreed.

I inhaled the fresh air. Out here, in the open, I detected a slight off-island accent in Sister Agatha's speech. No matter. The island had always been a sanctuary. People from all over the world were drawn here in their quest for inner peace. Big Brah said all who came here to live in aloha belonged to our island ohana.

Sister Agatha started walking toward the lanai. "Come, Brother Rex will be pleased to see you," she said.

We followed her up the three short steps to the lanai. Brother Rex set down his reading glasses on the open book and looked up at us.

He regarded Big Brah and me with soft, blue eyes. "Koa! Umi! Sister Agatha, I can't thank you enough for bringing them to me!" he said.

Sister Agatha stood by his wheelchair and looked lovingly down at him. "You bet," she said, softly.

The lanai had outdoor chairs and a table. Sister Agatha gestured for us to sit. Big Brah and I wanted to be near Brother Rex. We pulled up a couple of chairs and sat down.

"You get started, I'll be right back," she said.

She entered the home through the front door. After she left, there was a brief silence. Brother Rex was moved seeing us.

When he spoke, there was a tremble in his voice. "I knew your parents, your grandparents, they were good people, the accident was such a tragedy. I always tell my parishioners your story, how courageously the two of you've overcome adversity, you're an inspiration to us all!" he said.

Well, I got my courage from Big Brah. He was one of a kind. He made all of us Waialeales look good. Big Brah smiled and bowed his head modestly. Brother Rex remembered something else. He also smiled.

He said, "I even knew your great grandfather, Kahua Waialale. I remember the first time I met him. I was a little boy, fresh from the mainland, new on the island, unused to its ways. I was in grade school, and our entire school was invited to the opening of the Island Hospital. Kahua Waialeale was there. He was a lot like you, Koa! Big, strong, a whirlwind of energy and good humor, a true leader! I was shy, the other boys wouldn't stop teasing me.

"I didn't know how to eat the pork laulau. I was hungry, I struggled to open up the weird, inedible ti-leaf wrapper, I was embarrassed, my ears burned.... Fortunately for me, great Kahua was there.

"Your great gramps was busy talking to all the important grown-ups who'd been invited. He kept talking to them, but as he strolled past me, he kindly stopped to open the wrapper, good-humoredly mimed me how to eat the laulau, patiently waited to make sure I ate it properly. The pork flavored by the taro leaf it's cooked in, I'd never tasted anything like it in Indiana or Kansas or New York.

"I loved the laulau instantly. Great Kahua nodded approvingly, patted my head affectionately and left, all without a word being spoken by either of us. But his aloha, his compassion touched me, I got such a boost of confidence and courage, great Kahua made the island feel like home for me. I grew up, I made the island my home. I've loved the pork laulau ever since, it's my favorite dish!" he said.

The front door opened. Sister Agatha stepped onto the lanai with a plateful of scrumptious looking scones.

She set the plate down on the table. "Help yourselves!" she said.

Big Brah leaned to his side, took a scone and ate a bite.

"These are good!" he said.

Sister Agatha smiled. "Yes, they're lovely. When I was young, I was homesick, I used to crave these scones. I'd just come to the island from Britain," she said.

Britain. That explained her faint off-island accent.

She said, "I was learning to surf from my friend, Leilani. I told her about the scones. She was so sweet, she learnt how to make them, she baked them for me.

"I've never tasted better scones, I've never been homesick again. It's been years, Leilani married, had children, grandchildren. What a joy it was to babysit each one of the kids! My dear friend Leilani still bakes me these scones, bless her heart!"

Obviously, Sister Agatha had come to the island to live in aloha. She belonged to our ohana. She left us again only to return with an exquisite, well-loved porcelain tea set on a tray.

She put the tray down on the table. "A couple more minutes for the tea to steep," she said.

She sat down, folded her hands neatly on her lap and looked expectantly at Brother Rex. Brother Rex lifted his reading glasses to close the book on his lap and placed the glasses on top of the closed book. He was getting ready to tell us the important thing he knew about the murder.

He said, "I wanted to see you as soon as I heard you were investigating the murder. I knew Izor well. He always trusted me, spoke with me. I know he dropped out of college to get married, he got into trouble in his business, but I never thought he'd end this way."

Listening intently, I reached for a scone. All this about Izor we had learned from Lei Bomino and Maria Gomez as well.

Brother Rex said, "But lately Izor was coming around,

he had a new energy, a new sense of purpose. He told me he'd uncovered the source of his troubles, he couldn't decide what to do about it, he was torn."

New energy, new sense of purpose, torn? These were new. The scone nearly stuck in my throat. I gulped it down hastily.

Brother Rex said, "I tried to help Izor, what I could, but he wouldn't tell me what it was he had uncovered, who or what it was that was the source of his troubles. Not knowing frustrated me. I pressed him hard to confide in me, but he was adamant. Papa Bomino, big brother Romo, Izor, Ohia, the stubborn streak runs in the men of the family, I didn't know what more to do."

Sister Agatha sighed. She lifted the tea cozy off the teapot, set the cozy aside and poured the rich brew into the cups. "You did everything you could. It's terrible, Izor's life snuffed out, so cruelly...."

Brother Rex said, "I wish I'd tried harder."

"You did your best," she said.

Brother Rex said, "Perhaps if I'd uncovered the source of his troubles, even a hint of what it was, was it a thing or a person, at home or at work, or did he think it was something deep inside him...perhaps Izor would still be alive!"

"The goddess works in mysterious ways," she said.

Mysterious, indeed. For example, despite the situation, the scones tasted strangely good, and the brew was perfect.

Brother Rex folded his hands wrinkled with age and service. "I feel bad, I feel responsible, I had to tell you this about Izor...hope this helps you in your investigation," he said.

Agreeing, Sister Agatha nodded. With sudden

vehemence she added, "We want you to bring the killer to justice!"

Bring the killer to justice. All of us felt strongly about justice.

Big Brah had listened wordlessly. "I can imagine how you feel," he said.

We thanked the couple and headed out. On the drive back to the coastal highway, Big Brah was thoughtful. Somehow the peaceful surroundings of the church had quietened me. I sat silent, enthused by what we had learned.

Brother Rex had known something important. The victim's state of mind just before the murder. Izor Bomino had found the source of his troubles right before his untimely death. He had developed a new energy and a new sense of purpose, but he was torn. It raised an even more important question.

Who or what could be the source of Izor's troubles? Big Brah proposed we visit Izor Bomino's business. Sounded like a good place to start looking for Izor's troubles. Big Brah was like a boy scout, always prepared.

He had already researched the business. Sometimes Big Brah never slept. Izor Bomino's high-end lumber business supplied costly hardwoods to upscale developers. Izor had a sales office downtown. The lumber yard was at a different location. The sales office was closer. Big Brah decided to start with the sales office.

Back on the coastal highway, we drove south to the island's delightful little downtown, our destination Global Quality Lumber's sales office. The sun was behind dark clouds. You couldn't tell the time of day.

The truck's dashboard clock showed noon. The streets here were lined with plumeria trees. Their branches bare, the trees waited silently for summer and yellow, white and pink fragrant flowers. The storefronts were as unique as the stuffs they were selling.

Art gallery. Tattoo shop. Island wear. Food, or as we call it on the island, grinds. Pet shop. Global Quality Lumber's sales office was an undefinable single-story building. The small parking lot in the front had a single car. A good-looking red sedan.

The sedan had a red on white "I ♥ my ohana" sticker on its chrome bumper. Heartwarming. We parked next to the red car. The neat red tile roof had weathered many storms, its color faded. The clean white paint on the sidewalls had cracked and yellowed with time. The display window had venetian blinds. The slats were tilted closed. The inside wasn't visible. But the wood door was solid and the "We're Open" sign on it encouraging.

As we entered the office, the door chime echoed hollowly in the big, empty room. The strong citrus scent of an air freshener did little to dispense the musty odor that permeated the surroundings. The office had been closed up for more than a day. Ceiling lighting illuminated the place. The hardwood floor had area rugs. At the back, there was a closed door to the rest of the office. A glass cabinet occupied the entire wall to my right. I was drawn to the display cabinet.

On the island, we loved our surfboards. The glass cabinet had models of footlong surfboards with labels showcasing different kinds of local tropical lumber. Koa, monkey pod, ohia, kiawe, mango, ironwood, kamani, tamarind, sandalwood and others. Interesting. The sitting area in the middle had inviting low sofas, chairs and a glass-topped center table.

The base of the center table was a marvel. The wooden

base was in the shape of a monk seal. The monk seal was skillfully carved complete with whiskers, fore flippers and hind flippers. On the island, we loved our monk seals even more. There was a neat stack of metal filing cabinets against the left wall.

Place to store the paperwork. Nice office Izor had. He wouldn't be back in his office ever again. Cruel. The door at the back opened.

A man with short, black hair entered the room. He was dressed formally in a sky-blue shirt, navy blue trousers and black work shoes.

He smiled, pleasantly. "My name is Keanu, how can I help you?" he said.

Big Brah told him our business. Keanu's smile vanished like the sun had behind dark clouds outside.

Keanu looked nervous. "I'm just an intern here, I don't know much…." He gestured toward the door at the back. "Our individual offices are back there, mine's the office next to the rec room.

"On the morning of the murder, I was hard at work in my office. I was thinking, the boss is late, and he's never late, strange. Aunty Julie, she's worked here for ways longer, she'd called in sick, you know, the flu, so I was alone. I heard the door chime, someone came into the front office.

"Thinking it must be the boss or a customer, I came out to look. It was a cop instead. He didn't look like a cop, he wasn't in uniform or anything. His name was Loni. He had a thick mustache, he looked sour. He was looking for Ohia Bomino. I was shook.

"I told Loni, Ohia didn't work with his father. From the family tidbits the boss threw at me, I'd heard Ohia was personnel manager at the famous Aloalo Resort." He stopped unsure of the effect he was having on us.

Aloalo, Hawaiian for hibiscus. I loved the flower.

Big Brah nodded, approvingly. "The Aloalo Resort. Everyone knows the resort, we're all proud of it," he said.

Emboldened by Big Brah's approval, Keanu said, "I told Loni about Ohia. Loni was about to leave, when I remembered to ask him, what it was about. Loni told me, the matter was confidential, he couldn't tell me now, he had to see Ohia first. I thought Loni wanted to see Ohia about some personnel problem at the resort. Police trouble, maybe.

"An hour later, Loni calls me, tells me the boss is dead, murdered, and just like that, he hangs up. I didn't know what to do. I wished Aunty Julie was here, she knows everything, she'd know what to do. But she sounded terrible when she'd called in.

"I panicked. I didn't know if I still had a job or anything. I put up the closed sign, locked up and left." Shaking his head at the memory, Keanu paused.

Big Brah could tell where on the island you were from just by how you spoke. Softly, he said, "You live east side, but you've also lived on the west side, haven't you?"

Keanu started. "Yes, I-I used to live on the west side, long time back, not any more. I live in Aunty Lena's hostel now, you know who she is?"

Everyone knew Aunty Lena. Aunty Lena loved ohana, but she had no known relatives. Aunty Lena ran a hostel. She welcomed young men and women who needed a home. She provided them with boarding, nourishment and special Aunty Lena nurturing. They were her relatives. They were her ohana.

Big Brah nodded. "I know Aunty Lena," he said.

Keanu said, "Aunty Lena's shocked."

Knowing Aunty Lena, I figured she would be shocked. She was a feisty woman. She burned whenever she heard of any injustice anywhere in the world. The island was her first love, and this happened on her island.

Keanu said, "She can't believe something so violent happened on our peaceful island."

"That sounds like Aunty Lena," Big Brah said.

Keanu said, "Aunty Lena got me this job. She knows Aunty Julie. On the morning of the murder, when I got back to the hostel, Aunty Lena saw me back from work so early, she was surprised. She was getting ready to scold me to get back to work. I told her about all this. She had me pray. The entire day, I spent like that, praying with her."

Aunty Lena cared deeply for her ohana. The young men and women in her ohana came from troubled backgrounds. She believed they needed more chances to learn from their mistakes. They would grow up right, given a second chance. Her kindness kept her full of hope. What had troubled Keanu?

Keanu said, "Then Mrs. Bomino called us last evening. She told me, she'd be looking after the business, we'd be fine. We had to remain open for our clients, so here I am, carrying on as usual."

Big Brah nodded, sympathetic.

Keanu grew self-conscious. He gestured toward the sitting area. "Where are my manners? Please, sit down," he said.

We all sat down. Keanu fidgeted. He adjusted his sky-blue shirt's collar. He tugged at the ends of the shirt's short sleeves. He smoothed down the front of his shirt, where no such thing was required.

Big Brah must have sensed Keanu's discomfort. "What

makes you nervous?" he asked, pleasantly.

"Oh, it's nothing. Aunty Julie is still out sick, she knows a lot more about the business than I do. I've been working here only a few months. But it's weird to be in the office and not have Mr. Bomino around. He was always here."

"He was always here, but the business wasn't going so well lately," Big Brah said.

"Oh, I know nothing about it," Keanu said, quickly.

Too quickly. No doubt he did know something. How was Big Brah going to get the information out of him? Gently, of course. Big Brah got up. He ambled over to the metal cabinets stacked against the wall.

He tapped on the metal cabinet nearest him. "Tell me, are all the business records filed away in these?"

Keanu leaped up from his chair. He strode toward Big Brah, purposefully. "You can't touch those papers, even the cops can't touch those papers without a warrant!"

Whatever Keanu knew about the business and was hiding from us had to be in those files.

Big Brah must have realized that too. He made a soothing motion with his hands. "You're right," he said.

Keanu didn't say anything, but he was still nervous. Fidgeting, he waited for Big Brah to sit down again. Big Brah strode back to his chair. Keanu also returned.

Big Brah settled himself, calm as ever. "It's important I know what kind of trouble your employer was in at the time of his death. Now, I'm working on behalf of the Bomino family, I can always ask Mrs. Bomino, she'll be happy to grant me permission to search every file."

Keanu sank back in his chair. A sullen look came over him. "Go ahead then, call Mrs. Bomino. If she instructs me to show you the files, I will," he said.

"But I don't know what I'd be looking for. On the other hand, it's clear to me you already know what it is, and which file to look for," Big Brah said.

Keanu said, "I don't know what you're talking about."

"I'll tell you what I'm talking about. If I ask Mrs. Bomino, she'll instruct you to tell me all anyway," Big Brah said.

Keanu gulped, nervous.

Persuasively, Big Brah said, "Save me the effort of calling her."

Keanu still didn't say anything.

Big Brah said, "I don't even need to see a file, just tell me."

Keanu was in great pain. He scrunched up his face. He was close to giving in.

Big Brah said, "Why do you want me to call her while she's grieving?"

"But I promised Mr. Bomino I'd never tell anyone, and he's dead, what am I to do?" Keanu said.

Big Brah reasoned with him. "I'm trying to find the person who killed Mr. Bomino."

"I only work here!" Keanu said.

"If Mr. Bomino could speak now, he'd want me to know," Big Brah said.

Keanu curled up and clutched his head with both hands. "Okay, okay, I'll tell you what you want to know."

Chapter 6: Dump Trucks, Cranes and Mixers

Always patient, Big Brah sat back and waited for the truth.

Slowly, Keanu let go his head and straightened up. "This is about one of our biggest clients, a big-name developer," he said.

There were many developers on the island.

"You know, the big-name developer who built the Aloalo Resort?"

I leaned forward.

"Bo Digalo," Keanu said.

Bo Digalo was indeed the big-name developer for the Aloalo Resort. The most expensive and popular resort on the island. The Aloalo Resort had been Digalo's first project. Powered by the success of Aloalo, Digalo had been in business for close to three decades. I looked at Big Brah. He was nodding already.

Big Brah said, "I've not met Mr. Digalo, but I know who he is."

Keanu spoke slowly but clearly. "It happened only last week. Mr. Bomino had instructed me to organize the files. I was going through them, I came to the file on Digalo Construction. In the file, I found a recent letter, it was from Mr. Digalo himself.

"In the letter, Mr. Digalo accused Global Quality

Lumber of supplying him cheap lumber, but charging him for high quality expensive hardwood, in other words, cheating! I was surprised, I took the letter to Mr. Bomino. He knew.

"Mr. Bomino made me promise I wouldn't talk to anyone about it, you know how fast word spreads on the island, and I agreed. He told me he was concerned, and he was taking care of the trouble. He made me file the letter away. That's all I know, believe me."

Big Brah and I exchanged glances. Could we believe Keanu?

Nervously, Keanu looked from Big Brah to me, then back at Big Brah, again. "You believe me, don't you?"

Neither Big Brah nor I said anything.

Keanu licked his lips, still nervous. "I'm telling you, I don't know anything else. Verify it in anyway you like."

Keanu had refused to tell us about the letter, initially. But then, Keanu was being loyal to his employer. Both Big Brah and I knew something about loyalty. My instinct nudged me to believe Keanu. Someone who could verify Keanu's story came to mind.

I spoke up. "Aunty Julie should know all this, shouldn't she?"

Big Brah looked over at me. He nodded, approvingly. Both of us turned to Keanu.

"That's right! Aunty Julie was in the room the entire time!" Keanu said.

I looked at Big Brah. Time to raise the serenity factor in the room. Time to put Keanu at ease.

Big Brah said, "When is Aunty Julie expected back in the office?"

Keanu said, "She'll be back tomorrow. Aunty Julie and the boss go a long way back, you must see her."

Reassuringly, Big Brah said, "Sure, I'll see Aunty Julie, tomorrow."

The serenity factor in the room rose. The long-gone, sunny smile returned on Keanu's face. "See, I knew you guys would figure things out, you're detectives."

Big Brah smiled, amused.

Keanu was remorseful. His sunny smile wavered. "I should've told you all from the beginning," he said.

Big Brah's easy smile widened. "Keanu, mahalo for telling us everything," he said, all sincere.

Keanu sprang up, obviously eager to end the conversation. Waiting for us to leave, he adjusted his shirt collar and smoothed down the front of his shirt, nervous again. Whatever was making him nervous, Big Brah and I couldn't do any more about it. Outside, the sky was still dark, but it wasn't raining. Big Brah and I got into the big truck. We had filled up on the scones earlier. We didn't need lunch.

He said, "We're already downtown, Digalo Construction's office is close by, let's go see Digalo."

Digalo's office was just a few blocks away. On the short drive over, Big Brah was silent, and I was thoughtful. We were going to meet Digalo. Big Brah must have taken Keanu's story seriously. And, why not?

Izor had confided he had uncovered the source of his troubles to Brother Rex. Brother Rex regretted not learning what the source or the trouble was. Then, referring to Digalo's accusation of cheating, Izor had told Keanu he was taking care of the trouble. So, the source of Izor's troubles could be Digalo, no? From outside, Digalo's office looked showier compared to Izor's.

The parking lot was much bigger, with many more vehicles entering, exiting or parked. The office building was a solid, two-story structure. The building was stamped and claimed with a large, fancy wall sign displaying "Digalo Construction" and a slogan, "Proud to Serve the Island." A shiny revolving glass door beckoned.

Two men in hard hats entered the building through the revolving door. Big Brah and I followed. The reception area was cool, big and bright. A sharply-dressed receptionist behind an L-shaped desk had her eyes on a screen. The two men in hard hats passed her desk, talking intensely about their project.

The receptionist didn't look at them. The two men were regulars here. Silently, Big Brah and I approached her.

She turned to look at us, promptly. "How can I help you?"

Big Brah slid her a business card over the desk. "I'm investigating the murder of Izor Bomino, I want to speak with Mr. Digalo about it," he said.

She glanced at the card. Her eyes widened. She nodded quickly, and then disappeared into the inner office. Soon she returned, followed closely by a big man. Big Brah thanked the receptionist. Relieved, she went back to her screen. The big man was dressed formally in a shirt and tie and trousers with suspenders.

The big man had thinning hair combed over carefully. He had a pudgy, round face and a prominent nose. His mustache was neatly trimmed. He moved his bulk energetically around the front desk. His big shoulders, arms and legs all moved, and his big belly jiggled.

He stretched his hand out, a big grin playing on his round face. "Big Brah, it's a pleasure to finally make your acquaintance, I'm Bo Digalo," he said.

Big Brah shook hands, quietly.

Bo Digalo turned and proffered me a hand as well. "You must be Umi, I've seen you brahs in the news!"

His hand was soft for someone in construction. He ushered us into his big private office. My feet sank into the plush carpet. A trendy chandelier and a wide bay window brightened the room. The spotless window framed a view of the familiar mist-topped green mountains. Digalo had us sit down in comfortable chairs at a large desk.

On the wall behind the desk, a huge framed photograph was prominently placed. A young, lean and long-haired Bo Digalo and the island's beloved mayor of the time waved at the camera. Grinning big, both of them were swathed in leis and good cheer. It was the grand opening ceremony of the Aloalo Resort. The desk had replicas of construction machines.

Dump trucks, cranes, mixers, you name it, you got it. Delightful. Next to the toys, there were plans, prints, drawings and a new construction tablet. Business was booming. Digalo retreated behind his desk, settled down in his executive chair and rocked back and forth.

The grin was still on his face. "You say you're here to investigate the murder, but why have you come to me?" he said.

"You may know something important about Izor Bomino, you did business with him," Big Brah said.

"I did, I did do business with him, for a long time. I'm really sorry the man had to go like this, but I know nothing about the murder," Digalo said.

"You had issues with Mr. Bomino," Big Brah said.

The grin on Digalo's face threatened to fade. "No, not really, just regular business stuff, no big trouble," he said.

Big Brah said, "You were having trouble with the lumber Mr. Bomino supplied you."

Digalo's grin got totally wiped out. He squirmed in his chair. "But that's business confidential information, how did you get it?" he said.

Patiently, Big Brah said, "I'm investigating this case on behalf of the Bomino family, Izor Bomino's affairs are now my concern."

Digalo resumed rocking. "Of course, of course, I'm not thinking right, thanks for telling me. Sorry I wasn't forthcoming right away. I'd rather not be associated with murder in any way. I was merely protecting myself. Murder isn't good for business. Hope you understand."

"I understand, but you wrote to him only last week," Big Brah said.

"I did, what about it?"

"You accused him of cheating," Big Brah said.

Digalo bristled. "I didn't just accuse him, I told him he cheated, because he did! I wanted my money back! My workers installed the inferior wood, they put in many hours, but they had to tear down their work. A total waste of time and money. I have an irate client threatening to sue me. This was big trouble, yes."

"Yes, big trouble," Big Brah said.

Digalo waved a hand at us. "But not big enough to kill a man!" he said.

"No?"

Digalo waved both hands frantically. "Never. I'd never do such a thing." He put a hand on his chest. "My whole life, I've served the island and its people. Taking a life, no, that's not me, besides...."

"Besides?"

Digalo sighed, heavily. "Besides, I have troubles of my own. My wife, I loved her, this week, she left me. She left me with only a note stuck to the refrigerator, no explanations. I was clueless, I thought she was the love of my life. I was gullible." He put a big hand on his chest over his heart. "It hurts inside, but I show it to no one." He paused for effect.

Compassionately, Big Brah nodded.

"I'm mourning. I don't want anything to do with this murder."

"I understand," Big Brah said.

"You know what I do when it hurts this bad inside? I work harder. I work harder to serve the island and its people, that's the kind of person I really am!"

"Noble, very noble." Big Brah agreed.

Satisfied Big Brah saw the hurt inside, Digalo softened. His grin returned. "I can help you," he said.

"I'd appreciate any help," Big Brah said.

Digalo leaned forward. He lowered his voice. "I know the murderer," he said.

Startled, I nearly fell off my comfortable chair.

Chapter 7: The Lumber Yard

Big Brah regarded Digalo, silently. I was at the edge of my comfortable chair.

"He's Izor's ex-employee, very disgruntled. You may have heard of him, I don't know?"

Big Brah shook his head.

A disgruntled ex-employee. Didn't sound too promising. I settled back in my chair.

But Digalo provided a stronger motive. "Izor didn't just cheat me, he cheated this fellow. I'm not, but this buggah may be…revengeful."

Say, what? Revenge got my attention.

Digalo said, "He's in construction now, he subcontracts, my contractors hire him, I meet him often. In front of me, in front of others, he's sworn to kill Izor many, many times. I'm sure he's the murderer."

Well, then. I was back on the edge of my chair.

Digalo was triumphant. He raised his voice. "You want to know who the murderer is?"

Big Brah nodded.

Digalo almost shouted. "Yo Bipo!"

The name didn't ring a bell. But Big Brah would want to meet Bipo. Big Brah thanked Digalo, and we left. Outside, daylight had faded, and the lights in the parking lot had turned on. I was slow getting back into the big truck, thinking. Yo Bipo. He had sworn publicly to kill Izor.

I was curious to learn Bipo's story. "Like Digalo, Bipo's also in construction, he's bound to have an office around."

Big Brah shook his head. "We'll be back downtown tomorrow to meet with Aunty Julie, we'll see Bipo then. The baseball cap found at the crime scene, if Loni finds DNA on the cap, it's going to be interesting. Kali will have talked to Loni about it, she'll have the news. Right now, I need Kali."

Big Brah needed Kali, always.

"Let's go home, I'm hungry," he said.

The thought of food made my patient stomach growl politely. I was starving. A surprise waited for us at home. Kali was already there. I should have known. Miraculously, when Big Brah needed her the most, Kali was always there. She swung the front door open for us, a radiant smile on her pretty face. She had her cooking apron on.

She took one look at our faces and said, "I knew you'd be working and hungry, so I finished work early and came over. I've made your favorite ahi poke, with spicy mustard, as you like it, am taking suggestions for sides."

"Steamed rice," I said. "Salad," Big Brah said.

"Good, you can tell me about your day over dinner," she said.

It was good to be home. The evening was dark outside. The lights made the kitchen cozy. We gathered at the round table. Kali's spicy ahi poke was out of the world awesome. Each creamy forkful of the fish packed flavor. I filled her in on the day's happenings.

Kali listened attentively.

I said, "We didn't find anything more about Antonio Gomez's feud with Izor Bomino, but that doesn't mean anything. Gomez is still a suspect. We didn't get to meet

Papa Bomino and big brother Romo either, but we'll keep trying.

"From Brother Rex and Sister Agatha, we learned Izor had found out the source of his troubles, but Izor was torn, he didn't know what to do about it. Izor knew something that was trouble for someone else, so his murder wasn't a random accident. We tried to track down the source of his troubles, and we got more suspects.

"Bo Digalo. Izor cheated him, Digalo demanded his money back. Moreover, Digalo's wife left him this week, the event could have triggered something in him, people do crazy things during such emotional times.

"But Digalo denies any knowledge of the murder. Instead, Digalo believes Bipo murdered Izor. Digalo could be deflecting suspicion away from himself, we'll know more, when we meet Bipo, tomorrow. Keanu...him, I don't know if he's a suspect.

"But something about the murder's making Keanu nervous. I'll make up my mind on Keanu later. We'll meet with Aunty Julie tomorrow, let's see what she has to say."

Kali said, "I know Aunty Julie through Aunty Lena. Aunty Julie is a no-nonsense woman."

Big Brah nodded approvingly at me. "I think you've nailed the investigation so far." He looked at Kali. "About the baseball cap found at the crime scene, did you get a chance to contact Loni?" he said.

She set her fork down and looked solemnly at us. "I didn't have to contact Loni, he dropped by my office to discuss the cap. He has a viable DNA sample from it."

Big Brah had told me, if Loni found any DNA, things would turn interesting. I listened.

Kali said, "Loni wants Ohia to volunteer his DNA sample, so the analyst can try for a match."

I shivered. I should have seen this coming.

Kali said, "Now, it's a difficult situation. Loni's sure if he asks Ohia to volunteer his DNA, Ohia is going to say no."

Likely. I nodded. Big Brah listened.

Kali said, "So, Loni wants your help."

Didn't he always? I grinned. Big Brah smiled. And Big Brah always helped.

Kali was very protective of Big Brah. She sighed. "Koa, this time, I warn you, you don't have to do what Loni wants."

Big Brah smiled bigger. "Fear not, dear Kali, tell me," he said.

"Loni wants you to persuade Ohia to volunteer his DNA," she said.

I gasped. The audacity. *Really now, Loni.*

Big Brah shook his head, chuckling. "If there's no match, Ohia walks free. If there's a match, I catch the killer. Let me guess, Loni thinks it's a win-win situation for me."

Kali's eyes widened in admiration. "Those were Loni's exact words," she said.

I knew it. Big Brah could handle Loni, anytime, anywhere. Big Brah and Kali gazed at each other for a long while.

I took the opportunity to register my opinion. "I think it's too early, we've got other suspects," I said.

Both Kali and Big Brah turned to look at me. Big Brah nodded. "Yes, it's early, but that isn't the only problem. The bigger problem is Ohia hasn't told us the truth. On the morning of the murder, after meeting with his father, it took him 50 minutes to get home. The same drive took us just 15 minutes."

I said, "The first thing Ohia should volunteer is the truth."

Big Brah looked at Kali. "Tell Loni, I want to help him, but I have to see Ohia first, then I'll decide how to help."

We were going to help Loni. But, how? All three of us exchanged thoughtful glances. Soon, Kali left. The following morning, Big Brah and I returned to the kitchen table. Clouds concealed the sun outside.

Muted daylight streamed in through the kitchen's tall windows. The incoming air was cool and refreshing. We finished a nourishing breakfast. I was curious to learn how we were to help Loni.

Big Brah answered the question. "Let's get the truth out of Ohia," he said.

I heaved a deep breath. "How?"

"Surprise him."

I nodded, vigorously. "Solid technique. If you want the truth from people, don't give them time to think up lies," I said.

"We're detectives, Umi, we search for the truth, always."

"But, how do we surprise Ohia?" I asked.

Big Brah chuckled. "Uncle Maka," he said.

Uncle Maka had the buzz about everything on the island. For as long as I remembered, he had always had a head of white hair and a kind smile. He was Aunty Lena's boyfriend, so Big Brah and I knew him, loved him. Uncle Maka was also the concierge at the Aloalo Resort.

He had worked there since the resort opened. He knew the resort better than the island. Big Brah called Uncle Maka about Ohia. The murder was the biggest buzz on the island. Uncle Maka was most willing to assist.

Ohia hadn't worked yesterday, bereavement, and he

would be taking the next few days off. But today, Ohia had come in to take care of a few things. He was at work. Big Brah took directions to Ohia's office. He thanked Uncle Maka, told him I owe you one and hung up. He didn't bother warning Uncle Maka not to tell anyone about the call. Big Brah trusted Uncle Maka's discretion.

Big Brah and I drove to the resort, our goal to surprise Ohia and get the truth out of him. A light rain had started, the visibility low. The Aloalo resort was a sprawling architectural marvel on a hillside overlooking the gorgeous Honu Bay. The misty rain hid the bay from view. The resort's gardens were landscaped, lush and chock-full of perennial blooms.

The resort had every amenity, swimming pool, spa, boutique, restaurants, gym, everything. We parked at the back. Ohia's office was in a separate building behind the main structure. The office door had his name on it and below it his designation. Personnel Manager. Big Brah knocked, and as soon as we heard a "Come in," we entered. Ohia was at his desk, doing paperwork. He looked up. Curly hair. Sharp nose. Jutting chin.

Ohia frowned, surprised. "What're you doing here?" he asked.

Big Brah said, "Loni's analyst has extracted DNA from the cap found at the crime scene, Loni wants you to volunteer a DNA sample."

Ohia rose from his chair. He looked bewildered. "What does that even mean, a DNA sample?"

"It means an analyst will collect a sample of DNA from you. They have their means, a cotton swab in your mouth, a prick of your blood, or even strands of your hair will do, it depends on the preference of the analyst."

Ohia sank back into his chair. He planted his elbows

on the tabletop and held his head with both hands. "Oh, what am I going to do?" he said.

Sternly, Big Brah said, "Start by telling us the truth."

Ohia looked at Big Brah, startled. "Why're you talking to me like that?" he said.

"Because you're running out of time. If you volunteer the DNA and there's a match, the cap is yours, the police have a solid case against you. If you refuse to volunteer, Loni only suspects you more. Either way, you're in trouble," Big Brah said.

Ohia said, "You're supposed to keep me out of trouble."

"I will, but I need to know the truth about what happened the morning of the murder," Big Brah said.

"I already told you what happened. Dad and I had a great meeting. We parted friends. I only wish I hadn't left him, just stayed with him a while longer...I could've saved him. If I was there when the killer showed up, I'd do anything to protect Dad! If only I'd been a little less selfish.

"I was just so happy at getting my way, and Dad, as usual, giving, letting me have my way, letting me start my own business, getting on with my life with Kela, I had it all. I was happy. I rushed away to share the news. Now, I don't have him. I wish I could've saved him, that's all."

"No, that's not all, for example, you're not telling us who you rushed away to share the news with," Big Brah said.

It's got to be Kela, I thought. A man has to share such news with his woman.

Ohia said, "I don't talk to Mom about money matters, always Dad, so I didn't speak to her about it when I got home. I was going to take Kela out to dinner, break the news to her in a celebration after work. Didn't happen. I didn't get to share the news with Kela at all that day, Loni showed up here with the awful news."

"It took you 50 minutes to get back home, the same drive took me 15," Big Brah said.

"Oh." Ohia trembled. He covered his face with his hands.

At last, his hands slid off his face. "I should've known you'd figure it out…okay, I'll tell you what really happened."

Big Brah waited, patiently. I watched, intrigued.

Ohia looked remorseful. "I'm sorry, I can explain. First of all, you have to understand a few things about my family. Mom, Dad, me, Uncle Romo and Papa Bomino, we're all like one family, even if we don't live together. We love each other. Second, we all love our privacy.

"We don't like anyone prying into our lives, so of course this murder is like the worst thing that could've happened to us. Finally, for me, Uncle Romo isn't just Dad's big brother, he's always been like a second father to me.

"Uncle advised me to ask for my inheritance, so I could start my own business. When Dad and I were arguing over my inheritance, Uncle tried to convince Dad to give me my share. My dad listened to Uncle, after all, Uncle was his big brother. Uncle even arranged my meeting with Dad that morning. So, naturally, after meeting with Dad, first I went to Bomino Court to tell Uncle the good news.

"You're right, I did share the news, it was with Uncle that I did. It took me about 15 minutes to get to Bomino Court, try it, confirm it yourself, if you like. Uncle was home, he was eager to find out how it went, I told him the good news. I spent about 15-20 minutes with him, and about the same time to drive back home to Mom. There, that should account for the 50 minutes."

"You could have told us this the first time around and saved us all the time," Big Brah said.

"Yes, I should have told you the first time, I regret it. But I didn't want the police or you to disturb Uncle. With Dad gone, Uncle's taking care of Papa Bomino, all of us. Obviously, Uncle couldn't have killed Dad. Uncle was waiting for me in Bomino Court the entire time I was meeting with Dad.

"He'd needlessly be asked questions, his privacy ruined. I wanted to save him from all of that. I couldn't save Dad, but, at least, I can save Uncle." Ohia was close to tears.

Big Brah sighed. "You did good to protect your ohana, I would too. But remember I'm on your side, I'm working on behalf of all of you, don't hide anything from me, okay?" he said.

Tears rolled down Ohia's cheeks. He just shook his head. "What do I do about the DNA sample?" he said.

Big Brah went around the desk and placed a hand on Ohia's shoulder in support. "Tell Loni you're willing to volunteer the sample. If it isn't your cap, there will be no match, and Loni will stop suspecting you. You've got nothing to fear."

Ohia tried to smile through his tears. "I'm glad Mom hired you, Big Brah," he said.

"I'm glad I can help," Big Brah said.

I was happy for Ohia. Big Brah had asked Ohia to volunteer a sample of his DNA. Ohia would soon cease to be a suspect, officially. Excellent. Outside, a rainy mist enveloped Honu Bay.

I loved to see the bay's cheery blue expanse on a sunny day. The memory of the sparkling waters warmed my heart, as Big Brah drove the big truck out of the resort in silence. I reflected on Ohia.

After meeting with his father, Ohia had driven to Bomino Court and seen his uncle. Ohia was an alibi for big brother Romo. A bonus. True, big brother Romo had never been on my suspect list. With an awesome big brother like mine, I just couldn't suspect big brothers. Why it took Ohia 50 instead of 15 minutes to get back home was also explained. Good. Big Brah was protecting the Bomino family honor.

It was best if both Ohia and his uncle were innocent without a doubt. Of course, Big Brah would still have to meet big brother Romo, you know, the method. I was just happy we had gotten the truth out of Ohia.

Back on the coastal highway, pleased with the way the morning was going, I said, "What next?"

Big Brah was also upbeat. He said, "I know we have to go downtown to meet Aunty Julie, but first let's go see how Lei Bomino's taking the news, I don't want her to worry, since—" and here he did a shaka, a hand gesture we islanders used to show aloha for each other "—we're on it!"

So it was in a positive mood we arrived at Lei Bomino's residence. She was home. The carport had the lone SUV same as the first time we were here. Next to the carport, in the parking space for visitors, light rain pattered on a sports car. Our client had a visitor.

We parked next to the sports car. Silently I asked Big Brah if he had any idea who the visitor could be. He extended his lower lip and shook his head to say no idea. We stepped out in the light rain.

The way you handled rain on the island was different. You never hurried out of it no matter how urgent your affairs. If it was raining and you had to be out in the rain, you took it slow, you sauntered, you strolled, you ambled. Too many of our visitors tried to outrun the rain and slipped and slid and fell.

Sure-footed, I followed Big Brah to the wide lanai of the big house, the raindrops refreshing. Lei Bomino opened the glass-and-wood front door as she had last time.

She looked better. Her salt-and-pepper hair was done in a neat bun. Even the dark circles around her eyes didn't look so bad. She was strong. I was glad she was coping with the situation.

She had the hint of a smile on her face. "Ohia just called, he told me the news, I'm so relieved, I can't wait to have him be done with all this."

"Yes, he'll be done soon, I don't want you to worry," Big Brah said.

"Come in," she said.

With his usual politeness, Big Brah said, "You've got a visitor, hope we aren't intruding."

She said, "Not at all. Big brother Romo is here, he'd like to meet you."

Right on. Big Brah had to meet big brother Romo. Here was the opportunity. Our morning had just gotten better. We entered the comfortable living room with its big windows and hardwood furniture. Framed family photographs decorated the walls. The rooster wall clock showed twenty minutes past eleven. A slight, older man rose from an armchair to greet us.

His mostly gray hair was combed neatly. He had no beard or mustache hiding any part of his face. Stylishly dressed, he wore an off-white shirt with light green patterns on it, light green trousers and wing-tips. He had on smart gold-rimmed glasses and an elegant wristwatch with a gold band. He shook hands with both of us. His grip was firm. He took the time to meet my gaze.

His voice, when he spoke, was level. "Big Brah, Umi, it's a pleasure to meet both of you, Lei told me...."

He wasn't tall. He wasn't short. He was just sane. He looked every bit the angelic big brother he reputedly had been to Izor. I think I was slightly in awe of him. After murmuring pleasantries, all of us sat down. Big Brah and I sat on the couch. Across the coffee table, big brother Romo reclined in the armchair. Lei Bomino sank into an accent chair. Both of them faced us.

Big brother Romo said, "I'm so glad you advised Ohia to do what the police want. I know the chief, he's a good man, I trust the PD to do the right thing. Ohia is innocent, I know it.

"He was with me, right after he met with Izor, I'd know if he'd killed his father! If anything, our Ohia is hot-blooded, he can't act that cool. If he'd done such a thing, I'd be able to tell from his face, his speech, his body language, but I saw no such thing. He was just happy, I guarantee it."

Big Brah nodded, agreeing wholeheartedly. "Yes, sir, I'm sure Ohia is innocent."

"Well, I'm glad that's out of the way, how's the real investigation coming along?" big brother Romo said.

Big Brah never discussed an investigation with anyone but Kali and me. His demeanor full of regret, he said, "I have a policy not to discuss an ongoing investigation."

Immediately, big brother Romo made a contrite face.

"I'm sorry, I didn't know, I won't bother you then," he said, graciously.

Big Brah said, "Thanks for understanding, how's Papa Bomino doing?"

Big brother Romo said, "Not so good, I'm afraid. He's still in intensive care. The doctors aren't allowing anyone to see him, except Sister Agatha, who prays. They're monitoring his vital signs, he's aging, but he's strong inside, he loved Izor."

Caringly, Big Brah said, "Hope Papa Bomino gets better soon."

Big brother Romo shook his head and then sighed. "This has been such a shock. I'm glad we have you to take care of us."

With the clients taken care of, I was dying to get back on the trail of the suspects. Outside again, it was drizzling, as Big Brah and I drove downtown in the big truck. Like Big Brah, I was eager to meet Aunty Julie and learn what she had to say about Izor. Soon Big Brah and I entered Global Quality Lumber's office.

The door chime jingled. This time the door at the back opened promptly. Instead of Keanu, a woman stepped out briskly. She had short, brown hair and reading glasses balanced on her nose. She had on no makeup, and her neat formal office dress had no frills. A wristwatch was her only accessory.

Her demeanor was solemn but welcoming. "I'm Julie, you must be Big Brah and Umi. Keanu told me you'd be coming over, I was waiting for you," she said.

Kali had warned us Aunty Julie was a no-nonsense woman. Big Brah was on his usual best behavior.

"It's lunchtime, we must all be hungry," he suggested, politely.

She tilted her wrist, peered at her watch and frowned.

"Why don't we talk story over lunch somewhere, my treat?" Big Brah said.

She smiled, charmed. "I have an hour for lunch, no more," she said.

No better place downtown to eat or drink than the Tavern, the happening place on the island. The Tavern opened for lunch and stayed open late night. It was the place islanders went to for office lunches, dates, dances, meeting friends, enjoying powwows, parties and a general good time. We drove her there in the big truck.

Even this early the parking lot was nearly full. The Tavern's neon sign shimmered brighter in the rain. We strolled in through its inviting sliding doors. In the foyer, colorful screens displayed the specials of the day.

The lunch special was one of my favorites, Asian-style fried chicken. The aroma of food was everywhere mixed in with the gentle sounds of an island reggae beat, conversation and laughter. As we ambled past the screens, I let my eyes adjust to the near darkness.

Dimly lit, the bar was to our left. A smattering of islanders occupied the barstools and tables. Early birds. Ahead, the dance floor was quiet. Not for long. It would get noisy soon. We turned right.

Brightened by overhead lights and open windows, the expansive dining area came into view. The sounds of conversation and laughter soared by several decibels. The aroma of food reached mouthwatering levels. It was Friday. The place was packed with office-goers glad the work of the week was almost over and the fun of the weekend was about to begin.

Many tables were placed comfortably apart and interspersed with potted palms. The decorative palms brought nature indoors. A local family owned the Tavern.

The men carried in the supplies at the back and cooked in the kitchen. The women pretty much managed the rest of the place efficiently. One of them was Kali's friend, Mohua. Mohua was petite and always cheerful. She knew us. What we did. She gave Aunty Julie a sharp look from behind her desk, decided our guest was harmless and came out to greet us.

She held three menus and smiled brightly. "Table for three?" she said.

Aunty Julie and I nodded. Big Brah said, "Yes."

Mohua took us to the table Big Brah preferred. The corner table at the back of the large dining area, hidden by a lush palm. We sat down. I liked the privacy the palm fronds provided. Big Brah looked out the window at the green mountains and the cascading waterfalls in the distance and took a deep breath. The view relaxed him and helped him think, since he was not in his kitchen anymore. Mohua took our orders.

The lunch plates came with two scoops of rice, a salad and a drink. Aunty Julie ordered fried Ono fish, I chose fried chicken and Big Brah the pork laulau. All of us wanted iced tea. While we waited for the food, we chatted. Aunty Julie told us the story of her life. She lived with her dog, Ami.

Her home was modest. She had worked her entire life, never married. Her work was her life. Before she met Izor, she had worked a number of jobs. When she met him, she was ready to settle into a job.

She said, "Izor was a good employer, he was moody, could be difficult sometimes, but he always came around. It's what I liked about him. He had a good heart, he was flexible, and when you work together, that's important."

Our food arrived. I worked on my salad. Fresh. The conversation turned to the investigation.

Big Brah said, "Keanu told us about the problem Izor was having with Digalo."

Aunty Julie chewed on her salad, frowning and shaking her head. She swallowed, then said, "Keanu's new, inexperienced, he shouldn't have talked about it, he was told not to."

Big Brah defended Keanu. "He was really reluctant, he didn't want to talk about it, I persuaded him to tell me."

She said, "Well, then, you know. It's true. The quality of the lumber Digalo got was inferior, not what he'd paid for. He didn't realize it until later. He had trusted us, we'd never failed him before." She sighed.

Always hospitable, Big Brah refilled our glasses with more iced tea from the jug Mohua had thoughtfully left us.

Aunty Julie said, "Sorry to say, but this wasn't a new situation for Izor, or me. We'd had a similar case a while ago. How it happened, I don't know. We keep the lumber in the yard before it's shipped, and I don't go there too often. Neither did Izor. That's one thing about Izor, he was emotional, easily deceived. Keanu too had been deceiving Izor.

"I'm friends with Lena, I know you're close to her, she looks after Keanu. She wants him to have a better life than the one he's had before. She told me about Keanu. Izor and I were looking for an intern, the work was getting too much for me to handle alone. I recommended Keanu to Izor. Izor could've hired anyone, but he wanted to help. Izor took Keanu on.

"Izor mentored Keanu, and Keanu hid the fact he gambled away every penny Izor paid him, Keanu was in debt! When Izor found out, he was angry, he scolded Keanu. Keanu was arrogant, he's young, he talked back, was rude, and the two had a terrible argument. I brokered peace. Keanu gave up gambling, but I believe he still holds a grudge."

Grudge enough to kill Izor perhaps, I thought. Motive. On the morning of the murder, when Loni arrived at the downtown office, Keanu had told us he was working alone. No alibi. Silently I added Keanu to the list of suspects. Aunty Julie was giving us solid information. No nonsense. I liked Aunty Julie. I savored the fried chicken. It was as good as it got outside of Big Brah's kitchen.

Aunty Julie sipped the cold brew and came to a conclusion. "I think Keanu would've told you about the problem with Digalo."

Surprised, Big Brah looked at Aunty Julie.

"Whether you persuaded him or not!" she said.

Big Brah said, "Okay, this time Keanu may have spoken too much, but he wasn't there, when the problem first happened."

She said, "I was there, I know what happened. Essentially, what happened to Digalo had happened back then as well. An important client like Digalo had complained he'd received inferior quality lumber instead of quality hardwood. Bipo was like a Keanu back then. Izor suspected Bipo had made the substitution, then sold the hardwood for cash to someone who wanted it cheaper. Izor had to fire Bipo.

"Bipo was bitter about it, but I couldn't feel too sorry for Bipo. He was still young, he could start over easily. That he did, he started over, this time in construction, and really, if it wasn't him, I didn't know anyone else who could've done it. If I were Izor, I'd have done the same. But

Izor's dead, killed."

There was a long silence.

Aunty Julie sipped more iced tea. "I won't be surprised if Bipo's still bitter," she said.

Bitter Bipo. Digalo had mentioned him too. Twice mentioned, Bipo had to go on the suspect list as well. I sipped the cold, sweet tea, satisfied. The meeting had been productive so far.

Not surprisingly, Big Brah said, "Bipo must have an office downtown."

"He does, his office is on the same street as Digalo's, right at the end, you know, where the old mill used to be. Bipo Construction," she said.

Mohua brought us our bill. Big Brah paid. Mohua smiled at the generous tip and left. On the drive back to the Global Quality Lumber office, Big Brah thanked Aunty Julie for her time and stories. Aunty Julie was pleased.

She told us to ask her anything, anytime. "Izor didn't deserve to die. I'll tell you anything you want to know, I'm in the office or I'm home, I rarely go anywhere else. I know it won't bring him back, but I want you to find the person who killed poor Izor," she said, in her no-nonsense way.

Our goal was to find the killer. "We will," Big Brah said, reassuring.

After dropping off Aunty Julie, I expected Big Brah to drive over to Bipo Construction.

But Big Brah said, "Bipo got fired for replacing the wood. Must have happened at the lumber yard. Let's go check out the lumber yard, finish finding out how the business works."

I agreed. "We'll get a better idea what Bipo's job was."

"Then we meet Bipo." Big Brah drove the truck out of downtown.

From the coastal highway, we took the exit for the lumber yard. After a few homes, the inland road climbed. We drove through wilderness. Trees reached for the sky. Thick bushes competed with the abundant tall grass for the ground.

Soon we were on more level land and in another clearing. Tall grass and wild bushes still lined the road. A high fence enclosing the compound of the lumber yard started on our left. We reached the beginning of a driveway. The driveway led up to a metal gate.

Big Brah slowed the truck down. The metal gate was as high as the fence. The gate was closed. A signboard outside had "Global Quality Lumber" in bold and below it in cursive "Fine and Exotic Lumber for Construction and Furniture." Instead of entering the driveway, Big Brah drove the truck forward.

The road narrowed to a single lane. No one was around. We followed the road as it curved around the lumber yard. Big Brah glanced at the high fencing.

"Take a good look, Umi...for any way to get in...or out," he said.

The fencing consisted of a four-foot wall with another four-foot barbed wire fence on top of it. It looked pretty impenetrable. We circled the back. Sounds of machines working emanated from the other side of the fence. A movement caught my attention. A fork lift carried lumber. The place was open for business. Soon we were back at the entrance.

This time, Big Brah turned the truck onto the driveway. He brought the truck to a stop outside the metal gate. The rain was taking a break. The gate with its large concrete posts looked sturdy. The left post had a video intercom. On the decorative post cap, a camera swiveled. Someone was looking at us. A speaker was installed below the camera.

A man's voice sounded. "Welcome to Global Quality Lumber, this is Garth, how may I help you?"

Big Brah stuck his head out of the truck's window, introduced us and explained the purpose of our visit.

Garth sounded hesitant. "Hmm...I know who you are, Big Brah, but this is so unusual...since you're working for Lei Bomino...uh, okay, I'll open the gate for you, drive right in, I'm in the office to your right."

The metal gate opened. Big Brah drove the truck into the yard. The metal gate closed behind us. Ahead, the driveway continued all the way to a shed with a hanging sign on it. The sign read, "Pickup." A warehouse rose next to the shed. The yard on both sides of the driveway had several big, robust bins.

The bins had lumber stacked in them. A forklift carrying lumber sped out of the warehouse and headed to the shed. To our immediate right was a log cabin. It had to be the office. Big Brah parked the truck in front of the log cabin.

We got out. The cabin's door opened and a tall, lanky man emerged. He was dressed in a shirt, blue jeans and sneakers. Somehow the combination of short hair, beaklike nose and thick beard made him look like a bird. Garth. With big strides, his long arms swinging, he came out to meet us.

Big Brah shook hands with Garth. "Sorry to bother you, but this is an important part of my investigation," he said.

Garth said, "Murder, terrible business, I really liked Izor, he was a good, kind employer. I'll do what I can to help you, where would you like to start?"

Big Brah pointed. "How about the pickup shed and warehouse over there, then maybe your office?"

Garth said, "Sounds good, follow me!"

We followed Garth to the pickup shed. Outside the shed, he said, "Why don't you guys look around, ask me any questions afterward? I have to go have a word with the crew." He left us.

The pickup shed had a roof and no walls. Curiously Big Brah and I strolled around it. The shed had eight, green metal bins, with the numbers 1 to 8 painted in black and white on the sides of each bin. Some of the bins were filled with lumber. Some were empty. We would soon learn why. Afterward Big Brah and I ambled into the brightly lit warehouse through a wide, open entrance.

The warehouse had an open beam ceiling with light fixtures hanging from the beams. The smells of sawn wood, varnish and oil filled the air. Lumber was stacked in shelves and bins, all neatly labeled and numbered. Big Brah and I walked the aisles looking at the lumber.

Lumber in deep, rich shades of red, ebony, white, yellow and brown, all colorful. Lumber in all shapes and sizes. Machine-cut lumber, squares, slabs, blocks, burls and pieces that still retained their natural shape. I was impressed. We headed out.

Garth was waiting for us outside. "Come, let's go to my office," he said.

Inside his office, a small screen on the wall displayed the live feed from the camera at the gate. The room smelled refreshingly of coffee. In a corner of the room, there was a coffeemaker with paper cups. The office had a window looking out at the bins, pickup shed and warehouse.

The light from the window was insufficient. Bright

overhead lights were on. Garth's desk and chair was next to the window. The top of the desk was crowded with hand-sized blocks of wood, samples no doubt, a desktop computer, a printer and a phone.

On the wall behind the desk, there was a corkboard. Several sheets of paper, the print on them faded, were stuck to the corkboard with colorful pushpins. Garth gestured at a couple of chairs and invited us to sit.

We sat down. With usual island hospitality, Garth got us coffee. He poured some for himself. He sat down at his desk, facing us. He sipped coffee. He peered around for a place to set the cup down on the crowded desk, found an empty spot and set it down. Satisfied he sighed.

He said, "Fifteen years ago, I was on the mainland, I worked a sales job. It was a recession year, the job wasn't much. I was tired of my mainland life, all the materialism, consumerism, I dreamed of a simpler life, a slower pace. So I came to the island. I was young, jobs hard to get. Izor hired me, made my island dream come true. I've worked here ever since." Garth paused to blink back tears.

Garth looked away and then he looked at me and tried to smile. "I've lived on the island long enough to know your name Umi rhymes with roomy."

I smiled, pleased. Garth was growing his local roots strong.

Garth said, "We've had trouble, a couple times, which place doesn't? But Izor always trusted me, never a bad word, always kind, and now this...."

There was a silence. Big Brah broke it. "You've been around a long time, tell us how things work," he said.

Garth rested his elbows on the top of the desk, interlocked his long fingers and smiled. "That's easy. Our clients are mainly construction companies or furniture makers. Have you been to our downtown office?"

"Yes."

Garth said, "They work with the clients, marketing, sales, orders. Once they have a sale, I get a copy of the order. It's usually Aunty Julie, sometimes Keanu."

"We've met them," Big Brah said.

"Good. They bring me a copy of the order, or I go up there, grab the orders myself." Garth tapped the desktop computer with a long finger. "I enter the order number into this computer, check the inventory, then if need be, call a supplier. The exotic stuff is hard to get, sometimes the delivery is in batches, over a period of time. Based on what I got on hand and what I'm getting from the supplier, I give the client a delivery date. Once I'm sure I have the lumber, I take a copy of the order to the crew, they get the order ready."

Garth looked out of the window. Big Brah and I followed his gaze.

Garth pointed to a forklift delivering lumber to a numbered bin in the pickup shed. "That's them working on an order, they stack the wood into the metal bins in the pickup shed. You may've observed, each bin has a number. For large orders, there's usually more than one bin, for a small order just one. One of the crew brings me back the numbers on those bins.

"The crew members are mostly young, don't last too long on the job, they're on to newer, more interesting things fast. Also, it's easy to make a mistake.

"The mills stamp and label but the lumber often looks the same to someone who doesn't know. For example, wenge, which is cheaper, may look like ebony, very expensive.

"Similarly, cumaru and teak. I could go on, but you get the picture. So, once I have the bin numbers, I go check the crew got the order right. I've been doing this so long now, but even I can make a mistake, it's easy. I'm always extra careful.

"Then I come back here and enter the bin numbers for each order into this computer. I let the client know the order is ready for pickup.

"We help load the trucks, and it's costly to have workers waiting around, so we restrict pickups to Thursdays. On Thursdays, I let the trucks in through the gate, print the order with the bin number on it, go out and give the driver the papers. The crew helps load the truck, the driver hauls it away, easy." Garth finished.

Big Brah nodded, slowly. "Sounds foolproof, so how did Digalo Construction's order go wrong?"

Garth frowned. "Beats me, I've thought and thought about it. I checked the bins, I swear I made sure the crew got the lumber right. I remember giving the trucker from Digalo Construction his papers just as usual, I just don't know what happened."

Big Brah said, "It's happened before, were you here then?"

Garth made a face. "You mean the time Bipo got into trouble? I was quite new at the time, I don't have a clue. I only know what Izor told me. You saw the barbed wire on top of the wall? Izor had it installed after the incident, also the metal gate.

"Back then, we only had the wall and a latched gate to keep out feral animals. I'd just arrived from the mainland, I wasn't used to the island's loose security. Easy, Bipo could've just driven in and stolen the lumber."

Big Brah said, "But the barbed wire and the gate made

no difference this time, the lumber got stolen anyway."

Sadly, Garth nodded. "True," he said.

True, how the lumber got stolen was a mystery. But we had learned how the business worked. Big Brah had to be satisfied. It was time to see the man who had been fired for the first theft. Bipo. We drove back downtown. Bipo Construction's office was on the same street as Digalo's but at the very end.

The painted sign by the street that read Bipo Construction was weathered and rusted. The office was a modest trailer. The yard was littered with junked machinery and leftover construction materials. Parking was streetside. Like Digalo, Bipo was in construction, but he wasn't quite as successful as the older man. Not yet.

As we got out of the truck, a man in a hard hat emerged from the trailer's only door. He turned away from us to punch a keypad mounted on the wall. We entered the driveway. The man in the hard hat turned around and saw us. Big Brah asked him if he knew where we could find Bipo.

The man shook his head vigorously, grinning. "It's Friday, he leaves early. We all do, I'm the last one out, had to finish paperwork, I just punched in the lockup code." With typical island openness, he added, "Bipo lives by Waikahe Beach, you can always find him there."

Waikahe Beach. Interesting. I knew the nearby homes, mostly rentals. The crime scene was maybe a 5-minute walk from the neighborhood. Bipo lived there. Suddenly he was number one on my suspect list.

I didn't know if Big Brah shared my perspective. As we drove to the Waikahe Beach neighborhood, Big Brah had a serene expression on his face. He was thinking. Not surprising, he did a lot of his thinking, while he drove.

And not surprising, he didn't like being disturbed, while he was thinking. I looked out of the window and enjoyed the views of the island, until we reached the beach neighborhood.

Here, Big Brah drove the big truck slowly in deference to the playing children, friendly dogs and laidback island birds. One time he had to stop to let the playing keiki cross the road.

We drove by homes. Small homes. Big homes. Which one did Bipo live in? Clean yards. Cluttered yards. We were almost done looking. A yard with a rusty, discolored mixer and a crane came into view. This had to be it. Behind the junked machinery was a small home with a lanai.

Big Brah braked the truck to a smooth stop on the rain-slicked road. "We're here," he said.

Big Brah and I walked to the lanai. The front door was closed. From behind the front door, loud music thumped. Big Brah rang the doorbell a couple times. Finally, the music stopped. The door opened. A woman stood in the doorway, panting. Black activewear. Sweat glued bangs of dark hair on her forehead. Her face glistened.

She smiled at us, her nose wrinkling sweetly. "Sorry, did I keep you waiting? I have the music on loud when I work out, I don't always hear the doorbell." She paused to examine us more closely. She must have realized she didn't know us. "Are you here to see Yo?" she said.

"Yes." Big Brah introduced us and told her we were investigating Izor Bomino's murder.

Her eyes widened. She was about to say something. A lean man with shaven head and a braided goatee appeared behind her. He saw us.

His smooth face twisted into a grimace. "I know

nothing about the murder," he said.

She opened her mouth to say something.

He put a hand on her shoulder, warning her not to say anything. "We don't know anything about the murder," he said.

If he was denying any knowledge of the murder this vehemently, he obviously knew plenty about it.

Chapter 8: Love Therapy Works

The woman turned back to look at the man. "Yo, what's the matter with you, it's Big Brah and Umi, let them come in first!" she said.

Still grim, Yo relented. "Sorry, come in, I didn't mean to be rude, this is Maile, my wife," he said.

The modest living room was lived in and cozy. The two small windows had colorful curtains with heart patterns. The curtains fluttered in the breeze. A rug with heart patterns covered most of the floor. The rug was presumably used for working out. The coffee table had been moved to the side. There was a phone hooked to external speakers on the coffee table. The couch was well-loved and comfortable.

Big Brah and I sat on the couch. The loveseat cover had two large red hearts embroidered on it. Covering up the red hearts, Yo and Maile sat stiffly next to each other in the loveseat.

Yo said, "I was just saving you time, cuz seriously, I know nothing about the murder."

"You did know Izor Bomino," Big Brah said.

"Know him? I worked for him, so yeah, I did know Izor," Yo said.

"All I've come to do is talk story about your experiences with him, so I can understand the man better and figure out what got him killed," Big Brah said.

Yo's stiff shoulders relaxed visibly. Carefully he said, "You've come to the right place, then."

Big Brah said, "You must know plenty about Izor."

"Yes, plenty. He wasn't always bad. When I started, he had a young family, he was kind to me, he hired me. I was younger, greener, I trusted him. I was also ambitious, I wanted to get ahead, make money, gather power, get famous. Izor mentored me, taught me the lumber business. At first it was great. Aunty Julie was there. I don't know why everyone calls her Aunty Julie." He laughed softly, blowing out a breath in short gasps.

Big Brah didn't miss the irony. He smiled, amicably. "Everyone calls me Big Brah," he said.

Yo said, "I guess it's an island thing. Anyways, as I was saying, Aunty Julie was also there, she knew the business as well as he did, maybe better. I learned from her. Things were going well. Then, I think what happened was Izor turned greedy.

"I suspect he had some bad habit, something so bad, he couldn't tell anyone about it. He must have needed extra money to feed the bad habit. Behind my back, he sold cheap lumber, passed it off as expensive lumber, and it was a huge contract, so it was a lot of money. What do you expect? Cheaters never prosper. Izor got caught. Things turned bad.

"He accused me. He told people he was sure I'd done it. Of course I hadn't, I've never pilfered a penny in my life. At first, I thought he couldn't be serious. Then I realized maybe he'd been so kind to me all this while, so he could have me around to blame, in case he got caught.

"I denied doing it. Izor didn't believe me, even Aunty Julie wouldn't listen to me. They fired me."

Big Brah and I listened attentively.

Yo threw up his hands. "Total injustice. I burned inside. I suffered. But I kept my cool. I'd saved up some money. I survived on it. You know, the universe, when it runs you over like a dump truck and flattens you, it knows to give you a break afterward. One night I was drinking at the Tavern, I met Maile." He wrapped an arm around her shoulders.

She snuggled closer to him, happy to hear his story, even if she had heard it before.

Yo squeezed her even closer. "I fell in love, my life changed, I could only imagine my life with you, Maile. What I'd been through...didn't matter. All that mattered was the present, sharing every moment of my life with you, and the future. The past with its bitterness, I left it behind me. Done. Pau!

"I lost all my ambitions for money, power, fame. All I wanted was love. I wanted to secure our future together. I stopped drinking. I got a job in construction. Our love was like mana. The energy gave me new life. I worked hard. Soon I had my own company. And Maile, you've helped me every step of the way, I couldn't have done it without you.

"So, yeah, Big Brah, I was bitter once, but it's a distant memory now. I have love, I have a life, I can't be bitter, ever."

Looking at them cuddled together on the loveseat with two red hearts, the hearts now hidden, I couldn't help think they were a loving couple. His story rang true. Still, he had been too quick to deny any knowledge of the murder. Whatever it was Yo was hiding, Big Brah wasn't getting closer to it.

Big Brah congratulated both of them on finding each other. "It isn't always easy finding love, when you do, hold on to it. It's what Kali and I do. Most of all, I like how you've turned your life around after an adversity, it's something I admire," he said.

Husband and wife exchanged looks. She to say you were worrying about nothing. Big Brah understands. He to say phew, you were right. Big Brah must have realized he wasn't going to get to the whole truth.

He thanked both of them for their time. "You have a great story, I'm in awe," he said.

The couple held hands. They glowed with pleasure. We left. Back inside the big truck, I tried to provoke a reaction out of Big Brah.

I said, "Okay, am I to take Yo out of the suspect list?"

"Not so fast, Umi, both Yo and Maile are hiding something," he said.

Big Brah and I don't always agree on everything. Triumphantly, I slapped the armrest. "I knew it!"

I was still in good spirits at dinnertime. We had covered a lot of ground during the day. Moreover, Ohia would be in the clear soon. Kali would have the latest from the PD. Her office was in the same county building as the PD's. She picked up all the PD news. But she was in a different mood when she showed up. First of all, she arrived late. Unusual.

When I heard her truck, I ran to the front door to greet her. She blew in same as usual, but instead of her customary brisk hug, she lingered. Something was bothering her. Her hug had all of her love and reassurance, only more. I appreciated it. Then she was gone to the kitchen.

By the time I entered the kitchen, she was already in Big Brah's arms. Somehow, I knew they would be in each other's arms longer. I sat down at the round table.

Something else was amiss.

The cats were nowhere to be seen. They always came downstairs when Kali arrived home. They were starved of company. Big Brah and I hadn't been home for a long stretch. Yesterday, when we were out, Kali had been there, so the cats were happy. Today they expected her back, but she hadn't showed up early. All three of us had been away. The cats sulked. A pointy trident of guilt stabbed me.

The guilt trident had been flung from the top of the stairs. Poli`ahu. She sat very still with all the regality of a chiefess on a throne. Pristine white fur. Large green eyes watched us. She had an air of outrage, tempered with resignation at her fate and a faint hope that in the future all would agree leaving her alone was unacceptable. And Wiliwili?

He had to be in his favorite hiding place. The walk-in closet in my bedroom. Kali breezed over to the refrigerator and flung it open. Big Brah thoughtfully kept a big airtight container full of her favorite lilikoi ice cream. Kali took out the container.

She got herself a spoon and started on the ice cream. "I'm so hungry, famished, I can't wait!" she said.

Big Brah and I exchanged looks. We were not brothers working in the detective business for nothing. We knew something was bothering her. Big Brah went to Kali and kissed her forehead tenderly.

She slurped ice cream. "I need this," she said.

We knew what was bothering her. It happened, every now and then. She must have gotten a nasty phone call or a sarcastic text message or something to remind her of her family back on the mainland. She would share it with us. Soon. Big Brah worried about her.

Big Brah knew it was good for her to be away from

her bad family. It was the only way for her to survive. But everyone needed a good family, a loving family, an ohana with aloha. Big Brah tried hard to make her feel we were her family now. Kali knew it.

Her lingering hug for me and her extra long hug for Big Brah said it all. She had made the decision to leave her unloving family years ago, when she first flew to the island. Aunty Mahina had always been a free spirit. The rest of the family didn't get along with Aunty Mahina. Showing exemplary courage, Kali broke with her family. Her compassion drove her to care for her lonely aunt. Big Brah also knew Kali was very young, when she made the big decision.

Just in high school. Kali was still coming to terms with it. Not easy with her bad family members bullying her. Telling her she had become as bad as the aunt they had shunned. Telling her she had run away from them. Telling her she didn't care for them. Filling her with self-doubt. Amazingly Kali never retaliated.

She dealt with their taunts and insults with great fortitude. But she had a soft heart. Sometimes, she wished they were kinder, gentler, different. She suffered. Big Brah suffered with her. It was human. For a moment I fervently wished they were married already. What would make her feel better? I had to get the cats downstairs. But, how?

It was true what people said about cats. Cats owned you. You didn't own them. Cats told you what to do. You didn't tell them what to do. They came to you. You couldn't summon them. But I had my ways of summoning both of ours.

I whistled softly for Poli`ahu. "Twinkle, twinkle little star."

Poli`ahu held on to her aloof chiefess impression.

"How I wonder what you are," I whistled.

It was her favorite song. Her ears twitched.

"Up above the world so high."

She bounded down the stairs.

"Kohu kaimana i ka lani."

She was in her chair next to me, purring. She couldn't resist her favorite song. Affectionately, I petted her soft silky fur. Next, Wiliwili. I sprang up and raced up the stairs.

At the top of the stairs, I swung left toward my rooms. Big Brah and Kali had rooms on the other side. Careful not to be heard, I padded across the expansive sitting area with its gorgeous views of the beach and ocean. Wiliwili knew my walk-in closet was his sanctuary. He knew I would never disturb him when he needed his alone time.

Unless there was an emergency. I entered my bedroom. I had left the window open. A breeze rustled the palm fronds outside. I peered into the darkened closet.

Wiliwili lifted his head, startled, then regarded me curiously with his golden eyes. "Meow."

"Sorry, brah!" I scooped him up into my arms and raced back to the kitchen.

Kali had abandoned the ice cream container on the kitchen counter. She was at the table, fussing over Poli`ahu. She swept Poli`ahu into her arms, held Poli`ahu like a baby and rocked her. Poli`ahu meowed adoringly. Big Brah patiently put the ice cream container away. From my arms, Wiliwili stretched out a white-mittened paw toward Kali, longingly.

Kali set Poli`ahu down, took Wiliwili from me and cuddled him. He purred. Poli`ahu landed furry kisses on Kali's legs. Kali laughed, delighted. She was feeling better.

Big Brah knew what I had done.

He came over and fondly ruffled my hair. Poli`ahu approached me, meowing. I had used the power of the song on her. She gazed at me with her green eyes. Then she brushed my leg with her snowy-white tail. A tail hug. My heart had been in the right place. I was forgiven. Wiliwili butted his head on my ankle, playfully. I had rushed him down, but for a good cause. We were brahs. *Cats don't hold grudges anyway.*

Kali settled the cats into their chairs. Both of them basked in the glow of her love, purring, the past forgiven and forgotten. When Kali was happy, she loved to clown.

Playfully, she rubbed her tummy. "Mm, the ice cream hit the spot, I needed that. By the way, I got an invitation to a wedding today, my niece's, on the mainland. The wedding was last month. They sent the late invitation just to make me feel I wasn't part of the family. Well, the jokes on them, my family's right here!" Her big, brown eyes filled with unshed tears.

Big Brah was an ocean of love and tenderness. Swiftly he gathered her into his arms and hugged her close.

I threw my arms around both of them. "Group hug!" I said.

Instantly two strong arms, his firmer, hers softer, included me. *Love therapy works, always. My ohana.* Soon we feasted on a superb dinner. Milkfish curried in coconut milk and Big Brah's special vegetable fried rice. The drink was utterly tropical. A soothing blend of lilikoi and guava juice and almond milk. I was ready to deliver my daily report on the investigation to Kali.

I put away the plates quickly and returned to the round table. I pulled my chair back a little. I liked to have space around me when I spoke, otherwise my hands moved and knocked things over. Drum roll. I reported.

Finally, I said, "To summarize, both the older employees, Aunty Julie and Garth told us Izor was kind, a good employer. We have a new suspect, Keanu, he has a motive now, Aunty Julie says he argued with Izor over a gambling problem. Digalo, we didn't dig up," and here I couldn't help grin at the wordplay, "anything new on him, nor did we find anything new about Antonio Gomez or his feud with Izor. The Bipos?

"Yo Bipo has a motive, he was involved in the same kind of scam as Digalo, except Digalo's the client, and Bipo was the employee who got the blame for it, and was fired. Bipo thinks Izor cheated to feed a bad habit, something no one else has told us. What makes Bipo more suspicious, he lives minutes away from the crime scene, and both he and Maile are hiding something."

Kali was impressed with the progress we had made. She told us what was going on at the PD. "Loni even cracked a smile at me, you know how he is, always brooding, so that was pleasant and weird at the same time. Ohia volunteered his DNA sample. Loni was super happy. He told me to thank you for convincing Ohia. To celebrate, he'll ask his wife to make you her yummy cupcakes and musubis," she said.

Big Brah chuckled. "When will the results of the DNA match be available?"

"A week from Monday. It's taking longer because it has to be done off island. Moreover, the chief doesn't want to make a mistake, the murder has got a lot of attention in the media lately, the chief insisted on getting the match tested from two different labs.

"The chief has also invited you to the PD. He's scheduled to meet with Loni to discuss the results and next steps. The chief wants you to join him and Loni, since you've been so helpful," she said.

The chief wanted both Big Brah and Loni present, when he made the important decisions. You don't become chief unless you are smart. The chief was also a shrewd judge of ability. He knew Loni was good but Big Brah was better. The meeting was a week from Monday.

We would have to wait. Bummer. But the wait gave us ample time to nab the real killer. Things were working out. Another heartening fact was the weekend was here. I wished for relaxing ohana time.

As if reading my mind, Big Brah made Kali an offer. "If you stay the weekend, I'll drive you to work Monday morning," he said.

I thumped the tabletop approvingly. "Yes, stay," I said.

She looked at all four of us adoringly. Contented, she laughed. "I will," she said.

I was glad Kali stayed the weekend with us. Loving and caring, Kali and Big Brah made such a good couple. Together they cooked up my favorites for a Saturday brunch. Blueberry pancakes with lilikoi ice cream. Fluffy eggs and cheese baked in ramekins. Crispy hash browns. The storm had passed.

Another storm was due in a few days. We spent the day outdoors, the winter sun warm on our backs. We tended to the garden, made each other laugh and talked story. In the evening we cooked laulau together for a late, late dinner. I loved hanging out with Big Brah and Kali. Besides, it was good to take a break from the grim events of the week to relax. Sunday, we attended Izor Bomino's funeral prayer, so things turned solemn.

To pay our respects, together we went to the Pono Church. Big Brah dressed the traditional way to honor

Izor and our ancestors. A red-feathered mahiole, helmet, decorated his big head. An ahuula, cape, made of feathers adorned his wide shoulders, and he traded his cargo shorts for a kapa malo.

Big Brah was handsome no matter what he wore. Kali looked pretty in a simple black muumuu accessorized with a fresh ti-leaf lei around her neck. I had on clean shirt and trousers. At the church, family and friends had gathered on the black stone platform. The wide platform had pillars reaching up toward the endless sky. No rain was expected. There was no canopy over the platform.

Brother Rex, in his wheelchair, faced all who had gathered. His white beard was freshly trimmed for the occasion. He conducted the prayer, his voice deep and clear accompanied by the music of the turbulent Waikahe River. Silver-haired and somber, Sister Agatha stood next to him in silent prayer. His voice trembled at times, but she managed to keep up her beatific smile. Afterward, they mingled with the gathering in the covered courtyard. As we prepared to leave, Sister Agatha found us. Big Brah asked after Papa Bomino.

She said, "Papa Bomino is better, he's still in intensive care, he couldn't possibly come. I did ask him if he was okay with the funeral prayer today, and he told me yes, was all he could say."

Big Brah said, "He's getting better, that's good, can I see him soon?"

"He's very weak. Other than the doctors and nurses, Romo and I are the only ones who can go near him," she said.

We thanked Sister Agatha. Lei Bomino, Ohia and big brother Romo looked grief-stricken, as they stood outside the covered courtyard tearfully thanking everyone for coming. With comforting hugs, we shared their sorrow. Kali then talked with Lei Bomino. Big Brah and big brother Romo listened on attentively. Ohia pulled me aside.

He put a warm hand on my shoulder. "Everything's going to be all right, won't it?" he said.

He was older than me and a lot taller. He looked like he needed reassuring.

I did my best. "Big Brah told you to volunteer the DNA sample, and you did."

Ohia removed his hand from my shoulder, looking troubled. "Yes," he said.

"You can count on Big Brah to keep you out of trouble," I said.

He looked out over the raging waters of the river. Thoughtfully, he rubbed his jutting chin. "Hope things work out, Umi," he said.

"Of course things will work out," I said, confidently.

The next day, things started going wrong.

Chapter 9: The Tutu Pika Effect

The morning started good. Big Brah, Kali and I were in the kitchen, the mouth-watering smells of scrambled eggs, hash browns and toast in the air. We finished eating. Big Brah's phone jingled. Big Brah answered.

He listened. "I'll be there," he said.

He hung up. "That was Aunty Julie, there's been a break-in at Global Quality Lumber's sales office, come on, we better go," he said.

All three of us hopped into the big, black truck. Kali got off at the gray county building. I sat alert in the backseat all the way to the Global Quality Lumber office. From outside, the place looked about the same.

Red tile roof, display window with venetian blinds and solid, wood door. The blinds were closed and I couldn't see the lights inside. The music of the door chime sounded ominous, as we entered the office. Inside, the ceiling lighting shone down on a mess of files and documents on the hardwood floor.

The neat stack of metal filing cabinets against the left wall was in disarray. Some of the cabinets were open, others closed. The sitting area in the middle with its low sofas and monk seal center table looked untouched. To my right the display cabinet with foot long surfboard models was also intact. The burglary had to be about all the important business records stored in the filing cabinets. Looked bad.

The door at the back opened. Aunty Julie emerged. She wore a formal office dress. Her short, brown hair was messed up. Beads of perspiration had formed on her forehead.

She pointed at the files and documents strewn on the office floor. "All our business records, the mess! I wanted you to see it first, I'll start cleaning up later."

Big Brah frowned. He got down on the floor. Without a word, he went through the mess, reading, examining. I craned to look over his shoulder. The record of a sale to a customer dating back years. The recent record of a payment to an employee. All mixed up. There was no way Big Brah was going to find anything of use.

He rose. "What happened?" he asked.

Aunty Julie said, "Yesterday, after the funeral, I wasn't feeling so good, I came in here to let it finally sink in, Izor was gone. I left the front blinds open for the morning, and Keanu even if he comes in before me, he never closes the blinds. I came in this morning, as usual. First thing I see soon as I got out the car, the blinds were all closed. I thought, unusual."

"Where's Keanu?" Big Brah said.

"He's late, he hasn't come in yet," she said.

"Okay, go on," Big Brah said.

She said, "Next, I open the door. The lights turn on. I almost screamed. If Izor saw the mess, he'd be livid! He was always so careful to have everything documented and filed away."

Big Brah said, "How did the intruder get in?"

Without a word, Aunty Julie walked us to the back of the office, out the door, past the individual offices and to the rec room. Small and lit up by overhead lights, the rec room had a TV, a microwave oven and recliners. The coffeemaker had a pot of coffee on it. The smell of coffee filled the air. The lone window was broken.

Aunty Julie pointed to the shards of broken glass on the hardwood floor by the window. "The window was broken, then forced open," she said.

Big Brah examined the window, then the shards on the floor. "Who else has the keys to the office?" he said.

"Both Keanu and I have duplicates, Izor had the master key. For safety, he used to keep it at home, I don't know where, but both Lei Bomino and Ohia know about it. So if Keanu or I ever lost our duplicates, we could ask anyone in the Bomino family for it."

"Can you tell what is missing?" Big Brah said.

She thought for a moment. "Nothing else has been stolen, not even the TV in this room, it wasn't a random burglary. Someone was looking for something in those files," she said.

We returned to the front office to stare down at the mess of files and documents on the floor. "What could the intruder have been looking for?" Big Brah said.

"These files are business records of all our valued clients and employees," she said.

The door chime sounded, as the door to the front office opened. Keanu entered, a travel mug in his hand. His short hair was tousled, his shirt was buttoned unevenly and the laces of his left shoe was undone. He had dressed in a hurry. He saw us and froze. Then he took his time to sip his drink, presumably coffee, from the travel mug.

He made a satisfied face then sauntered toward us smiling. "What's going on here?" he said, trying to appear casual.

Aunty Julie was oblivious to Keanu's attempt at

appearing casual. "Keanu, I'm so glad you're here, someone broke into the office last night," she said.

Keanu looked surprised. "I can't believe it, why would anyone break in?" he said.

"We don't know, yet," she said.

Keanu stared down at the files and documents on the floor. "Did the burglar do this?" he asked.

"Yes," she said.

"Wow. It'll be impossible to know if the burglar took any documents, they're all so messed up," he said.

"I came in early, I called Big Brah," she said.

Keanu did a shaka for Big Brah and me. "Well, I'm glad the pros are here to investigate!" he said.

Big Brah turned to Aunty Julie. "Will you be able to tell if any file, any record is missing?" he said.

She thought for a moment. Then she took a deep breath and exhaled slowly. "I know these files, they've been my life for years, I'll know if anything is missing."

Keanu said, "Wait a minute now, for real?"

Aunty Julie smiled at him. "I was already working here when you were born, Keanu, I can do it." She turned to look at Big Brah. "But it'll take me a while to sort out this mess, I'll be working late."

Big Brah was no stranger to sorting out messes. He encouraged her. "I'm sure you can do it. We'll be picking up Kali in the evening, we'll stop by then to cheer you on."

With the intent of cheering on Aunty Julie, Big Brah, Kali and I visited the spacious office in the evening. The lights were on. Some of the files and papers strewn on the floor had been stacked up in neat piles. Others still lay scattered. The metal filing cabinets were all still opened and closed haphazardly. Aunty Julie emerged from the back to greet us, reading glasses balanced on her nose.

She had freshened up and her short, brown hair was in place, but she looked tired. Kali spent a lot more time with Aunty Lena than Big Brah and I did, even though technically Aunty Lena was known to us first. Kali knew Aunty Julie through Aunty Lena. Following island etiquette, Kali and Aunty Julie chatted first. Big Brah listened on attentively. I admired the footlong surfboard models inside the display cabinet.

Finally, Aunty Julie included us and said, "I sorted some of the papers back together."

Big Brah continued to listen attentively. I abandoned my perusal of the model surfboards and paid attention.

Aunty Julie said, "My eyes hurt, I'm done for the day."

"Wasn't Keanu assisting you, where's he?" Big Brah said.

"Keanu wasn't feeling so good, he's also been through a lot lately. First the murder. Today the burglary. I told him to go home, rest, he left early. We'll both be back at it tomorrow." Aunty Julie sighed. "Besides, my dog Ami will be waiting for me, I don't like to be too late for her dinner and walk. I'll continue tomorrow. So far, I haven't found anything missing."

"Mahalo for all your hard work today," Big Brah said.

Perplexed by first the murder and now the burglary, I followed Big Brah and Kali out of there. I was still puzzled when we gathered at the round table for dinner. Were the murder and the burglary connected? If so, how? I hoped Big Brah or Kali would have some answers.

Big Brah and Kali had whipped up grilled ahi steak with a special wasabi sauce, sautéed vegetables fresh from the garden and steamed rice. The food cheered me up. We hadn't made any progress on the investigation. I had nothing to report to Kali.

Instead, I said, "What do we do next?"

Big Brah frowned. "I understand the victim well enough now to move forward in an informed manner. Our method has produced suspects: Digalo who claims he was cheated, Bipo who may be revengeful, Keanu who could be holding a grudge."

"What about Antonio Gomez?" I asked.

Big Brah shook his head, slowly. "I don't know he's got such a good motive, a feud with a neighbor? I'm not saying, passions do flare up between neighbors, but I can't believe it will result in murder. So, at least for now, unless fresh evidence presents itself, I think we can ignore Gomez," he said.

No Antonio Gomez? We didn't have to deal with his rudeness. In a way, I was relieved. "We focus on Digalo, Bipo and Keanu then?" I asked.

Big Brah said, "Yes, our next step will be to verify each of their alibis, we're going to meet them again."

My feet tapped the floor. "Tomorrow, we meet them tomorrow?" I said, eagerly.

Big Brah disappointed. "Before we meet them, I want to move the focus of the investigation to a different angle, the stone dagger used in the murder," he said.

The stone dagger. I was listening.

"If we can trace its sale, meaning, if we can find out if any of the suspects bought the stone dagger, we have our killer," he said.

Why didn't I think of that? Well, that's why we got Big Brah.

"Now, Tutu Pika still makes stone daggers the old way, the quarry up north has been in his family for generations, Poha looks after the quarry." Big Brah glanced at Kali.

Kali didn't always know all the details about our family on the island. She nodded, smiling. "I remember Poha, he's cute," she said.

On second thought, Kali knew everything, always. Poha was one of my favorite people on the island. Big, brawny and simple, Poha was actually Tutu Pika's nephew, but Poha was raised in Tutu's household, so Tutu looked on Poha as one of his own.

Big Brah continued. "I remember, when I was a boy, Tutu Pika used to teach us children about the craft. I learned a few basics from him, but he's the expert. I say we go see him tomorrow, trace the stone dagger's origin. Kali, we need photos of the murder weapon, so we can show Tutu Pika."

Promptly Kali said, "I can get you photos, I have some on my phone."

We had a new trail to pursue. My heart beat faster. And, a visit to Tutu Pika's was always fun. With digital photos of the murder weapon transferred to Big Brah's custom-built tablet, Big Brah and I started work early the following morning, ready for some fun.

Swiftly Big Brah baked haupia pies and we packed them in boxes to bring along. In the big, black truck, we headed over to an older neighborhood. Tutu Pika lived in an ancestral home along with his large family. Tutu Pika used to be our grandpa's friend.

Tutu Pika had given us love like we belonged to his family, more so after we lost Grandpa, our tutu kane. Tutu Pika was not related to us by blood, but we were ohana. Big Brah and I left the coastal highway and drove along a country road. We reached a neighborhood with huge lots.

The ground was wet from an early morning shower.

In the slanted rays of the morning sun, the grass was silver and green. We turned into Tutu Pika's driveway. Mango and lychee trees flourished on both sides of the driveway. The mango trees were bursting with clusters of buds and blossoms. I loved the sweet, tangy smell of the blossoms.

I inhaled deeply. We turned a corner. Homes came into view. The old-style, single-story home in the middle that was Tutu's. Around the older home, four modern single-family homes. The family had expanded.

Children still not school-going age played on the common grounds, shouting out to each other in excitement and laughing out of pure happiness. The sight and sounds of their merriment made us exchange glances and smile. Big Brah parked the truck outside Tutu's home. We got down. We were like celebrities here.

The children swarmed Big Brah. He lifted each of the keiki high into the air, had them "fly, fly" then brought them down smoothly. The children squealed in delight. Big Brah handed each of the keiki a box of the haupia pie he had baked for them. Their delighted squeals turned to shouts of joy. The bright one in this lot was Akamai.

Akamai was going to start school in a few months. He had a big head teeming with ideas, and he was the keiki leader. He took directions fast. He knew things some grown-ups struggled to understand. Precocious. Wise beyond his years. Big Brah said Akamai was a lot like me.

Like me, Akamai hero-worshipped Big Brah. Akamai and I had an elaborate shaka. You raised your right hand, palm inward, extended your thumb and pinky and curled up your middle fingers to make your shaka. Touched your shaka over your heart for ohana, swung your shaka in an arc for island and shook your shaka for justice. Akamai wanted me to stay and play.

I told him another day. Instead, I made Akamai an offer. Would he join Big Brah and me while we talked with Tutu Pika? Little Akamai was a huge Big Brah fan. He wouldn't be able to resist my offer. Sure enough, Akamai agreed. He told the others what to do while he was gone. Very importantly, he turned back to me. I told him to take us to Tutu Pika.

Akamai ran ahead, pausing to squint back at Big Brah to make sure we were close behind. The front yard of Tutu's home was littered with toys, new and old. The wide lanai was also cluttered. Akamai led us into the home through the front door.

The formal living room was an uncluttered oasis, the walls adorned by stone carvings. The stone carvings took your breath away so exquisite was the workmanship. They were both real and abstract and in various shapes and sizes.

Full-sized mynahs, a miniature monk seal, a volcano with human hands reaching up to the sky, a stone dagger. My pulse quickened. The stone dagger looked like the murder weapon. A framed photograph of the master craftsman, Tutu Pika, being honored by the island's honorable mayor was displayed prominently alongside the products of his craft.

Tutu Pika sat in a rocking chair on the back lanai. He had only a few gray hairs left on his balding head. Each of them had been brushed back with pride.

He was frail, thin, bent over with age and pleased to see us. "Koa, Umi, sit, sit, by your presence, you've brightened up the morning!" he said.

The lanai had an interesting array of hand tools lined up against its wall. Every kind of chisel and hammer used to cut, carve and shape stone. I looked at them wondrously. Big Brah and I sat down on a couple of chairs. Akamai seated himself on top of the lanai stairs. He sat sideways, so he could admire Big Brah. At the same time, he kept an eye out in case any of the other children came wandering back. A likely event.

Tutu Pika leaned back and rocked himself contentedly. He knew Big Brah would definitely have something interesting to talk about. "What brings you here?" he asked, eagerly.

Big Brah said, "You hear of the Bomino murder?"

"I did, I did, it's on local TV all the time, I hear you're investigating the murder?"

"Yes, I am, and I need your help," Big Brah said.

"How can I help?"

Big Brah worked his tablet and brought up a photo of the murder weapon. He maximized the image and held it up where Tutu could see it best. "This is the murder weapon."

Tutu squinted at Big Brah's tablet. "I see it," he said.

"Do you recognize it?"

Tutu squinted at it some more. "It's definitely not one of mine...or anyone else I know."

Big Brah made a puzzled face. "How can you tell?" he asked.

Tutu said, "Let me explain, our ancestors used to make stone daggers with hand tools. Nowadays you can make stone daggers with machines, daggers that can be made faster and with finer finish. But each machine-made dagger looks and feels exactly the same. To escape the monotony, you want a handcrafted stone dagger. Each dagger is unique. Why?

"Because each craftsman has a unique style, you

know, things like the sureness of his or her hand alone, reflected in the smoothness, depth and accuracy of a cut. A whole lot of things go into style, and most of them result from the strengths of the craftsman.

"But it's important to remember, style can also show up as a weakness, say a tendency by a junior craftsman to leave behind tiny, tiny blemishes. Those blemishes will also form a pattern, just as sure expert strokes do, and all of the pattern is the craftsman's style. So I can tell the murder weapon isn't mine."

"Do you recognize the style?" Big Brah asked.

"The craftsman isn't anyone I've worked with or known. I have a good memory. I remember."

Big Brah was impressed. "What else can you tell us about it?" he said.

Tutu took the tablet from Big Brah. He held it up close to his eyes. "I recognize the stone, it's the same everyone uses, it's from our quarry up north. This was made locally."

Big Brah looked interested. "Locally? What kind of craftsman could have made it?"

"I saw several small blemishes, so I'd say an amateur, or someone who got stuck at an early level of the craft and never learned thereafter, a beginner who produces flawed work."

Big Brah nodded. "Or someone who does stone work for a hobby with hand tools bought from a hardware or specialty store?"

Tutu thought for a moment. His face lit up with a smile. "Could be, as you say a hobbyist, there are many on the island. I used to correspond with some of them, now I text them!"

Big Brah smiled too, his tone lighthearted. "Recently,

has any of them acted weirdly?" he said.

Tutu cackled. "No weird, weird is ordinary on island!"

"Okay, fine, no one's been weird," Big Brah said.

"Everyone was okay, now this murder, I want all this to end."

"You'll tell me if anyone is being weird, right?" Big Brah said.

"Right."

There was a comfortable silence. Nearby, a rooster crowed. The sun was higher, stronger. In the distance, the ocean was a deep blue.

Tutu Pika grew animated. "You go see Poha, he's been learning a lot about the quarry. Could be, he's even seen the murderer!" he said.

"Mahalo for all your help and expertise," Big Brah said.

Tutu Pika glowed with pleasure. He tottered up. "Not so fast, I won't let you go," he said.

Big Brah and I looked at each other. Even Akamai in his short life knew what was coming. He gazed up at Big Brah in open admiration. We followed Tutu Pika into his workshop right next to the lanai. The large room had its windows open bringing in the ocean breeze and the scent of daytime flowers. Tutu Pika had several places he used for work.

A variety of lamps lit up the workplaces. Hand tools and pieces of stone art were everywhere, on the floor, on the furniture and on the wall shelves. The numerous sets of tools were always in precise order, the order he last used them in, and he never forgot the order. So, it worked.

Tutu Pika spoke to Akamai and me. "I never allowed the other keiki to come inside, only Koa."

I looked at Akamai. He was to my right, away from Tutu and Big Brah. He had a look of wonder on his young face. He was looking around, his eyes wide. I suppressed a smile. Clearly, he hadn't been allowed inside the workshop before today either. There was a row of chisels coming up. He would have to watch out.

Tutu Pika continued. "Koa was unlike all the other children. He was quiet, he listened, he observed, he learned. For example, he always knew the order I put my tools away. Moreover, he had the good sense never to mess with them. That's more than I could say about the others!"

Akamai had been listening intently to Tutu Pika. Tutu was walking toward his favorite corner of the workshop by an open window. Two things happened simultaneously.

Akamai stumbled over the set of chisels and knocked them out of order. Guilt-stricken, he looked up at me, panic in his eyes. Luckily, Tutu Pika also arrived at his favorite corner. He was focused on the stone carving of the goddess and the kahuna.

Big Brah and Tutu Pika admired the beauty of the masterpiece. I had a decent memory. I used it to recall the order the chisels had been in. I swiftly put the chisels back in place. Akamai and I made the same face. Phew!

Tutu turned to Akamai. "If you continue being good like Koa, I'll let you come inside, would you like to help?" he said.

Close to tears happy, Akamai nodded his big head vigorously. Satisfied, Tutu Pika gestured toward the stone carving of the Goddess of True Love and the Powerful Kahuna. He had told us the story behind his masterpiece before.

Tutu Pika said, "You see this, Akamai, it's my favorite piece to work on. Koa had brought Kali over to see me, the grandfather, the tutu kane, as family tradition demands. I was so inspired by the couple, I set out to carve the goddess and the kahuna as a wedding gift that very day!"

Although the wedding had not happened yet, the gift had come along nicely. All of us commended him on his work.

At last, his voice full of feeling, Big Brah said, "We'll have to take your leave now, Tutu."

Tutu looked at us. His love for us filled his eyes with tears. He blinked them away. "Remember, at the quarry, you'll have to look for Poha. You know how shy he is, he doesn't like being seen," he said.

Big Brah and I hugged Tutu affectionately. Akamai lived here. He didn't have to hug Tutu with us. He could hug Tutu anytime he wanted. But he did what we did. He hugged Tutu very respectfully. And then Big Brah did a shaka for Akamai. The shaka made Akamai's day. He grinned from ear to ear.

Grateful, Akamai hugged me fiercely. "Mahalo, Umi!" he said.

Fondly, I ruffled his hair.

Tutu Pika patted my back, smiling. "Umi, you got a great memory, and the big Waialeale heart," he said.

I was close to tears happy. Big Brah nodded, approving.

Tutu Pika said, "Akamai, I feel like working, go get me my water!"

You needed the water to carve stone. Akamai was taking Big Brah's childhood place with Tutu Pika. We headed to the door.

Outside, on the lanai, Big Brah said, wistfully, "Yeah, I used to bring him his water too!"

From behind us, through the open door, I heard Tutu

Pika caution Akamai. "This time, don't stumble over the chisels, Umi won't be there to save you."

Big Brah and I exchanged shakas and smiled. Tutu Pika and Akamai were fond of each other. They would do just fine. Back in the big, black truck, Big Brah still had the smile. I was inspired happy. It was the Tutu Pika effect. Added to the happiness was the excitement of following the trail of the stone dagger. The stone for the dagger had been quarried locally. Had Poha really seen the murderer? Big Brah and I headed north on the coastal highway, our destination the quarry.

I knew of the quarry, but I hadn't been there. Curving sharply, the road turned steep up the mountains. Big Brah handled the turns expertly. The truck sped smoothly up. We bounced along a dirt road for half a mile. The vegetation cleared and the quarry came into view. Here, the mountain, bare and rocky, sloped gently.

Unlike most quarries, there were no cranes, no rock breaking machines, no machinery, only jagged, broken stone. The side of the mountain had always been harvested for the stone by human hands. Poha did the harvesting now. Tutu Pika had taught him. The quarry was deserted.

No car. No soul. Our truck trundled along the dirt road, the quarry now on both sides of us. Tutu had told us we would have to look for Poha. We all knew Poha was shy. Poha had to be hiding somewhere close. But, where? The dirt road got worse.

I scanned the mountainside. The mountainside had dark, hollow eyes. Scary. At first, I shrank back in my seat. Then I looked closer. The hollow eyes were shadowy openings to caves. Phew. The truck lurched and jolted forward.

The road deteriorated fast. Big Brah gripped the steering wheel with both hands. Soon he braked the truck hard. The truck skidded to a halt. It was the end of the dirt road.

Perplexed I looked around. The sun baked the surroundings. "Where can Poha be?" I asked.

"Hmm." Then sudden inspiration hit Big Brah. "Umi, those caves back there!"

He got the truck turned around. We bounced all the way back. The caves were above us. We jumped out of the truck.

We trekked up the mountainside. The rocks, hot from the sun, radiated more heat. I sweated. Up close, it was very clearly a cave. Big Brah ducked inside.

I simply walked in. The insides of the cave was cloaked in darkness. My eyes had to adjust to the dim light. It was way cooler here. The cave provided much relief from the hot sun. Big Brah was right. The caves were the place to be on a warm day.

At last, the reddish-brown rocky walls, the ceiling and the floor were visible. The floor sloped up gradually. Our ancestors used tools made of stone. They used the hard basalt to make their stone tools. They would come up here to the mountains from the coast to quarry the hard basalt. Then they camped in these caves. There were signs of human habitation from long ago.

The rocky floor and the wall at the back had been smoothened to make it more comfortable to rest and relax. The nights got cool up here. A fireplace had been built with rocks on the hard floor. Everything was covered in dust. A barely discernable movement on a side wall caught my attention.

Inch-long cave wolf spiders crawled on the reddish-brown rocky wall, their body colors matching the color of the wall. They didn't have eyes, these spiders, but they sensed our presence. Unafraid, they crawled down the wall toward us. They were happy to have a visitor.

I was happy to see them too. The cave was empty, otherwise. Big Brah must have made the same discovery. Disappointed, I was about to turn back. A faint scraping sound from behind alerted me. Suddenly I was aware of a presence lurking behind me.

I spun around. A giant of a man stood outside, blocking the cave entrance. His shoulders were immense, his arms and legs the size of tree trunks, his hair and beard grown wild. He had shaggy eyebrows and a flat nose. I didn't know how much of us he could see in the dim light. But I had seen enough. I sprang forward at him. *Attack.*

Chapter 10: Pigs, Spiders and Pohaku

I slammed my right fist into the giant man's big belly. My punch had force and my knuckles were hard. He doubled up. I rejoiced. Relentless, I swung my left fist as hard as I could to match the force of my right.

He caught my fist one-handed. Bewildered I tried to free my fist. His grip tightened. He had been faking it when he'd doubled up. My punch had made no impact on him. Sure enough, he straightened up effortlessly.

Summoning all the strength I had, I swung my right fist at him, again. He caught my wrist midair with his other hand. I struggled. He let go of me. Failed at combat, I was already embarrassed. I tried to run.

Now he did something even more embarrassing. He grabbed me again, this time from below my armpits. He pulled me out into the glaring sunlight and threw me up into the air. I had seen Big Brah playing with the little kids at Tutu Pika's only a couple hours ago!

That did not make it any better. "Let go, Poha, you big brute!" I yelled.

Poha giggled like a little girl. He caught me easily and swung me around, again and again, until I finished yelling. Then he set me down. He had a deep voice that emanated from the middle of his ginormous chest.

He admonished me. "You know the rule, Umi. Until

the day you beat me in combat, I make you fly, fly!"

He and I had been doing this since I was a little keiki. "You won't make me fly, fly for too long then," I said, like I did every time.

Poha broke out into peals of laughter. His laughter was contagious. Soon I was laughing too. Big Brah came out of the cave. He exchanged shakas then hugged Poha fondly.

Big Brah gestured toward the cave opening. "We figured you'd be resting inside," he said.

Cheerfully, Poha gestured toward one of the other caves down the road. "I was, in the other one." He stretched his giant body in the relaxed way our cats did when they woke up from a good nap. "I was napping, the sound of your truck woke me up." He made a regretful face. "Sorry, it took me a while to get here!"

Poha was excited to have us at the quarry. He grinned. "I don't get visitors too often, one, maybe two in a month," he said.

Grinning, Poha gestured toward the ocean shimmering blue down in the distance. "Our ancient ancestors used to live on the coast, over there. They'd climb up here, work for a few months, carry the stone back to the villages, where they carefully carved tools out of the stone. The tools were the backbone of island economy. They were used to make everything else. Cloth, kitchen utensils, building material, fishing equipment, you name it, you got it."

I gazed at him in awe.

Poha chuckled. His chuckles also rose from the center of his ginormous chest. A dreamy look came over his rough features. "Ancient islanders even used tools made of the stone from this quarry to sculpt the lava rock, pohaku, the one I'm named after. Irony, isn't it? Me, the pohaku from the shores, I've come up here to the stone on the mountain to be sculpted."

To be sculpted. I'd known him all my life. Met him at every birthday, wedding and funeral our families had or were invited to before and after he started living here. Once in a while, Poha floored you with something so deep. His dreamy look faded.

He returned to reality. "Come, you must see my home. Like our ancient ancestors, I love to live up here. You'll love my hale!"

He led us up a mountain path. We left the quarry behind. Tall grass and wild bushes grew on both sides of the path. Soon we walked under the cool shade of trees. A mountain stream gurgled to our left. Ahead of us, feral pigs rustled the tall grass. A baby boar, distinguishable by his developing mane, scampered out of the grass snorting loudly. Poha knelt down.

He held out his big arms. "Pua'a!" he called out.

With a thunderous snort, Pua'a jumped into Poha's waiting arms. Human and best friend cuddled. Poha rose, Pua'a in his arms. Lovingly he carried Pua'a for several yards then Big Brah wanted Pua'a. Big Brah took Pua'a into his arms and let out a soft "aww...." Of course, Big Brah let me have Pua'a too.

I staggered around with Pua'a wriggling and snorting playfully in my arms. Finally, I set him down. Pua'a shook his small, curly tail happily. He trotted away in the direction of the mountain stream.

Fondly Poha looked on after Pua'a, like a father letting his son go. "Yes, it's a warm day, drink lots of water," he said, protectively.

Pua'a wiggled his ears and disappeared from sight. We

laughed. Poha had a way with animals. His hale was in a small clearing. The modest home was built on stilts. Steps led up to the front lanai. Easily we followed him up the steps.

The lanai was a spider haven. It was shaded from the sun at that time of day, and it had chairs. Big Brah and I would have sat down there, but Poha insisted we see his entire home first.

The sparsely furnished living room had a square rug, a large recliner, a coffee table and a bookcase. A rugged tablet with a blank screen rested on the coffee table. The living room had plenty views of both the mountains and the ocean. A giant bed occupied most of the bedroom.

Through the bedroom's window, the startling, blue sky was visible through the new foliage of trees. In the kitchen area, I breathed in the fresh, mountain air and heard the sweet music of songbirds. To make it perfect the bookcase in the living room was full of good mystery novels.

I lingered by the bookcase and looked for titles I hadn't read yet. There were many. Poha had good taste. We returned to the lanai. Small, brown boy garden spiders and big, gold and black girl garden spiders basked on their intricate webs. I sat down. The webs near me bobbed, as the shy critters withdrew.

"Wow," I said, looking around, "this is awesome!"

Big Brah seated himself. He nodded, approvingly. "I can get used to this!" he said.

Poha sat down in a big, wooden rocking chair, rather like the one Tutu Pika used, except Poha's was much bigger and it looked like he had made it himself.

He looked pleased. "Not everyone gets me, I knew you two would!"

Big Brah leaned back in his chair. His face went under a web. Instead of withdrawing, a big gold and black girl spider dropped onto his wide forehead. Amazed I watched. The spider made her way to his temple. Big Brah put his hand there. She scampered onto his hand. Big Brah brought her in front of his eyes and the two of them gazed at each other for a while in mutual awe.

"She's beautiful," he murmured. Using the Hawaiian word for beautiful, he said, "She's nani." Then he talked to her. "Hi, Nani!"

All critters responded to Big Brah's aloha for them. We were all one ohana. Simply amazing. Poha put big hands on his plump thighs and looked from one to the other of us enthusiastically. Living up here as he did, it didn't look like he had heard about the murder.

"I haven't been down to the coast in a while, what's the news?" he said.

Big Brah let Nani crawl on his bare forearm. "The news is bad. Someone killed Izor Bomino, did you know him?"

Poha's innocent face filled with regret. "Sorry to hear, can't say I knew him though."

"I'm investigating the murder."

"Then I know justice will be served," Poha said.

"The murder weapon was a stone dagger."

Poha's eyes widened. "Unusual," he said.

Big Brah said, "Tutu Pika recognized the stone, told us it was from this quarry."

Poha frowned. His face wasn't used to frowning. It looked as if he was freaking out. He wasn't, really. "I can help you find the killer," he said.

He got up and went into the living room. He returned with the rugged tablet I had seen on the coffee table. He sat down.

He held the rugged tablet up. "See this thing? I convinced Uncle Pika to invest in one of these, it costs. There used to be a handwritten log. Uncle had an employee and when the employee left for the next island, the log either went with him or it was just lost.

"Don't know what happened, the old log is gone. But if anyone bought stone from me these past four years and some, their name and address, it's got to be in here!"

I sat up. Big Brah continued to gaze admiringly at Nani crawling on his forearm. He held his hand out, palm up. I did the same. Nani crept carefully onto my palm. She crawled to my wrist. It tickled. She nuzzled my wrist. So sweet.

In the while, Big Brah must have done the math. "If you get only one or two visitors each month, you can't have more than hundred names. It won't take long, mind reading them out?" he said.

I let Nani go gently back to her web. Poha read out the list. I recorded him on my phone in case we needed to hear the list again. Granted there were a few other familiar names, but so far as we knew those people had nothing to do with Izor Bomino. Only two names really stood out.

Yo Bipo and Bo Digalo. The trail of the stone dagger was leading us back to the suspects. Another name popped up. Antonio Gomez.

I groaned. *Not him.* But anything for the cause of justice. Poha finished reading the list. I knew he would want us to hang out with him some more.

Preemptively Big Brah got up. "Poha, we'd love to hang out with you some more, but another day, we have work to do," he said.

Poha said, "Aww...I was just going to cook something so we could party."

All of us laughed. Still chuckling, Big Brah and I descended the steps of the home and headed back to the quarry. We'd left the big truck there. Yo Bipo and Bo Digalo were in construction. They may have had valid reasons to buy the stone. But Antonio Gomez had also bought the stone.

Big Brah said, "I want to know what Antonio uses the stone for, since he won't tell us, we ask Maria. Maybe she'll be more forthcoming."

Apprehensive, I said, "I hope Antonio's cooled down."

"If we hurry, we may just be able to find out what we want, leave before Antonio returns from work," he said.

No Antonio? That sounded even better. I hoped Big Brah was right all the way to the Gomez home on Bomino Court. The sky was blue and the light still good. We parked outside the home and followed the stone path to the lanai. *Hope we don't have to confront Antonio.* Big Brah rang the bell.

To my immediate relief Maria Gomez opened the front door. The last time I had seen her she was dressed for the outdoors. In her home clothes, pink top and long skirt, and her straight long hair done in a loose ponytail, she looked softer, gentler.

Her wide forehead furrowed at the sight of us. "I'm so sorry about last time, I don't know what came over Antonio, he's never behaved so strangely. But I really can't let you in, he told me not to engage with you in any way."

Solemnly Big Brah said, "That's unfortunate ma'am, I know he bought stone from the quarry."

Maria Gomez shrunk. Her body stooped, the lines on her wide forehead deepened and she looked scared.

Big Brah reassured her. "All I want is to find out what he uses the stone for...."

She recovered. "Oh, you know about the stone, you won't get my Antonio into trouble, will you?"

Big Brah shook his head to emphasize. "No, ma'am, if your husband is innocent, he has nothing to fear from us."

She ushered us into an enormous living room. The room had two levels. Lamps lit up every corner of the lower level with military efficiency. The couch and armchairs had monotonous brown covers. The tall windows had glossy blinds. The blinds were closed. There was no clutter anywhere. The higher level was dark.

In the wash of the light from the lamps, I saw the dining area's crystal chandelier, large rectangular table, chairs and wall cabinets to store dinnerware. Everything looked normal. She sank into an armchair and gestured for us to sit down.

She said, "Please, make yourself comfortable, I'm so glad you came back, I wanted to apologize for Antonio's bad behavior. He's never been like that, it's not like him at all. Worse, he won't even tell me, even after you left, he wouldn't tell me a thing!"

Then I saw it. The windowless wall to my left had a display. The display pieces were arranged in precise rows and columns. Each piece was balanced on a hook for the blade and a tiny block of wood to rest the handle. The display pieces were stone daggers.

I froze.

Big Brah glanced my way. He had seen the stone daggers displayed on the wall. But as usual he didn't show any reaction. He sat down in an armchair and gestured for me to sit, as if everything was okay. I sat down, slowly. Maria Gomez must have observed me staring at the stone daggers.

She said, "Those daggers are Antonio's hobby. Ancient islanders, your ancestors," she paused to smile at Big Brah and me, "used to make them. Now that we live here, they're our ancestors too, Antonio loves to uphold tradition. It's his way of giving back to the island he loves so much."

Her words demonstrated Antonio's love for the island and the traditions of our ancestors, our kupuna. Big Brah nodded, approvingly. The threat of Antonio's imminent arrival ignited my imagination. I imagined Antonio, buff and crew cut, stride to the wall, carefully choose the sharpest dagger, smirk, hide it in his pocket and stride away intent on killing his annoying neighbor and ending the feud once and for all. Sinister.

She continued. "Our visitors love the daggers. I told you, I run a charity to clean up Waikahe Beach periodically. We did a cleanup only last Saturday. Afterward I hosted a little party."

"Mm-hmm." Big Brah nodded approvingly, again. He was big on taking care of the land, our aina.

She pointed to the dining area. "I put all the food there. Everyone was here, everyone. There were people from all over the island. Strangers who were on the beach joined us, and we had a sweet couple visiting from California. All of them spent a lot of time admiring the daggers, Antonio's handiwork. Now, I understand a stone dagger was used for the murder," she said.

Softly Big Brah said, "Yes."

I sat up.

She said, "Listen to me, it simply couldn't be one of Antonio's, all he does with the daggers he makes is hang them up on the wall, believe me!"

While Antonio had carved dagger after dagger, Maria

was sure none of Antonio's daggers was the murder weapon. What was Big Brah making of this? Big Brah sat still, unresponsive. I counted the seconds. A minute elapsed.

A worried frown came over her angular face. "Antonio will be back any moment now," she said.

I panicked. I jumped up.

Big Brah stirred. "Mrs. Gomez, you've been a huge help, can't thank you enough for the work you do for our aina, keeping the Waikahe Beach clean."

She smiled, pleased.

Big Brah got up. "We'd better leave before your husband gets home," he said.

I nodded vehemently.

"I'm sorry, I don't know what's come over my Antonio," she said.

Big Brah would figure out what had come over Antonio. *But, not now.* We had the information we needed. Antonio had used the stone from the quarry to make daggers. Sinister. We made a fast exit. Once we were back inside the cozy confines of the big truck and cruising down the coastal highway, I heaved a sigh of relief. We had made it without having to confront Antonio.

Big Brah blew out a long breath and grinned. "You were jumpy in there, had to get you out fast!"

Nothing ever spooked Big Brah. I said, "There was something spooky about those daggers."

He patted my shoulder reassuringly. "Whatever it is about those daggers, we'll find out the truth," he said.

Curious, I said, "What's the matter with Antonio?"

Big Brah said, "Antonio must have warned Maria not to tell us about the daggers. And it also explains why he lost it when he saw us with her the other day, he didn't want her to blurt out the truth to us."

That sounded right. I was thankful Big Brah had got us out of there without an encounter with Antonio.

I was still feeling grateful when I reported to Kali over dinner at the round table. "Keanu didn't get any stone from the quarry, I'm happy to take him out of our suspect list. He just needs a break.

"Certainly, between Digalo and Bipo and Gomez, we have our murderer. They were the only ones who bought stone from the quarry. But we'll need proof if we're to accuse upstanding members of the island community of murder. Buying stone from Poha isn't enough.

"But tell you what? One thing's for sure. We're close to catching the killer."

The next morning, I was rudely reminded how far we really were from catching the killer. It happened in the kitchen. I was at the round table working on a cheesy spinach omelet, buttery garlic toast and chilled rice milk. Nom nom. I was about done. Kali was staying with us through the week. Before leaving for work, she was bidding adieu to the cats. Big Brah and Kali had finished breakfast. Big Brah's phone jingled.

Big Brah listened to the caller and frowned. He turned away to look out of a window. Big Brah asked a question, listened some more and hung up. He didn't move or say anything. He continued to stare out of the tall window. Obviously, he was thinking. He came over to the round table, still frowning. He never frowned that long. This had to be big.

Big Brah said, "That was Aunty Julie, she says Aunty Lena called her this morning. Keanu is missing."

Chapter 11: Machete and Red Fish

I gaped up at Big Brah. "Missing? This is so sus."

Big Brah's face showed regret. He said, "Aunty Lena says Keanu left her a note saying he's going away."

"Going away, why?" I asked, amazed.

"Due to Izor's untimely death." Big Brah shook his head.

The spear of disappointment hit me hard.

Next to me, Kali spoke, her voice full of concern. "Keanu. Aunty Lena loves him, he's her ohana. He'll be all right," she said.

Big Brah put the phone away. "The goddess protects those who live with aloha, so Aunty Lena is good. Question is, what's in Keanu's heart?" he said.

I spread my hands. "I just struck Keanu off the suspect list last night, I even mentioned he needed a break, and now, missing."

Both Big Brah and Kali fell silent.

I blew out a breath. "Do you think Keanu's guilty?"

Big Brah lifted his big shoulders then let them drop. "Can't say, Umi, he may or may not be guilty, but he's closely associated with the victim."

I said, "But he didn't even buy any stone from Poha."

"We should consider other possibilities. Anyone on Poha's list could have bought the stone, made the dagger and sold it to any gift shop, perfectly legitimate business. Keanu could have just bought the dagger from a gift shop," Big Brah said.

I had been eager to find a killer from Poha's list. Digalo or Bipo or Gomez. *Back to reality.* I'd been wrong about Keanu.

"What do we do?" I asked.

Big Brah glanced at my empty breakfast plate. Satisfied I'd finished eating, he nodded. "First, we go see Aunty Lena, she's super wise, she'll have insights. Then I want to check out the note Keanu has left and find out if anything's missing from his room."

Keanu was racing back to the suspect list, for real. I groaned. In the big, black truck Big Brah dropped Kali off at the gray county building. Big Brah and I headed to Aunty Lena's. I worried about Keanu the entire time. After the truck crested a steep climb, Aunty Lena's hostel came into view.

The hostel was situated on a level lot. It was a two-story building with lots of rooms and bathrooms. At the back of the building, Aunty Lena had stopped the progress of a wild canyon with a fence. She lived in a cottage next to the hostel.

Petite and feisty, Aunty Lena burned if she heard of an injustice on island, off island, in the past, present or future. This early in the morning she was in the hostel's ground floor kitchen making pancakes, eggs and coffee for the residents. Her children. She worked by the hot stovetop burners. A nearby window provided cool fresh air.

She had flour on her hands, flour on her apron and a faint coat of flour on her round glasses. She poured batter onto a hot griddle. 6 pancakes at a time. Her children had to be fed. They'd be downstairs soon. She couldn't interrupt the breakfast routine. No problem. Big Brah and I stood on either side of her. We chatted.

Aunty Lena flipped a pancake. "Caught me by surprise! Keanu had problems in the past, you know, like a lot of my children, especially when they come at an older age. Keanu came to me when he was seventeen, he was from the west side.

"His family still lives there, they don't want him, I take care of him. He was into gambling, keeping bad company. I had him finish high school. Through Julie, I got him a job with Izor. I thought Keanu was over gambling. But I was wrong.

"Keanu got into trouble with Izor over his gambling debt, so much trouble, I got to know Izor. Izor was a good man, what a terrible way to die!" She paused to look sharply at first Big Brah then me. "You better find the killer."

I put on my most confident expression.

Big Brah reassured her. "Justice always wins, Aunty," he said.

Reassured, Aunty Lena flipped all 6 pancakes. Impressive.

Big Brah asked, "The fight Keanu had with Izor, could it have prompted Keanu to kill Izor?"

Aunty Lena shook her head. "Never. Whatever else he may be capable of, Keanu isn't a killer, he didn't kill Izor."

"Why did he go away then?" Big Brah said.

"I don't know, you'll have to find that out yourself, here's his note." She extracted a folded sheet of paper from her apron pocket and showed it to us. The lined sheet had been torn neatly from a notepad.

I read the legible handwriting easily. "Dear Aunty

Lena, I'm always grateful to the goddess, I have you to take care of me. This is about Izor's murder. I have to go. I don't want you to worry. It's all my fault. I can't stay out of trouble. Sorry. Keanu."

She tucked the note back into her apron pocket. "Izor told me he feared Keanu might steal from the business to pay for his debts. I told him what I just told you. Never. Whatever else he may be, my Keanu isn't a thief. Izor believed me, you bet he did!" she said.

I didn't know anyone who didn't believe Aunty Lena. Big Brah wanted to see Keanu's room. Aunty Lena insisted we eat first. We'd already had breakfast. But no one could say no to Aunty Lena. Without a murmur, we feasted on her sweet macadamia nut pancakes. Only when she was done making the last pancake did she walk us up the stairs to the second floor.

She said, "Keanu returned from work early yesterday. When he didn't come down for dinner, I wondered why. He's usually the life of the dinner table, joking and wisecracking. After dinner I came upstairs to check if he was all right. His door wasn't locked, I called for him, no answer, something was wrong. The others were still downstairs, I was alone. I opened the door, the room was empty! I found the note on the study table.

"Keanu's been in trouble with the cops in the past. But I was sure he had done no wrong this time. Writing me, his aunty, a note and going away for a few days. No crime. He's a big boy, he can take care of himself. I wasn't gonna call the police on him. But still, what do I do?

"In the morning, I had to inform Julie, Keanu wasn't gonna show up for work. I told her about his note, how Keanu was shook. A murder's hard, specially for young people."

We walked down a corridor. Big Brah said, "Can you tell if anything is missing from his room?"

"Anything missing...hmm, why didn't I think of looking? See, you're the detective, I'm not. I just worried my poor Keanu's missing. I should've thought to look if he took anything with him. Of course, his car's gone, it's his first car, it's his favorite thing, his toy. He's worked very hard to own that car, he's only a few months away from paying it off, I'm proud of him. It's a red sedan. I gave him one of my 'I ♥ my ohana' stickers, he stuck it on the rear bumper right away."

I remembered the good-looking red sedan parked outside Global Quality Lumber's sales office the first time we met Keanu. Instead of just days it felt as if it had been a long time ago.

Aunty Lena opened a door and took us into Keanu's room. "I've taught him to organize his room, I'll know if anything is missing," she said.

It was a nice corner room. The late morning light streamed in through the window. The window had a view of the deep canyon at the back of the building. Pure nature. The front of the building was also visible. The asphalt of the deserted approach road sloped away. Keanu had taken the lonely road out of here. *Why?*

Aunty Lena adjusted her glasses and examined the room. The room had a comfortable bed, rug, study table, chair, wall closets and shelves for storage. The study table was where Aunty Lena had found Keanu's note.

She said, "He's taken his ukulele, his green tent, his sleeping bag, his fishing lines and his backpack beach chair. If I hadn't read his note, I'd think he's gone fishing!"

"Does he have a friend?" Big Brah said.

Aunty Lena thought for a moment. "Keanu's friendly,

but he doesn't have a close friend."

"Could he have confided his troubles to the others here?" Big Brah said.

"Keanu's been here the longest. No one else knows what he does more than me. He tells his Aunty Lena everything."

Big Brah inhaled deeply, then exhaled slowly. He fell silent.

Aunty Lena drew closer to Big Brah. "Koa, do you think Keanu's in trouble?" she said.

Big Brah took his time to reply. Often, he had to meditate at the crime scene. "Aunty, I have to figure things out, I have to go back to Waikahe Beach," he said.

I knew what he meant. All of a sudden Aunty Lena looked weary. She took off her glasses.

Hot tears rolled down her cheeks. "I don't want him to be in trouble, Koa!" she said.

Big Brah hugged her. "The killer can't hide for too long," he said.

Aunty Lena separated and wiped her tears. "I know Keanu is innocent," she said.

Aunty Lena's love for Keanu was real. Why would Keanu run away from this? What could he be possibly running away from? I hugged Aunty Lena a big farewell. I loved her. I didn't want her to worry.

Outside, back in the big truck, Big Brah said, "I want to think things over, let's go to the crime scene."

No surprise. Big Brah was meditative all the way to Waikahe Beach. It was a clear day, the sun bright. The blue sky matched the blueness of the ocean. At the beach, the victim's truck had been towed away and the yellow police tape removed. Natural beauty had been restored. The Waikahe River, its waters deep, flowed into the ocean.

The deep river was perfect for Jet Skiers to venture inland. You got to see the beautiful tropical foliage and fern grotto. Jet Skiing was a popular sport for both visitors and locals. The beach was a sanctuary of golden sand baked by the sun. A clump of palms provided inviting shade. Big Brah and I sat on the soft sand under the leafy palms.

The endless ocean stretched in front of us. White-capped waves broke on the golden sand, a constant rhythm. The familiar smell of the ocean filled my nostrils. The touch of a breeze soothed my skin. Big Brah sat still, very still, his gaze faraway. He meditated. From time to time the drone of a Jet Ski going up or down the river interrupted the peace. I finished the mystery novel I had on my phone.

I started downloading another novel from the same series. *Poha's bookcase is a treasure trove of mystery novels,* I thought fondly. The download completed. It was getting dark.

Big Brah stirred. "Izor was all about family, he never shirked ohana," he said.

I agreed. "Even at work, he treated everyone like family."

"What bothers me most is the heartlessness. The killer murdered a father, a husband, a son, a brother," he said.

"The killer didn't learn the lesson of ohana!" I said.

"You're right, Umi, no ohana!"

We sat there in silent communion. The light around us faded, until I saw only the white caps of the waves.

At last, he got up. "Come on, it's time to get Kali," he said.

That evening Big Brah cooked but talked little. Kali

groomed Poli`ahu and Wiliwili thoroughly until their coats shone. Afterward the cats lay contented with no will left to move. I read.

Over dinner, I told Kali about Keanu. "Something spooked him, don't know what it was, but it made him bolt." I finished.

There was no getting away from the fact we were stuck. Even Big Brah didn't say much. "Umi's right, Keanu's running away from something," was all he said.

That night I lay awake in bed. I waited for the soothing rustle of the coconut fronds outside the bedroom window to lull me to sleep. There was one person who knew for sure who the killer was. The one who had killed. It was so weird. There was a killer hiding on an island full of good people. The thought kept me awake for a long time. Finally, I reminded myself Big Brah would catch the murderer. He always did. He always set things right. Then I slept. I dreamed.

My dreams often packed a revelation. In the morning, I had to tell Big Brah and Kali about my strange dream. I hurried downstairs to find them. They were in the kitchen quietly eating breakfast at the round table.

I joined them. "Before I forget, I have to tell you about my dream," I said.

Big Brah and Kali smiled and exchanged knowing looks. They enjoyed listening to my dreams.

I said, "Guess where I was? On a beach, it looked a lot like Waikahe Beach. Guess who else was there? Keanu! Guess what he was doing? Fishing! You know what was wild about this dream? Keanu has this huge fishing line that goes deep...all the way past the breakers. He catches this ginormous red reef fish.

"All of a sudden, this scary old man followed by

a scarier crowd appear out of nowhere, they all look like Keanu. They attack the red fish with machetes, it's gruesome. Like me, Keanu watches horrified. But guess what? The fish is magical.

"Each time the fish is injured, he heals himself. So awesome. The red fish jumps back into the ocean and swims away. End of dream."

Big Brah said, "How do you feel about the dream?"

"It was disturbing when it started, but in the end, it was awesome," I said.

Big Brah nodded absent-mindedly. "Good," he said.

Kali flashed me a smile and squeezed my hand. "Dreams!" she said.

Yes, dreams, especially dreams the rational mind found hard to explain. The dream occasionally playing on my mind, I worked on my college assignment. I liked assignments in the subjects I had chosen. To feed my curiosity, Big Brah and Kali constantly introduced me to different subjects. They encouraged me to study what I found interesting.

Sound advice. Helped me stay ahead with the course work. I was so far ahead in all my classes the Island College let me study on my own. So, I got to spend more time with family, on personal art projects and on investigations. I loved it. I sat at the kitchen table, my favorite place to do assignments. Kali left for work. Apparently Big Brah today only wanted to think about the investigation.

He messed around in the kitchen, doing chores only he knew about. It was past midday. The sun was warming up outside. Big Brah's phone jingled. It was on the round table. He put it on speaker, so I heard everything. It was Aunty Julie. I imagined her in her formal office garb, reading glasses and short, brown hair.

Her voice sounded excited. "Big Brah, I have news! I finished inventorying the files and papers."

"Well, congratulations, that was a lot of hard work!"

"Yes, thanks. There are just two files missing, one of a client, the other of an ex-employee. I told you about them at the Tavern."

"You mean Bo Digalo?"

"Yes, his is the only client file missing."

"And the other?"

"I told you about him too, the ex-employee, Yo Bipo."

"Why would anyone want those files?" Big Brah said.

"Well, Izor was a meticulous man, he liked things organized. He used to say he likes to forget about work things when he's out of the office, so he was careful about filing every little detail away. Not just the official paperwork, those we're required by law to maintain, but he'd write notes about a client or an employee, and then, he'd put those notes in the client or employee file as well," she said.

"Didn't he worry you or Keanu would read his notes?" Big Brah said.

I pictured her smile.

She said, "Yes, like you, I'd worry too, but Izor was naïve, he trusted both of us completely. He never thought we'd peek! He genuinely believed we'd only look at the files if he instructed us to do so, and I did. I looked into the files if he asked me to look something up. Or more likely, I'd need to look something up, and I'd ask him, and he'd just say yes. It was the same with Keanu, Izor trusted him too."

"Even if they had a fight over Keanu's gambling debt?" Big Brah said.

"Yes, even if, that's how naïve Izor could be sometimes about those near him. To the end, he trusted Keanu. The fight over the gambling debt was Izor trying to help out Lena. You know how Lena cares about her children, so Izor wanted to make a man out of Keanu, and good men don't get into debt by bad habits like gambling, he told Keanu. Keanu being young naturally rebelled, he wanted to prove his gambling wasn't a habit...." Her voice died out.

"Who would want those files?" Big Brah asked.

"I don't know," she said.

Big Brah thanked her for all her help. She wished us luck then hung up.

Big Brah said, "It's fair to assume Bipo and Digalo may know something about the missing files. Izor was a meticulous filer, he may have recorded something about his dealings with them in his files, something either of them may want to hide."

"Do you think they had the files stolen?" I said.

"Bipo could have stolen it himself, he knows the office. Digalo? I'd say he could have had it stolen," Big Brah said.

"What if both of them got together and did it?" I said.

"Could be, both of them have the same motive. Revenge. Their hatred for Izor could have brought them together."

I shivered. "Where does Keanu fit into all of this?" I asked.

Slowly Big Brah shook his head. Wryly, he said, "Keanu needs to grow up."

Of course, Keanu shouldn't have run away. *Grow up fast and return.* Meanwhile we had to find the killer.

"What do we do next?" I said.

"We eat lunch. Then we go talk story with Digalo and

Bipo. I want to know how they feel about their missing files," he said.

We were closing in on the killer. Digalo and Bipo. Could be either. Or both. Things had warmed up again. *Mahalo, Aunty Julie.* After lunch we visited Digalo's office. I was still upbeat. This time the receptionist at the front desk called Digalo on the office intercom. She immediately ushered us into his plush carpeted private office. Digalo was at his desk.

Digalo came around the outsize desk. He was dressed formally in shirt, tie and trousers with suspenders. Well-groomed, thinning hair carefully combed over and mustache neatly trimmed. His pudgy, round face had a plastic grin on it. He shook hands with us. Returning to his position behind the desk, he settled himself comfortably in his executive chair.

He gestured for us to sit down. "How can I help you, gentlemen?" he said.

We sat down under the light of the trendy chandelier. The air conditioner cranked on high. It was cold. I shivered. It was a clear, warm afternoon outside. The bay window framed the familiar green mountains. No mist on the mountain tops today. The fun collection of dump trucks, cranes and mixers was in a wire basket. Digalo placed his elbows on the desk's surface, clasped his hands and leaned forward expectantly.

Big Brah said, "Sorry to bother you, we're trying to tie up a few loose ends, I have questions."

"Don't speak in riddles, Big Brah. Tell me what your questions are, I'll answer them if I can, fair enough?" Digalo said.

"Fair enough! Recently there was a burglary in the office of Global Quality Lumber, do you know anything about it?"

Digalo's plump face clouded over. "A burglary! First a murder, then a burglary. You investigate crimes, Big Brah, I don't. I had nothing to do with any burglary, I didn't even know there'd been one."

"Even if one of the two missing files is of your business?" Big Brah said.

Digalo threw up his hands. "The file on my business is missing. Why am I not surprised? Those records proved Izor cheated me, I wrote to him about it, they'd want to lose that file! Well, let me tell you this, the law requires Global Quality Lumber to maintain the records of its business with Digalo Construction. If the file is missing, they're liable," he said.

"With Izor Bomino dead, I figure the only other person interested in the file would be you, Mr. Digalo," Big Brah said.

Digalo took a deep breath, closed his eyes and shook his head. He exhaled and opened his eyes. "No," he said, emphatically.

"No?"

"No, I'm not interested. Izor Bomino is dead. But Global Quality Lumber is still liable for its business with my firm."

Big Brah conceded. "It's true Global Quality Lumber is liable. But all the more reason for them not to misplace the file. Besides, you can still bring action against them, you have evidence the transaction happened, so what good will the missing file do to them other than bring embarrassment in court?"

Digalo tilted his head, stuck out his lower lip and waved a hand in the air. "That I don't know, it's an amateurish move, Izor's wife and son are new to this...."

"I'm confident Lei Bomino or her son Ohia had nothing to do with it," Big Brah said.

For the first time, Digalo looked genuinely troubled. "No, I mean, yes, I-I don't think Lei would do such a thing...or Ohia...he's a fine, young man, but there're others, maybe an employee?"

Gently Big Brah shook his head.

Frowning heavily, Digalo looked out of the bay window at the green mountains. "Lei has no experience," he said.

Big Brah fell silent.

Digalo's voice filled with concern. "Lei doesn't know how tough the business world really is," he said.

Digalo looked at us, his chin quivering with emotion. "She needs guidance," he said.

Digalo's concern for our client was genuine.

Resolutely Digalo rubbed his hands together. "Well, I don't know anything about the burglary," he said.

Big Brah thanked him. "Mahalo! Sorry to have bothered you, by answering my questions, you've helped a lot," he said.

Digalo's face cleared. He rose, smiling. On the wall behind him, in the framed photograph of a lean, bearded and long-haired Digalo with the beloved mayor at the grand opening ceremony of the Aloalo Resort, Digalo smiled the same way.

Graciously he said, "Anytime, Big Brah, I'm always happy to assist you in any way I can."

Graciousness notwithstanding, Digalo had drained some of the earlier upbeatness out of us. Outside, the sun was hot and the afternoon warm, muggy and energy-sapping. Big Brah had wanted to know how Digalo felt about the missing files. Other than Digalo's preposterous suggestion the Bominos stole the files and his strange but touching concern for our client, we hadn't unearthed anything else. Big Brah said every interaction with a suspect told us some part of the truth.

Sometimes it was a very small part but it was always there. You just had to think a little harder. But I couldn't think of a single good reason why the Bominos would steal the files.

Back inside the big truck, Big Brah confirmed my thinking. "I'm sure the Bominos didn't steal their own files, that's ridiculous," he said.

I said, "Digalo says he knows nothing about the burglary. Next, Yo Bipo, he was hiding something last time."

Big Brah blew out a breath. "Let's go see if Bipo's willing to tell us the truth this time."

By the time we parked by Bipo Construction's rusty, streetside sign, I was fully recharged. The sun beat down on the modest trailer, the office. There were more cars parked streetside than I remembered from our last visit here. The yard looked cleaner. All the junked machinery had been moved into a neat pile in the middle of the yard. What truth was Bipo hiding? We walked to the trailer. The trailer's door was wide open. Bipo was inside working at a table with a couple of other men.

Bipo's shaven head gleamed and his goatee was freshly trimmed. When he saw us at the door, he immediately told the others to carry on and hurried over to us. He shook hands with both of us, unsmiling. His bony hand was clammy. He was nervous.

He glanced over his shoulder at the other two men who were staring at us, then spoke to us with his voice low. "Why're you here?" he asked.

Big Brah also kept his voice low. "I'd like to ask you a few questions, outside, in my truck, if you will."

Bipo appreciated the privacy the truck would provide. His grim face showed relief for a moment. "Let's go," he said.

Still unsmiling, Bipo got into the passenger seat. I sat alert in the backseat, watching and listening. Big Brah started the truck, turned on the air conditioner and raised the windows. He turned sideways in the driver's seat and gazed at Bipo.

He said, "There's been a burglary at Global Quality Lumber, do you know anything about it?"

Bipo sat stiffly. He frowned. "No," he said.

"One of the two files missing is your employee file," Big Brah said.

Bipo shrugged, his thin shoulders rising and falling. "I'm not an employee, I haven't been an employee a long time now, long enough not to care about it anymore," he said.

"Still, of all the files, your employee file is missing," Big Brah said.

"I've nothing to do with Izor, not anymore."

"Agreed, but why would a burglar steal your employee file?"

"The burglar didn't just steal my file, there were others, you said so yourself," Bipo said.

"Yes, only one other," Big Brah said, dryly.

Bipo looked interested. "Okay, who else?" he said.

"A client, Digalo."

"Uh-huh. There you go, Digalo's a bigger fish than I am, I don't see you questioning him!"

"I just talked with him."

"Oh. Still. His file is missing too, does he know why?"

Big Brah shook his head. "Digalo says he doesn't know anything about the burglary."

"Then, why should I know? I know nothing about it," Bipo said.

Big Brah sighed softly. "Who else would be interested in your file?"

Bipo turned away from Big Brah. He looked out of the truck's window in the direction of the office trailer. I caught a glimpse of him in the side mirror. His eyes rested on the neat pile of junked machinery in the yard, and he had an intense look on his face. Then the intensity faded and a furtive look came over him. He ran a finger down his goatee as if trying to think up an answer. He was hiding something.

At last, Bipo said, "I don't know about my file. Digalo was a big client, but who'd want his file?"

Big Brah said, "Digalo believes Izor cheated him. Digalo's accusation is Izor replaced quality hardwoods with inferior lumber."

Bipo stiffened. "Does he now?" he said.

"It bothers you?" Big Brah asked.

Animated, Bipo turned to look at Big Brah. "It happened the exact same way when I was there, rare hardwood replaced with cheap lumber. I don't work there anymore, and it still happened, that proves it couldn't have been me. Both times, Izor cheated!"

"But this time he got killed. I have to find the killer," Big Brah said.

"I don't know about the killer, but it's obvious Digalo stole those files. He wanted the file on Digalo Construction secured to prove Izor cheated him. He decided my employee file may've had more information, since, you know, the last time Izor was caught cheating, I took the blame for it."

Big Brah said, "Was there anything in your employee file of interest to you?"

Again, Bipo turned away to stare out of the truck's window on his side. "No," he said, unconvincingly.

On our way back home in the truck, Big Brah said, "There was something in Bipo's employee file that was of interest to Bipo."

I agreed. "I felt it too, he was hiding something."

Surprising me, Big Brah said, "Both Digalo and Bipo are hiding things, we'll know exactly what, in time."

That night over dinner at the kitchen table, I filled in Kali on the investigation. "Keanu's still missing. Digalo and Bipo are being suspiciously secretive about things," I concluded.

Wasn't much. But Big Brah had been in worse. I was confident we would find the killer. Soon. In the morning, we got a break. The sun was out. It was another warm day. Kali was at work. Big Brah and I were home. We were in the living room, each in our own recliner.

Over the years, we had added our favorite things to the living room and made it the cozy haven it was. From where I sat, I had a serene view of the palms, the beach and the ocean. Poli`ahu and Wiliwili slept on the armrests of Kali's recliner. Big Brah was busy studying stone daggers on his tablet. I was deep in the mystery novel. Big Brah's phone jingled.

It was our client, Lei Bomino. She had found something of interest. She would find it easier to explain in person. Big Brah saved her the bother of driving over.

In no time at all, we were in her comfortable living room. The morning sun slanted in through the big windows. The room was filled with light and shadows.

The rooster wall clock was in the shadows. The sunlight fell directly on some of the furniture and the framed family photographs on the wall. A faint coat of dust had settled on them. Big Brah and I sat on the couch.

Lei Bomino chose the accent chair across the coffee table. It was a few days since I had last seen her grieving and tearful at her husband's funeral. Although there were more worry lines on her round face, the dark circles around her eyes had faded and her silver and black hair was pulled back in a determined topknot. She had found a sense of purpose. She was calmer now. She was also home alone. No Romo. No Ohia. The men were at work.

She said, "I'll be going downtown to the office from next week, so I've started preparing myself, gives me something to do, Julie calls it work therapy. I'll feel closer to Izor, looking after his work, something in me says he'd want me to." She paused to wipe the corner of her eye with a finger.

Big Brah nodded, sympathetic. "Work therapy," he said.

She said, "I really appreciate what you did for Ohia. He's hurting, he misses his father, he tells me to be strong. I know him, he acts mature, but he's soft inside, makes me proud though. Volunteering the DNA sample was such a load off his back, he's a new man, my Ohia. Now, he doesn't have to hide his head in shame, mahalo!" She looked at Big Brah then me.

She even cracked a smile. Displaying great inner strength, she said, "We'll get through this."

Big Brah nodded solemnly. "We'll get the results of the DNA match early next week, soon as I learn about it, I'll let you know," he said, helpfully.

She sighed. "Besides, things have been going wrong.

Keanu's missing, there's been a burglary...."

Big Brah said, "Why, yes, I had a question for you about the master key to the downtown office. Aunty Julie says your husband kept the key, is it somewhere here in the house?"

The rooster wall clock was in shadow. On the side table under the clock, the wicker bowl still had a handful of keychains and keys. She pointed to the wicker bowl. "We keep the master key to the office along with all our keys. I tied a red ribbon to the master key, you can see it. It's been there the entire time," she said.

Big Brah got up to examine the key. He held it up so I could see it too. The key had the manufacturer's name on its side. The single, brass key was tied to a red ribbon frayed at the edges from wear.

He said, "You sure the key has been here the entire time?"

"I put all my keys there, I use it all the time. If the red ribbon wasn't there, I'd know. So yes, I'm sure," she said.

Big Brah returned to the couch, defeated. "What is it you wanted to tell us?" he said.

Her face darkened with worry. "Global Quality Lumber was set up as a partnership. Izor had me as his partner. But I so rarely had to do anything, I know very little of the business. I'm going to be leaning on Julie a lot, she's been a good friend! In preparation for next week, I was sorting out our home paperwork and bills.

"Izor always took care of those in the same meticulous way he maintained his office, everything in perfect order. Maybe because everything was so well organized, maybe it was Izor's spirit guiding me, I got to look into a checkbook he was using recently.

"Only five checks had been issued from it. There were

copies of the used checks. To my surprise, all five checks had been made out to the same person, an ex-employee Izor had sworn never to do any kind of business with again, Yo Bipo!"

Big Brah frowned. "May I see the checkbook?" he said.

"Yes." She left the room, returned with a checkbook, handed it to Big Brah and resumed her seat.

Big Brah examined the checkbook. I craned to see what he was seeing. It was a customized checkbook the bank printed for its best customers. Big Brah had one like it for as long as I remembered. The checks had a background of lehua flowers, the address, phone and account number all printed out. The five copies were filled out in the same neat handwriting.

Even the signature was legibly "Izor Bomino." The checks were all made out to "Yo Bipo" and dated daily from March 3 onward. The last check was dated March 7, the day before the murder. Big Brah said life was easier if you knew math. I added up the amounts on each of the checks easily.

"Ten thousand dollars," I murmured.

Big Brah nodded approvingly. "That's what I got," he said.

Big Brah handed the checkbook back to Lei Bomino. "That's a lot of money, very short time, what do you think was going on?" he said.

Lei Bomino shook her head slowly. Her face reflected the pain she felt inside plain as the ocean reflected the moon. "Izor had sworn never ever to even speak to this man, why he'd do such a thing after all these years, I can't even begin to imagine, unless...."

"Unless?"

She shivered. "I don't like saying this, Yo used to be

like family, he's played ball with Ohia in the yard, he's come to my parties, I used to know him, but why'd Izor pay him money, unless…Bipo was blackmailing Izor."

I started. Bitter, blackmailer Bipo.

Chapter 12: Perseverance Pays

"Blackmail Izor, why?" Big Brah said.

Lei Bomino said, "Hmm, that I can't tell you for sure, recently there was another complication. Digalo accused Izor of cheating the same way another client had in the past. Back then I remember Izor had suspected Bipo, Bipo vehemently denied he'd replaced the lumber. So now, to keep Bipo quiet, Izor could be giving Bipo money. Not that I believe even for a moment Izor did anything wrong.

"But he was that kind of man, you know, he liked to pacify people rather than aggravate them. I'm sure he was trying to find out who the real culprit was in Digalo's case, in the while, he probably wanted to keep things quiet."

Big Brah thanked our client. "I'll ask Bipo about the money," he said.

To me, he said, "It's a Friday, Bipo leaves work early, if we hurry, we can catch him."

We hurried back to Bipo's office trailer. The door was open. Bipo was working inside with the same two men at the same table as last time. They were talking and doing some kind of interactive calculations on their construction tablets. Bipo's shaven head gleamed under the lights.

His thin, wispy goatee bobbed as he spoke. He saw us and he did the same routine as before. Told the men to carry on without him and scurried over to us. Silently Big Brah and I turned and simply trekked back to the big truck. Bipo followed us, wordlessly. Twice we had talked to Bipo, but he had kept his secret safe. This time he had something to answer. Goes to show, just keep trying. *Perseverance pays.* Bipo got into the truck confidently.

Twice before we had come to him. He had sent us packing both times. He was sure he would get lucky a third time. He wanted to get it over with. Bipo settled into the passenger seat with an air of impatience.

He turned to look at Big Brah. "What is it this time?" he said.

Big Brah took a deep breath and exhaled slowly. He gripped the steering wheel and gazed stoically out the windshield. "This time we know what you've been hiding from us, Mr. Bipo," he said, softly.

Bipo gaped at Big Brah. At last, he recovered. "I don't know what you're talking about," he said.

"I'm talking about the ten thousand dollars you got from Izor," Big Brah said.

"Yes, no, I, yes, yes, I got ten thousand dollars from Izor, I'm not denying, my bank will also confirm!" Bipo said.

Big Brah let the low hum of the engine and air conditioner fill the silence in the truck's big cabin. Then he said, quietly, "Mind explaining to me why Izor paid you?"

Bipo sighed. He made a pleading face. "I can explain, it isn't what you think, I wasn't trying to wrangle money out of Izor, quite the opposite. He wanted me to have the money!"

Big Brah said nothing. He continued to gaze out the windshield.

Distressed, Bipo wrung his thin hands. "Okay, I know it sounds wrong. Why would Izor want to gift me ten thousand dollars? After all these years. It's too good to be true, isn't it? My dad used to say, Yo, don't trust anything if it's too good to be true. I should've listened to Dad.

"You've seen where I live, the coastal trail is only three minutes from my home, I jog on the trail, every morning. Six days before the murder, I was jogging along the trail, beyond the bridge, Izor approached me. I was about to ignore him, jog away, when he thrust a check into my hand. I shouldn't have taken the money.

"He said, 'I know you're mad, hope this money will cool you down!' And he turned and jogged away. I looked at the amount on the check, and I scoffed at it. Two thousand dollars wouldn't begin to cover my losses due to him. But he did it again the next day. Another two thousand dollars. By the fifth day, I melted. He thrust the now familiar check into my hand.

"'Why're you doing this?' I asked.

"Izor smiled, all playful, like he used to, when I first started with him. He patted my cheek like old times, fond and cheerful. 'Tomorrow, I'll tell you why,' he said.

Bipo stared down at his hands. "But Izor didn't make it the next day, and now I'll never know why he gave me the money."

Big Brah turned to look at Bipo. "If you're innocent, you won't regret confiding in us," he said.

Bipo left without another word, slamming the door after him. Big Brah drove away.

I said, "His story is too weird not to be true, I don't think he could make it up."

Big Brah surprised me. "He's still hiding something."

Big Brah's sixth sense had to be tingling. I was sure he would get to the bottom of it. Soon. It was Friday evening. The weekend was here. He'd get time to think harder. We picked Kali up from work and drove home. Kali looked tired. Her big, brown eyes drooped.

She had worked herself way more than she should, one of the consequences of her interacting with her bad relatives. As we took the exit to our home from the coastal highway, Big Brah sniffed the moist, ocean air. He glanced at Kali. He must have decided she needed to rest and relax. A night ride on the ocean was one of Kali's favorite things to do when she wasn't working.

He said, "I propose we go canoeing tonight!"

Kali shed her tiredness like a warm jacket on a hot summer day. "Canoeing! Umi, did you hear that, we're going canoeing!" she shouted out, joyfully.

I love going out on the ocean, especially in the night. There is something surreal about the experience. I was already bouncing in my seat.

"Yay!" I joined in.

Our cool Kali was back. Fun. Back home, with the day ending around us in kaleidoscopic colors and the wild music of songbirds, we filled coolers generously with musubis, coconut water cans and other goodies from the refrigerator. Carefree. We all ran to our rooms to change into swimwear and an extra layer for the cool night breeze.

We gathered back in the kitchen, ready to head out to the boathouse. It was dark outside and I had my flashlight ready. I heard a car approaching fast on our driveway.

A visitor? *Please, not now.* Big Brah and Kali must have heard it too. We looked at each other uncertainly. The car halted in the front. Big Brah and I had our hands full rolling the packed coolers. Moreover, the kitchen door provided easier access to the boathouse. Kali signaled for us to carry on.

She headed toward the front door. "I got it," she said.

Both Big Brah and I knew she could handle anything as well if not better than us. So, we didn't worry. I sang a tune and Big Brah hummed all the way to the boathouse. I flipped the wall switch for the generator. The boathouse filled with light. Big Brah and I scrunched up our eyes to adjust to the sudden brightness. Then, as was our habit, with our eyes adjusted to the bright light, we took a moment to admire our boats.

The big boat's sizable v-shaped hull reflected the bright light. The wide deck with many seats was perfect for partying. Of course, Big Brah and Kali used the big boat for meditating out on the ocean. Next to the boat was the sturdy, outrigger canoe with its six seats and paddles. The canoe's booms and float were built to provide perfect balance. Big Brah and I had toiled making it. The canoe had started out as a science project.

I wanted to make a model of the outrigger canoe our ancestors had first used to find and populate the island. But with Big Brah nothing ever stays small. In no time the both of us were working hard on the real-life canoe. Big Brah was named after the koa tree. We used the wood from the koa tree to make the canoe. The wood was used by our ancestors too. It was tough. It was hardy. *Like Big Brah.* We set the coolers down on the canoe's two middle seats, cracked a couple of cans, sipped coconut water and waited for Kali.

Soon we heard voices from outside. Both women. One was Kali, for sure. The other voice also sounded familiar. Kali entered the boathouse with a woman in teal activewear. I recognized her instantly. Maile Bipo. So, it had been her in the car. What was she doing here so late?

I heard Kali say to her, "...what you have to ask Koa

sounds important, it can't wait, so come with us, it'll cheer you up, you'll get plenty time to talk."

Kali saw us and smiled brightly. "Maile's coming along," she said.

What important thing had Maile come to ask Big Brah? Big Brah and I tucked away the coolers under the seats, he calm, me curious. I sat on the bench at the front of the boat, the lookout. Maile climbed into the seat behind me. Big Brah was the steersman.

He took the stern seat. Kali sat in front of Big Brah. Big Brah and I paddled. Years of practice paddling together and our strokes were totally synchronized. Expertly Big Brah steered the canoe out of the boathouse.

The boathouse was built at the edge of an inlet. Effortlessly Big Brah navigated the canoe past the inlet to the open ocean. The canoe shot forward smoothly, gliding over the waves. The shore lights dimmed. The evening grew dark around us.

A canopy of stars sparkled in the moonless sky. Big Brah and I rested the oars and let the canoe bob at the will of the ocean. Water lapped against the canoe. Regardless of the time of day, being out on the ocean made me hungry. I turned around. Kali and Maile turned to face each other. They sat with their backs supported by the side of the canoe. In the gentle wash of light from the onboard night lights, a more recent upgrade to the ancient canoe, Kali promptly got food out of the coolers.

The musubis tasted delicious out here with the salty ocean spray all around us. I tasted the meat, the delicate seaweed and the chewy rice. Afterward the sweet-salty coconut water tasted better than ever. Eventually I looked at Maile. She was eating. Her dark hair was gathered in a high ponytail and wispy bangs covered her forehead.

She finished a musubi. "Mm...I never thought musubis could even taste this delicious, I feel better already. Mahalo, Kali!"

Kali smiled encouragingly at Maile. "What's bothering you?"

Maile grew solemn. Gathering her thoughts, she blinked several times. She looked uncertainly at Big Brah. "He's in trouble, isn't he, my Yo?" she said.

Big Brah took his time to reply. At last, he said, "I won't know if he's in trouble unless he tells me everything. Every time I speak with him, I get the impression he doesn't want to talk, as if he's hiding something."

Maile let out a dry sob. "I-I know he's in trouble. He told me how you've found out about the money he got from Izor, I had to come see you...why don't you think Yo's innocent?" she said.

Big Brah didn't answer her question. Instead, he raised a quizzical eyebrow. "Why're you asking me this?" he said.

She tried to explain. "You see, I love him. I know how he's suffered. The first time I met him at the Tavern, he was drunk and close to giving up. He'd been wrongly accused, all his hard work had brought him a lump of coal, he wasn't just tired, he was tired of life! I-I pulled him back from the brink.

"We loved each other. In the beginning he'd have episodes of depression. Our love was our sanctuary, everything was rosy as long as we were together. Things started to go well, Yo recovered. Then this terrible murder.

"He's on the verge of a depression episode again. I didn't want to leave him today, but luckily my parents, they love Yo like their son, they wanted to spend some time with him, and Yo wanted to hang out with them."

Big Brah took a thoughtful sip of his coconut water, as he absorbed what she had told him.

Her voice had a tremble in it. "I wanted to know what you think he's done wrong," she said.

Big Brah sighed softly. "I already told you, I won't know what kind of trouble he's in unless he talks freely with me." He looked toward the island silhouetted in the starlit night. "But, here we are, so far away from it all, why don't you tell me what you know? Maybe I'll be able to help you then."

She looked relieved. "Yes, I can tell you everything, I know everything Yo knows, it's better me than him. You see, when he's depressed, he gets upset talking to people."

Big Brah nodded, sympathetic. "I understand," he said.

Maile looked at Kali. Kali gave her another encouraging smile.

Maile took a deep breath. "Yo got ten thousand dollars from Izor, it's true, he showed me the checks. He told me not to tell anyone about it, not even my parents, he didn't know what Izor was up to. Izor used to be quite a prankster when Yo first started work with him at Global Quality Lumber. Most of his pranks were for fun, but when he accused Yo of cheating, all the fun was gone.

"Obviously Yo didn't trust Izor. The first check, Yo didn't even deposit it, but I think it was the second day, Yo got curious. He wanted to find out if the checks were for real, he deposited them. It took a day to verify. Both the checks were good! What was Yo to do? He's patient, he waited for Izor to explain. The day Izor died, just like the previous days, Yo went out to meet Izor...."

Say, what? Yo had gone out to meet Izor on the day

of the murder. It was a detail Yo had carefully never mentioned to us. It gets thirsty out here on the ocean. I chugged coconut water, engrossed. Big Brah didn't react in any way. Kali cracked open a coconut water can and handed it to Maile.

Maile sipped her drink. "Yo came back, earlier than usual, terribly agitated. His hands trembled, they were damp and cold, his face, I've never seen him more scared, he was just shaking all over, and at the same time, perspiring. Sweat on his forehead, sweat trickling down his face. I calmed him down, asked what happened.

"He told me Izor was dead, he hadn't killed Izor, Izor had been murdered. I asked him if he'd called 9-1-1, he told me no. When I reached for my phone, he wrapped his fingers around my wrist and shook his head pleadingly.

"I looked into his eyes, and I couldn't do it. I knew he hadn't killed Izor, he just didn't want to be involved in any way with Izor a second time. I sort of agreed never to talk about the money, Izor or that awful morning. But then you found out about the money, and here I am talking about it."

I felt sorry for her. Kali must have too. Both of us looked expectantly at Big Brah, assuming he would say something comforting to Maile. To our surprise he didn't.

Instead, Big Brah said, "Invaluable, by what you're saying, Yo was perhaps the first person to see Izor dead, I'm afraid I'll have to talk with him again."

"No, please, leave Yo out of this!" Maile was vehement.

Big Brah was equally insistent. It had to be his sixth sense at work. "I'm sorry, but he may have seen something or heard something important."

Maile closed her eyes, shook her head then blew out a breath. She was overcome with an emotion I didn't understand. She opened her eyes. Her chin was up. She was determined. She crushed the empty can in her hand and threw the crushed metal into the trash bag. She was desperate.

She said, "What's important, huh? Yo's employee file was stolen is important. You wanted to know if Yo knew anything about it, why don't you ask me the same question? You don't have to ask me, I'll tell you something about the file even Yo doesn't know.

"Yo only knows what he told me. He told me how Izor was meticulous and organized, Yo was afraid Izor would've kept records of the ten thousand dollars in his office files, Izor always did. Yo fretted about it. I wanted to ease his mind. Why should Yo suffer because of something Izor did? Yo had already suffered so much from Izor's previous actions! So I decided to end Yo's worry.

"Yo had told me about the office a thousand times. He'd told me where the filing cabinets were, everything, I knew to get in. I observed how worried he was the police would find the file, and it would get him into more trouble. Then you came to our home, told us you were investigating.

"Yo had a glimmer of hope the police wouldn't find him out, but when he learned you were involved, he worried a lot more. I couldn't bear to see him anxious. I asked him if he had the file, would that make him happy? He told me yes, it would ease his worries. We talked about it all weekend long.

"Sunday night, I waited for Yo to fall asleep, he sleeps at about midnight, but that night he was worried sick. He stayed up, I kept looking at the clock. Finally, at about 1 o' clock he slept. I let him get into deep sleep, took another half hour. Then it took me some time to get ready."

Maile smiled wanly likely remembering her own heroics. "I wore my black activewear, so I wouldn't be visible in the dark. I packed a flashlight, a rope and a Swiss knife. I'd never played burglar before, I didn't know what was appropriate, I used common sense."

Common sense? She had used common sense for the burglary. If only she had used common sense earlier. She wouldn't have attempted the burglary. A gust of wind, and a larger than usual wave rocked the canoe. Despite the rocking canoe, I listened with total attention.

There was a catch in Maile's voice. She said, "I let my love for him guide me. I left home after two. The streets were empty, I didn't drive too fast or too slow, I didn't want to attract any attention. Still, I got there in about 10-12 minutes. The parking lot was empty. I drove a block down the street, parked streetside. I used the sidewalk to skulk back to the building. It took me longer than normal. I was trying to stay in the shadows, away from the streetlights. I never really looked at my watch, but I'd say I was at the window of the rec room at about 2:30 in the morning. I used my flashlight to see.

"The window was broken. I was confused. I didn't know what to make of it, I took it as a sign the goddess was on my side. I climbed in easily, it was indeed the rec room with its TV and recliners, just as Yo had described. I padded to the front office. Another surprise.

"The files were on the floor, the cabinets a mess. I searched for Yo's file, I couldn't find it. Either someone had already stolen the file, after all the window was broken before I got there, or it was buried in the mess of files and papers on the floor. It was getting late, I feared Yo would be up, he'd miss me, look for me. I fled the place."

A bigger wave. The boat rocked wildly. I glanced at Big Brah. *Time to grab the paddles,* I thought.

But Big Brah sat there like a big rock, immobile. "Why're you telling me this?" he said.

"I'm coming clean with you...so maybe Yo won't be in...trouble," she said.

"Good, you're halfway there. Trouble is, Yo hasn't come clean with me, yet," Big Brah said.

Another big wave lifted the boat. The wind was really picking up. Big Brah moved fast. He grabbed a paddle and hurled me a glance to check whether I was ready. I was. Together we righted the canoe and paddled shoreward. Expertly Big Brah guided the canoe back to the boathouse. After Maile left, we finished emptying the coolers and doing a few other chores in the brightly lit kitchen. I asked Big Brah and Kali what they thought about Maile's story.

Kali sat down at the round table. She sighed softly. "Maile is sweet, she cares deeply for Yo," she said.

I joined Kali at the round table. "No doubt," I said.

Big Brah put away the coolers. He ambled over to the round table and stood over us. "We did get invaluable new information from Maile. The burglar had been there before her."

I was refreshed by the canoeing. "So, someone else stole the files," I said, brightly.

Big Brah looked significantly at both of us. "And Yo had gone out to meet Izor. Yo found Izor dead. Yo has been hiding this from us. He discovered the body. Pretty big."

I nodded.

"Right," Kali said.

Big Brah sat down. "The fallout between Yo and Izor wasn't a secret. With Izor murdered mysteriously, who else could have stolen Yo's file? Digalo could have wanted to find out more about the older scam, the scams were similar. Digalo's interest is clear. Yo made a good point. But we still don't know why Izor paid ten thousand dollars in five installments."

"According to Lei Bomino, it was blackmail!" I said.

"But Bipo says it wasn't blackmail. Izor was gradually making up for the injustice done years ago," Big Brah said.

Kali sat with her elbows on the table and interlaced her fingers. She rested her chin on her hands. "Anything Izor did just before the murder could be important. We have to find out why Izor paid the money."

Made sense. "But, how?" I said.

Big Brah closed his eyes, thinking. Kali gazed intensely at Big Brah. I waited.

Big Brah opened his eyes. "Izor was a meticulous recordkeeper. Maile and Yo, both of them, they made a mistake."

"A mistake, what?" I said.

"When Izor filed away Yo's records in his employee file, Yo was an employee. Maile made the same mistake, assuming Izor would have filed away why he was paying Yo in the same file," Big Brah said.

I saw where he was going with this. "Izor kept the checkbook he used to write out the checks to Yo at home," I said, excited.

Big Brah nodded, approvingly. "Izor wouldn't have filed away any recent record about Yo in the office," he said.

Kali clapped. "He'd keep the record at home!"

Big Brah had used his sixth sense. "Lei Bomino found the checkbook, she'll find the record for the payments, we'll know why Izor paid the ten thousand dollars," he

said.

"Yeah, whether it was blackmail payment or not," I said.

"It's not too late, I'm gonna call Lei Bomino. I'll request her to look for the record," Big Brah said.

"It's gotta be at home, his or hers," Kali said.

Excitement surged through me. I knew we were going to strike gold. But that night I was up for a long time thinking. Maile had found the office window broken, so if it wasn't her or Yo, who could have stolen the files? And why? The following morning Kali slept in.

It was her day off work. Big Brah and I finished breakfast. Big Brah's phone jingled. It was Lei Bomino. She was at the Bomino Court home, and she had found the record for the payments. Big Brah told her we would be over pronto. Bomino Court was quieter and even more picturesque than I remembered it from the first time we had come here.

The sun was out and the entire area was awash in sunlight. The homes looked out at the grassy rolling plains and the clear silhouette of the distant mountains. Big Brah slowed the truck. Ahead on the asphalt, a flock of doves basked in the sun, laidback and not at all prepared to move out of the way. Reluctantly they hopped to the side of the road. An enterprising couple flew alongside the truck.

Big Brah smiled and looked over at me. "The doves, they love us, Umi," he said.

I remembered Pua'a the pig and Nani the spider from our trip up to Poha's quarry. "As we love them," I said.

His smile widened. The low hedge of Izor Bomino's home came up first. Big Brah swung the truck in through the welcoming open entrance. The old swing and play structure were on the yard to our left. The large, two-story home with attached garage drew closer. All the doors and windows were wide open.

Lei was airing the home. The garage door was also open and the daylight strong enough to light up the inside. Unusual, the garage had no cars but an amazing collection of Jet Skis. Lei Bomino's SUV was parked on the side of the driveway. Big Brah parked the big truck behind her SUV. We got down.

I stopped to stare at the Jet Skis. There were well-loved older models and fun-to-ride newer models. A few of the Jet Skis were state-of-the-art. There was a total of fourteen.

Big Brah slowed down to a stop by me. "Nice collection," he said.

The front door opened. Lei Bomino stepped out to meet us. The dark circles under her eyes were back and her salt-and-pepper hair was all tousled. Even her muumuu was crumpled from wear. She hadn't got much sleep in the night.

She waved a dark blue file folder at us. "Mahalo for coming over," she said.

She must have seen me staring slack-jawed at the Jet Skis. Sadly she sighed. "Izor's hobby, he loved riding those Jet Skis, he'd always have them outside, never inside the garage, and a Jet Ski always in the truck, ready to go. We'd ride together sometimes, it used to be fun," she said.

She took us into a living room with hardwood floor and furniture. The sitting area had assorted chairs of varying sizes and designs.

She gestured at the armchairs for us to sit down. "Take your pick, each chair is special. You see, before Izor started Global Quality Lumber, he used to work in the family's high-end furniture business with Papa Bomino and big brother Romo. These chairs, he had them made with a lot of care for his own home. He cared a lot for his home, for Ohia, for me."

Big Brah fitted himself into a big armchair, while I did the same with a regular one. She handed Big Brah the blue file folder and sat down across from us.

She said, "Ever since you called last night, I've hardly slept. First, I went through my home, I found so many things, none of them of any value to you and the investigation, but you know, of so much sentimental value. I slept a few hours, then in the morning I came over to Bomino Court. Coming here brought back many more old memories, we used to live here as one big family, and just as you'd predicted, I found this blue file folder in his bedroom safe."

Solemnly Big Brah opened the file folder. I got up and stood behind his armchair, so I could see what he was seeing. There was just one sheet of paper. The sheet had a name written on top. I recognized the neat handwriting. Same as in the checks. Izor's, indeed. The name was Yo Bipo. Below the name, again in the same handwriting, a note.

Big Brah read the note out loud. "Paid $10,000 in 5 installments. Payments on March 3-7."

Lei Bomino said, "Hmm, after all these years...why would Izor pay Yo?"

Big Brah nodded. "Interesting timing. The last payment was made the day before the murder."

"Was it blackmail?" Lei Bomino said.

Big Brah closed the folder. "Hard to tell. Your husband doesn't reveal why he made those payments."

"That's all I could find," Lei Bomino said.

Big Brah thanked her. Disappointed, I returned to the big truck with Big Brah. Big Brah settled himself in the driver's seat, the blue file folder Lei Bomino had given us still in his hand. I belted up in the passenger seat. The sun was bright around us. The Jet Skis aired in the garage.

Next to me, Big Brah started. "I just realized, there may be more to this," he said.

Big Brah's sixth sense was at work. Big Brah rested the file folder on the steering wheel. He opened the folder. He examined the sheet of paper from the folder.

Big Brah was always careful not to miss anything. He flipped the sheet over. For a moment the page blurred, and I was connected to the dead man speaking from another realm. Then the blur morphed back to the page. There was another name at the top. Bo Digalo.

Below the name Izor had written, "Meeting at 7:45 a.m. on March 8, Waikahe Beach."

This was big. Temblors are rare on the island. Otherwise, I'd swear the big truck swayed like a boat on a stormy ocean. I was glad I was buckled up. Big Brah and I had met with Digalo twice. Both times, Digalo had carefully forgotten to mention he was supposed to meet with the victim precisely at the time and place of the murder. *Wow.*

Chapter 13: Cupcakes and Musubis

Within minutes Big Brah and I were out of Bomino Court and looking for Digalo. It was a Saturday. Digalo wasn't in his downtown office. The security guard knew where Digalo lived. She gave us helpful directions. Digalo's home was on a hill. In ten minutes, we were on a smooth, long driveway. The truck climbed the hill.

In the sunshine, the ocean sparkled blue, the sight fantastic. Up and ahead, the home with its wide arches, deep awnings and big pillars looked a fine work of architecture. On the island we liked our homes in all shapes and sizes, we knew how we liked them and we liked to tell our architects how. Digalo's home was exceptional. It proved his status as a big-name developer. The big truck continued to climb the hill. I heard the sound of someone mowing.

The pleasant smell of fresh-mowed grass filled my nostrils. The sound grew louder. A person in a yellow-and-black checkered pattern shirt rode a tractor-mower. Egrets colored as white as the ocean froth followed the tractor-mower. The birds eagerly gobbled up the critters the mower churned up. Checkered Shirt waved to us, friendly.

Big Brah stopped the truck. Checkered Shirt also stopped, turned the tractor-mower off and got down. On the elevated mower, he had looked bigger. But on the grass, I saw him fully. He was a small man. Grinning, he jogged up to Big Brah's window.

Checkered Shirt had bright, black eyes. "You look like someone I see on TV," he said.

Big Brah nodded.

Recognition lit up Checkered Shirt's eyes. "I know, you are Big Brah!" He looked toward me. "And you must be his assistant, Umi!"

Guilty, as charged.

Checkered Shirt said, "I'm gardener here, my name's Iggy."

Big Brah and I conveyed our happiness at meeting Iggy by declaring, "Good to meet you."

Iggy grinned contentedly. "I meet good people, I love it," he said.

How true. I shared Iggy's sentiment. I was loving it.

Suddenly Iggy's contented grin vanished. He seemed to remember something. "Bo tell me you question him about murder, is this true?"

Big Brah smiled, pleasantly. "Sure."

Iggy's eyes narrowed. "Bo good guy, he no hunt, he no kill nobody."

Big Brah didn't say anything.

Iggy squinted at Big Brah to make sure Big Brah was listening. "Bo, he always listen to me, always. I look after Bo."

Like the small suckerfish looks after the whale shark, I thought.

Iggy said, "Me his big brother, he my little brah."

Big brothers came in all sizes.

Big Brah smiled, amused. "Is Bo home, Iggy?" he said.

Iggy shook his head, shooting a silent arrow of disappointment my way. "Bo not home. He off island for the weekend."

My suspicion of Digalo grew faster than the bamboo grew in spring.

Iggy said, "Bo left message for you."

Big Brah must have also been disappointed. "What's the message?" he said.

Iggy pumped himself up. Maximum height. Maximum girth. He mimicked Bo. "Tell anyone who look for me, my wife left me. I mourn. Be back at work on Monday, 'til then I mourn!"

Sounded like something Digalo would do. It was a setback but Monday wasn't far away. Ohia's DNA match results were also due on Monday. To confirm Ohia's innocence, we would have to attend the chief's morning meeting. Then we'd be back on Digalo's trail. Big Brah thanked Iggy and we drove back home. First thing I noticed in our clean and organized garage was Kali's old, blue truck wasn't there.

Kali did grocery runs sometimes. We all did. I thought nothing of it. It was a Saturday, a weekend. The big, black truck could use a wash. I told Big Brah. He nodded and disappeared into the house. No doubt he had homework to do for the important meeting with the chief on Monday.

In no time I had the truck's black and chrome exterior shining. Kali hadn't returned. She rarely took this long for a grocery run, but I wasn't worrying. I sauntered inside. To my surprise, Big Brah was sitting at the kitchen round table, his face buried in his hands. He heard me and slowly lifted his head. His handsome face had concern written all over it.

He pointed to a folded sheet of paper stuck under the salt shaker. "Kali had to go," he said.

Bummer. No Kali. I read her note. "Got an email from

the mainland. This time they pointed out they sent me the invite, so the least I can do is send them a gift. They repeated that I'm a bad relative. I need to sort this out. Need time. Don't want to be a bother. I'm going to the cottage."

"Why do they keep bullying Kali? Ugh. She doesn't deserve it!" I said.

"True." Big Brah sighed softly.

Without Kali, Poli`ahu and Wiliwili grew droopy and sad. Big Brah made lilikoi ice cream. He knew Kali would need it. I read. We waited for her to come back. The day, then evening dragged by. No Kali. We slept. In the morning, Big Brah and I were up early.

It was a Sunday. We finished breakfast at the kitchen table. Still no word from Kali. It was a bright morning otherwise. The sun was out, the birds chirped and the fragrance of early blooms from the flower garden filled the house.

Big Brah must have noticed my gloomy face. "Don't worry, Kali's going to be all right," he said.

I was missing her. I said nothing.

The easy smile played on his face. "Let's go cheer her up," he said.

"Great idea!" I said.

But both of us knew Kali was not to be disturbed. Big Brah always said everyone needed time to meditate. Afterward you felt better. He had taught me to meditate. I knew it worked. Kali would get her time to meditate. Besides, this early in the morning, she was likely sleeping in.

I said, "What do you have in mind?"

"I made a fresh batch of lilikoi ice cream, you know how much she likes it, let's go deliver it to her, we'll leave it on her lanai!" he said.

Home delivery. We had done it before. I was up for it. We filled a container with the healthy, homemade ice cream. We put the container inside a blue cooler with a white lid and handle. I carried the cooler to the garage. The big, black truck still shone from the recent wash. We boarded the truck.

Big Brah nodded approvingly. I had cleaned the inside too. Soon we neared the cottage Kali had inherited from her grand-aunt. Island pines grew straight and tall all around us. Through the gaps in between the tree trunks, down a slope, I glimpsed a startling blue ocean. The road narrowed. The truck swished past a bridge over a gurgling stream. The cottage came into view. It was a sturdy, wooden structure with a lanai and a small garage.

Big Brah slowed the truck down. "The same plan. I'll drive closer, you hop on out, put the cooler on the lanai and race back."

I did a shaka. "By the time she gets the door open, we'll be gone," I said.

Big Brah did a reply shaka. "We don't want to disturb her, only help."

I had done this before. I was ready to go. We got closer to the lanai. My body tensed. The truck slowed down to a crawl. I hopped out, cooler in hand. I raced up the three steps to the lanai.

The lanai had quaint patio furniture: a table and chairs. I glanced at the front door. It stayed closed. We were going to get away with it. I set the cooler down gently on the table. I was about to turn away, when I noticed a decorative flowerpot on the table. The flowerpot had a folded sheet of paper wedged under it. The sheet of paper had my name on it!

Without pausing to think, I grabbed the folded sheet of paper and sprinted back. I dove into the truck. We sped away whooping. We'd done it. We had delivered the surprise ice cream. She'd find it, she'd enjoy it, but we hadn't disturbed her in any way.

I imagined seeing her again. She was always generous with her compliments. She'd be proud of us. Commend us on our speed, enterprise, innovation and stealth. Back on the coastal highway, I opened up the sheet of paper.

It was a note from Kali. "Koa, love you for your patience. Umi, I'll make it up to you. Love you both forever. Thanks for the ice cream! Kali."

I stared at the note for a long time. She had known we would be doing this. *How well she knows us,* I thought. Tears stung the back of my eyes. I blinked them away. I laughed and read her note aloud for Big Brah.

He chuckled deeply. He was always pleased when Kali surprised him. "She gets us, that makes you feel better, doesn't it?" he said.

Amazing. It did make me feel better. A lot. I was still in a good mood on Monday morning. Big Brah and I drove to the gray county building. Home to the PD and the medical examiner's office. Clouds had overrun the sun by the time we got there. We headed to the chief's office. The chief had a corner office. Everyone at the PD knew us.

We got to walk in and out. We belonged. The chief's assistant, the always smiling Mrs. Da Costa, sat in the outer office.

She waved us in with a smile. "Chief's expecting you, go right in," she said.

The chief's office had a friendly vibe. Bright, fluorescent ceiling lamps illuminated the surroundings. The walls were painted a stark white. But the walls were decorated with mementos and framed photographs of the chief, as he performed karaoke at numerous community gatherings all around the island. The chief rose from behind his desk to greet us.

The chief had a welcoming smile on his suave, clean-shaven face. He wore a blue shirt with a tropical flower print, black trousers and oxfords. He was small and dapper. His abundant silver hair was brushed in an eye-catching style.

Everyone recognized the chief by his hair. Rumor had it his hair had been the same since his high school senior year. Thirty-some years ago. He said he had brushed his hair the same way from the very day he decided to join the force. The hair on top of his head was crimped into five precise waves, and the hair on the sides and back of his head was trimmed short. I liked his style.

The chief glanced up at the office clock and waved for us to sit down. "Loni just called, he's running a few minutes late," he said.

The chief sat down. Big Brah and I settled down in chairs across the desk from the chief.

"His daughters!" The chief added by way of explanation for Loni's lateness.

Big Brah and I were well aware of Loni's fondness for his daughters. Sagely Big Brah nodded. I chuckled.

The chief said, "I can't thank you enough for assisting us in this investigation. Convincing Ohia to volunteer was a key part of it. You made the hard part happen, the rest comes easy."

The chief rolled his chair forward, rested his elbows on the desk and folded his hands. He sighed. "A crime like murder isn't good for our community. I'm responsible for safety on this island. It makes me feel bad when someone

I was supposed to protect dies. It's not a good feeling. I can't bring the man back to his family, but at least I can catch the killer. Both of you have helped me in this goal. I'm grateful to you, I'm proud of you!"

I was overwhelmed by the chief's words. Even Big Brah sat silenced. The office door opened slowly. Loni entered sideways, his shoulder forcing the door open. He held a large, purple gift bag in each hand.

As soon as Loni was fully inside the office, to my utter and complete astonishment, he cracked us a grin. His eyes had a strange light in them. He was animated. He held the purple gift bags high and danced into the room. He put the bags down on the chief's clean table with great familiarity. He wasn't at all his usual brooding self.

Triumphantly, Loni said, "Musubis and cupcakes for everyone!"

His girls had packed party plates, forks and paper napkins. All pink. There were cupcakes in one bag, while the other bag had the musubis. I took it Loni was showing his appreciation for Big Brah's effort to get Ohia to volunteer his DNA. Like the chief had done with words, Loni was showing his appreciation with cupcakes and musubis.

Me? I was ready to celebrate Ohia walking around a free man again. Without having to deal with the suspicion of having murdered his own father. We helped ourselves to the yummy treats. Smiling, Mrs. Da Costa got us a pot of coffee and cups. It was a party. At last, Loni sat down in the chair next to Big Brah. We settled down for the real business of the day. The results.

Loni swiveled his chair sideways to address all of us. "I have the DNA match results," he said.

This was the big moment. I looked at Big Brah. He sat

serene and unperturbed, his usual. I sat on the edge of my chair. My mouth felt dry. It was as if it was my DNA and not Ohia's that had been tested to match the DNA extracted from the baseball cap found at the crime scene.

Loni tugged at the ends of his unkempt mustache. He took his time. "I wanted to thank you, Big Brah, in front of the chief, for all you've done over the years for Homicide. You've been of great help, and in this investigation, you've been outstanding."

I was beginning to wonder. In the past, Big Brah had solved cases for Loni, yes. This time around he had done nothing of the sort. In fact, as soon as Ohia was proven not guilty, the pressure would mount on Loni to find the real killer. Loni sat straight up in his chair, his eyes stopped blinking and his face grew awfully solemn.

He said, "The DNA matches, Ohia killed his father!"

Chapter 14: The Other Girl

I slumped in my chair, dumbfounded. How could the DNA match? Ohia had told us, he had a cap like the one at the crime scene, but he had lost it. And he had definitely not worn it on the morning of the murder. It sure looked like he had lied to us. Astoundingly Big Brah chuckled.

He looked toward the chief and then at Loni. "I was sure the DNA would match, Ohia told me he had a cap like the one you found, he lost it. So I'm not surprised you got a match. But that evidence shouldn't make you conclude he killed his father."

Loni threw up his hands. "What else can we conclude? His cap was found next to the body!"

Big Brah shook his head, definitively. "I've got to know Ohia in the last few days, he's incapable of killing anyone, especially a man as close to him as his dad."

The chief was shrewd. "Why do you say that?" he asked.

"Because Ohia has a good heart."

The chief sucked in a quick breath. He didn't know how to argue against a good heart.

Loni said, "Oh now, we're going to ignore all the evidence, including DNA evidence, and go by your judgment of his heart?"

"It's not just me, his mother believes he's innocent."

"His mother!" Loni said.

"Also. Ohia met with his uncle shortly after the time

189

of death," Big Brah said.

"Did he now? He never told me, there's guilty written right there!" Loni said.

"His uncle told me Ohia arrived happy. Ohia couldn't have been happy if he'd just killed his father. I believe his uncle is right," Big Brah said.

"His uncle now, seriously? Of course his relatives will make up lies to protect him! That's where we in law enforcement come in. Ours is to see through their lies. Get to the truth."

Big Brah said, "The truth is, Ohia met his father at the beach. They reconciled."

"Reconciled? What were they fighting over? He won't tell me," Loni said.

"They were arguing over Ohia's inheritance," Big Brah said.

Loni said, "Inheritance. That's money! There's motive right there."

Big Brah shook his head.

Loni was jubilant. "Big Brah, you deserve more musubis and cupcakes. First you helped us with Ohia's DNA sample, and now this. The motive. Let's deliver justice! I say, we arrest Ohia right now!"

Big Brah fell silent. He was always right. But he was wise enough to know other people didn't know what he knew. A kind man, he didn't like arguing. He shook his head, again. "You won't be delivering justice by arresting Ohia, you'll be hindering it."

The chief looked from Big Brah to Loni. Whatever Loni's idle boasts, the chief was acutely aware of Big Brah's contributions to cases that had completely confounded Homicide and the entire PD in the past.

The chief said, "I think we should listen to Big Brah."

Loni protested. "I never get any support from you, Chief!"

The chief said, "Arresting Ohia will be big news, we can't have any doubts about his guilt."

Loni threw up his hands. "Go ahead, don't listen to me, listen to Big Brah...." He fell silent.

The cheerful Loni had been short-lived. He was sinking back to his brooding self again.

The chief leaned forward and looked intensely at Big Brah. "What is it you want to do, Big Brah?" he asked.

"Give me this week, until Friday. I'll find the real killer. If I don't, you can always arrest Ohia."

"What if Ohia flees?"

"I take responsibility. I'll make sure he doesn't, and if he does, I'll find him!"

The chief exhaled a long breath. "What do you think, Loni?" he said.

Loni sat silent, looking down.

Big Brah turned to look at Loni. "I know you want to deliver justice as much as I do," he said.

Unmoved, Loni continued to brood.

Big Brah said, "In delivering justice, we're brothers!"

Big Brah calling him a brother. Loni looked up.

Persuasively, Big Brah said, "It's just that you and I need to pull together to finish this investigation. It's true, the baseball cap found at the crime scene is Ohia's. But I can think of at least one other way it may have got there."

I had sat there, my head spinning the entire time. I had a sudden idea. "Ohia lost it on an earlier visit, he says he doesn't remember how or when he lost it."

Big Brah nodded, approvingly. "And, the murderer found the cap and planted it at the crime scene. To make it look like Ohia was the murderer."

Loni pulled at the ends of his mustache, thoughtfully.

Big Brah smiled. "There you go, see, if you think harder, you can probably come up with a reason yourself."

Loni looked miffed, but you could see he was reconsidering. Seeing Loni soften, the chief jumped into the conversation. Loni had just accused the chief of not supporting him. Time for some damage control.

The chief made a pleading face. "I can only give you 48 hours, Big Brah," he said.

Sensing the chief's support Loni found his voice. He looked from Big Brah to the chief, making sure both of them were with him on it. "Yes, Big Brah, if you don't come up with anything else by Wednesday, I'm arresting Ohia, is that clear?" he said.

The chief nodded. "That's reasonable, why don't we set a time?" He looked up at the office clock. "It's not ten yet, so we'll give you extra minutes." Displaying magnanimity, he leaned back in his chair and smiled at Big Brah. He didn't want to displease Big Brah either. "You got until ten o'clock on Wednesday to find, as you say, the real killer. After that the PD must act!"

The chief had a smooth style, always reconciling. I expected Big Brah to protest.

To my amazement, Big Brah said, "Sure, that works."

We had 48 hours to find the real killer. If we failed, Ohia would be arrested. Outside, in the sun, I shivered. We climbed into the big truck. It was toasty inside. Big Brah started the truck and cranked up the air conditioning. He didn't seem unduly worried about what had happened in the chief's office. He had a pleased smile on his face. He even hummed a tune.

Conscientious, I said, "Are we going to let the Bominos know about the chief's deadline?"

"Yes, of course, we must, we have to, but not right away."

Huh? Big Brah sounded flippant. I'd thought he would take the deadline far more seriously. We were nowhere near solving the murder. Ohia had only 48 hours left as a free man.

Perplexed, I asked, "What then?"

He was matter of fact. "We carry on the investigation, Umi," he said.

"As if nothing happened?"

He smiled bigger. "We can't deny we have a deadline, but we'd probably have found the killer by then anyway."

There you go. Big Brah the eternal optimist.

Big Brah said, "We can inform the Bominos later. With the deadline, our time is best spent chasing after the killer. Do you agree?"

Big Brah's optimism was beginning to rub off on me. Getting back to the investigation was far more urgent than informing the Bominos about the chief's deadline. *If we catch the killer the Bominos don't even need to know there ever was a deadline. Give them their peace.* "I agree," I said.

Big Brah said, "I want to know why Digalo was supposed to see Izor on the morning of the murder."

I was energized. I hopped onto my skateboard of optimism. "Why didn't Digalo tell us he was supposed to see Izor?"

Big Brah drove the truck out of the parking lot of the gray county building. "Let's go find Digalo," he said.

We drove to Digalo's office. Big Brah entered through the shiny revolving glass door. I swished in on my skateboard of optimism. The reception area was as I remembered it. Cool, big and bright. The sharply-dressed receptionist recognized us right away.

Her eyes widened at the sight of us. "Mr. Digalo called in to say he's working from home today, he knows you're looking for him, he's waiting for you at his residence," she said.

Big Brah thanked her. Digalo's home with its arches, awnings and pillars had lavish views of the ocean. The big truck rolled up the home's smooth, washed driveway. The driveway ended in a loop in front of the home. The center of the loop was set in decorative stone. The colorful stone was in the pattern of a flower.

The cuplike green calyx held a large whorl of red petals. In the center of the petals were yellow stamens with delicate filaments. An aloalo or hibiscus. Had to be a tribute to Digalo's first project, the famous Aloalo Resort.

Nice. We left the big truck on the side of the showy driveway. Up close, the patterns textured on the pillars of the wide lanai were ornate. We ascended the lanai's concrete steps. A small man in a yellow-and-black checkered pattern shirt opened the grand front door. I recognized him immediately. Iggy, the gardener. Iggy, the big brother.

As soon as Iggy saw us, his bright, black eyes lit up. "Me not just gardener, housekeeper too!" He must have remembered he'd also told us Digalo was gone for the weekend. "Bo back from trip, he wait for you, come, I take you to him!" he said.

Iggy took us to the east side of the home. We followed him into a covered sitting area overlooking a swimming pool. Digalo slumped in an oversized recliner. His huge body was draped in a rich silk robe with a black-and-white floral print. His round face was lined and droopy. His thin hair was unruly. He even had a stubble on his chin.

Digalo looked sick. He gestured for us to sit down. Big Brah and I sank into deep chairs. In front of us the still waters of the swimming pool reflected the cloudy sky above. Beyond the pool neatly mowed lush green grass sloped toward the ocean. The gray ocean churned a short walk away.

Digalo said, "I feel sick, you're looking for me, so I figure I'm in some kind of trouble. But I want nothing to do with this murder."

Big Brah made a wry face. "I wish I didn't have to involve you, Mr. Digalo, but you forgot to tell us something important."

"Something important? Like what?"

"Like you were supposed to meet the victim at around the time and place of the murder!"

Beads of perspiration formed on Digalo's forehead. Nervously he swiped his forehead with the back of his hand. He looked confused. "See, now, who told you that?" he said.

"Izor left behind handwritten notes."

Digalo looked alarmed. "Handwritten notes! What's he say?"

"He was to meet you at 7:45 a.m. at Waikahe Beach."

"Right...right! Yes, yes, I was supposed to meet with him. What else did he say?"

"Nothing else."

Digalo looked relieved.

"Did you meet Izor that morning?" Big Brah said.

"No, of course I didn't, I didn't go to meet with him."

"No?"

"No."

"What did you do then?"

Digalo took a deep breath and blew it out slowly.

"Okay, I'll tell you what happened. I'd accused Izor of cheating. He got back to me and asked we meet informally to discuss the issue about lumber quality. I didn't tell him, but I'd decided, mentally, I'd go. You understand?

"Nothing formal, but once I decide to do something, I do it. It's the kind of man I am. Anyway, I had decided to go. I'm confessing this to you, I needn't have, but I'm confessing this, to show good faith. Now, the meeting with Izor was in the morning, so I came home early the prior evening. I was not prepared for what I found stuck on the kitchen refrigerator. A message from my wife. She was leaving me. We've been married two years. And she was just gone. A wrecking ball had demolished my life!"

Big Brah said, "Your wife, did she tell you why she was leaving?"

Digalo grew emotional. "No, not a word! I was devastated. I didn't sleep the night. When morning came, I was a bigger mess. There was no way I could meet Izor or anyone else, you understand?"

Big Brah nodded, satisfied. "I understand, you were in no state to go out and meet with Izor. How about Iggy, was he around, can he say you didn't go out?" he said.

Digalo frowned. "Iggy comes in at 9 in the morning, leaves by 5 or 3 in the afternoon, he didn't witness any of my grief that night, or my actions the following morning."

Big Brah said, "Is there anyone else who knew you were home at the time of the murder?"

"I'm afraid not."

So Digalo had no alibi. Suspicious. I expected Big Brah to question him some more. Instead, Big Brah said, "Can we see your wife?"

Great idea. The wife knew the truth about the message on the kitchen refrigerator the evening prior to the murder.

Digalo gestured emotionally with his big hands. "Moa. Sure, if she'll see you, she doesn't talk to me! I was here every evening, we talked, we argued, why did she have to leave me with just a message? Maybe you can ask her and tell me!" he said.

Digalo's wife, Moa had taken up residence in an oceanfront townhome. She had rented the townhome. It had come furnished. Iggy knew where the rental was. He was helping move her stuff as and when she wanted. He sounded very pleased with himself, when he told us he was also the mover. On the short drive over, Big Brah listened to the weather report for the island on a local radio station.

Another storm brewed, stronger than the storm before. Indeed, the dark clouds gathered overhead spread all the way to the horizon. As we drove along a waterfront road, the agitated ocean reflected the darkness of the sky. Something was bothering me. But it would have to wait. Strangely Big Brah was in a good mood.

Big Brah flipped stations until he found one playing a Braddah Iz song. He had spent most of the weekend without Kali. He had suffered a serious reversal at the chief's office. He had a deadline to nab a killer. Yet he hummed along to Braddah Iz's rich rendition of "What a Wonderful World." The song ended. The commercials started. I couldn't hold back my concern any longer.

I turned the volume down. "Digalo says he was heartbroken, his wife left him, so he didn't go out to meet Izor. Do you accept the explanation?" I said.

Big Brah shrugged nonchalantly, quite

uncharacteristic of him. "It's as good as any."

I said, "What if the fact his wife left him drove him, in a fit of passion, to go out and murder Izor instead?"

Big Brah threw his head back and laughed out loud. "Umi, you have a great imagination, keep it that way, it's gotta be the mystery novels you read!"

Big Brah could laugh at my suspicion. But it bothered me anyway. "Instead of pursuing Digalo, why're we going to see Digalo's wife?" I said.

Big Brah grew solemn. "Digalo was home, every evening, every weekend. His wife knew that, she still left him, without talking it over with him. I want to know, why?"

We were still pursuing Digalo, indirectly. I should have known.

"It tells you something defining about Digalo," Big Brah said.

Following Iggy's directions, we found the townhome, no trouble. I rang the doorbell. A plump, middle-aged woman opened the door.

Dressed in a floral-patterned shirt, long shorts and flats, she had her shoulder-length hair colored brown and brushed back fashionably. For some reason she reminded me of Lei Bomino.

Quietly she said, "Iggy called, you must be Big Brah and Umi."

We mumbled our greetings. The living room had a cathedral ceiling, giving it the feel of a big room. Windows overlooked the ocean. Due to the dark clouds outside, the room got barely enough light through the windows. Packing boxes littered the tiled floor.

She said, "Watch out for the boxes, I'm still unpacking."

Big Brah and I made our way carefully past the boxes.

"When Iggy called, I was out grocery shopping, I got back as fast as I could," she said.

Big Brah and I sat in armchairs.

Moa sat lonesome in the loveseat. "How can I help you?" she said.

Big Brah said, "It's about Bo, he's shocked you left without talking things over with him."

Moa sighed. "He told you that?"

Big Brah nodded.

Moa shook her head and sighed again. "I can't believe he told you that, Bo knows why I left him."

"Why was that, ma'am?" Big Brah said.

"I left him the same reason his first wife left him," she said.

Big Brah said, "Do you know his first wife?"

She said, "Yes, Joanna, she's my friend. We hung out, went to school together. Joanna, me and this other girl, us three girls, we were best friends. Then Bo came into the scene, from nowhere, in junior year.

"Bo fell in love with the other girl. He fell hard. But the other girl, she wasn't available, she was already in love. So. Bo never could tell her he loved her. He married Joanna instead. I was a bridesmaid at the wedding. After struggling with Bo for good many years, Joanna left him, defeated.

"Bo came to me for comfort, rekindled an old friendship. Joanna warned me Bo had never stopped loving the other girl, our friend. Joanna had left him for that. But I didn't listen. Bo proposed, and caught in a romantic moment, I accepted.

"That our marriage lasted two years is testimony to how hard I tried. Bo still loves her, the other girl. He won't ever stop. I couldn't live with that anymore, I left."

A silence fell over us. Big Brah let the silence do the talking for a while. Then he said, gently, "This other girl, who is she?"

"Lei."

Chapter 15: Betrayal

Aghast, I stared at Moa.

Moa said, "Joanna, me and Lei, we grew up together, best friends. Lei fell in love with Izor Bomino. Then Bo came along, fell in love with Lei, but it was no use. Lei was still strongly in love with Izor. Bo married Joanna, then me, but he never stopped loving Lei."

I sat up. Moa had given us a stronger motive for Digalo. Jealousy. Digalo loved Lei. Moa left Digalo. Moved intensely and newly single, Digalo wanted to murder Izor. Digalo would finally claim Lei. Just as I had conjectured to Big Brah.

Moa said, "I'm glad you're investigating the murder, I feel really sorry for Lei."

Big Brah thanked Moa. We left. Outside, back inside the big truck, I wondered if I should bring up my conjecture about Digalo again. Uncharacteristic as it had been, Big Brah had already laughed at my idea. *Better not.*

Instead, I said, "Don't know why, I'd expected someone who'd married Digalo to be either gaudy, showy or temperamental. Moa was none of those."

Big Brah started the truck. "Moa was quiet, unassuming and practical. But Lei Bomino is the only person who can confirm Moa's story."

I belted up. "We had to tell Lei about the chief's deadline."

"Let's go see her," Big Brah said.

The lamps were on in Lei Bomino's comfortable living room. Not much light came in through the big windows. A cleaning aunty seated us on the couch and went away to get Lei. The rooster from the bamboo wall clock popped out and politely crowed five times.

5 o' cluck. The wicker bowl was in its place on the side table under the rooster wall clock. The brass key with the frayed red ribbon was still in the basket. The framed photographs on the wall had been recently dusted.

Big Brah got up to look at the family photographs. I joined him. I recognized Izor in the photographs from his likeness to Ohia. The same curly hair, the same sharp nose, the same jutting chin. Dancing with Lei at the Tavern.

Them playing baseball in the yard with little Ohia. The three of them with big brother Romo. With a bearded old man, presumably Papa Bomino. And with a lot of people who looked just like them. A family gathering. In each of the photographs, Izor looked young and happy.

Digalo had a lot to be jealous of. Again, the dark thought crossed my mind. Had Digalo killed Izor? Footsteps behind us and Lei entered the room. Work therapy had been good for her.

She had a spring to her step, and she greeted us with a smile. The smile erased the worry lines on her round face. Big Brah and I got back on the couch. She sat down in the accent chair across the coffee table, adjusted her muumuu and folded her hands neatly on her lap. I couldn't help seeing the striking hibiscus tattoo on her right forearm.

Big Brah had noted her tattoo the very first time we had seen her at our front door. It was a replica of the hibiscus in front of Digalo's home. Right there on his showy driveway. The exact cuplike calyx, large whorl of petals and delicate filaments of the stamens in the center. At the time I had assumed the decorative stone hibiscus in the center of the driveway loop was a tribute to the Aloalo Resort. Now, I was sure it was a reminder of an old flame. Lei.

Big Brah said, "I have some bad news, the DNA extracted from the baseball cap found at the crime scene turned out to be Ohia's after all."

The worry lines were back on her face. "What does that mean?"

"I have to find the killer by Wednesday, chief's given me 48 hours, else Loni arrests Ohia."

"Loni! What does he have against my poor Ohia?" she said.

Big Brah pacified her. "Nothing, Loni's just doing his job, let me do mine," he said.

Lei took a deep breath to calm herself. "Okay, I trust you, you'll find the killer by Wednesday?" she said.

"I will, but I need your help, can you answer my questions truthfully?"

Her brow furrowed. "Truthfully? Why, of course!" she said.

"Do you know Bo Digalo is in love with you?" Big Brah said.

Her jaw dropped. She looked bewildered. With an effort, she pulled herself together. "Is this...have you...oh, you have been talking to Moa, or was it Joanna, haven't you?"

Big Brah nodded. "Yes, ma'am, it was Moa."

She said, "I knew it! Don't listen to a word those two say. They're my best friends, no one knows them better than me, but on this, they're totally wrong. There was nothing between me and Bo. Sure, I was a high school senior, he used to become speechless and gulp when he saw me! So did half the boys on the island."

Big Brah said, "Still, Moa says she left Bo because she was convinced Bo would always love you."

Lei Bomino shook her head definitively. "Impossible. Unrequited love is no love at all. Bo can't just love me without me loving him back. I love Izor, you understand?"

Big Brah bowed his head. "I understand," he said.

Lei loved Izor Bomino. Understood. Big Brah and I drove home in the big truck. Daylight faded fast. We exited the coastal highway, swished past the familiar readerboard marquee sign and turned the corner. A beat-up truck was parked to the side of the driveway. Unusual.

The dilapidated truck carried a load of building blocks on its bed. Big Brah slowed the big truck down. His eyes narrowed. He drove the big truck forward carefully. A man stuck his head out of the beat-up truck's window and looked back at us. The wash of the big truck's headlights illuminated a shaven head and a goatee.

Yo Bipo. He saw us. He jumped out of the beat-up truck and slammed the door shut. He ran to the middle of the driveway, his thin body outlined by the big truck's headlights. He held up his arms and gestured for us to stop. Major emergency. Big Brah stopped the truck. Bipo came running over to Big Brah's window. His bony face had a mask of anger on it.

He shouted. "What have you done to my wife? What have you done to Maile?"

Big Brah got out of the truck. "You sound upset, why don't we talk about this in my office?"

Bipo was not done shouting. "I love her, I won't have

any harm come on her!" he said.

Big Brah nodded. "If the two of you are innocent, I won't have any harm come on either of you," he said.

Bipo sobered up. "Of course we're both innocent, the other option is impossible," he said.

Soothingly Big Brah said, "Then we're on the same side."

Bipo's voice turned even. "I want you to leave Maile out of this," he said.

Big Brah had Bipo come into the office. Big Brah sat at his desk. Bipo sat across from Big Brah. I took my place behind my desk. Under the soothing lights of the office, I watched them both.

Big Brah leaned back in his chair comfortably. "Now, brah, tell me, why are you angry?"

Bipo had gone from hot and angry to cold and angry. He sat stiffly. His face was now a true mask showing nothing.

He spoke, coldly. "I'm not mad, I just want you to keep Maile out of this," he said.

Anyone else would have mentioned Maile had come to Big Brah not the other way around.

But Big Brah chose not to mention it. "Why, what's the problem?" he said, gently.

Bipo said, "The problem, the problem is Maile has turned into a wreck, she's touchy, she's upset, she's crying at anything I say, like I'm going to jail or something!"

Big Brah sat up in his chair, squared his shoulders and placed both hands on the desk. Unexpectedly he said, "You brought this on her!"

Bipo turned frostier. "I brought this on her?" he said.

"Yes, brah, you didn't tell us the whole truth about your involvement in the murder," Big Brah said.

Bipo was icy cold. "Like what?" he said.

"Like you witnessed Izor dying or dead!"

Bipo melted like ice on a hot summer day. His shoulders drooped. He slouched in his chair. Lines creased his smooth forehead. He stared wordlessly at the gleaming surface of the desk for a very long time.

He said, "I-I never told anyone about it...only Maile... so she told you...."

Big Brah nodded. "Yes."

For a long moment, Bipo wallowed in the perceived betrayal. "She betrayed me...."

"I also know you didn't tell Maile the entire truth," Big Brah said.

Bipo looked up, interested. "How would you know?" he said.

Big Brah said, "From the tale you made up about the way you received the ten thousand dollars. No one else who knew Izor closely, his wife, his older brother, his son, his current coworkers, his neighbor, no one told me he was anything of a prankster. Only Maile did. I don't believe Izor was much of a prankster, I don't believe he'd just playfully give you ten thousand dollars without a logical and emotional explanation."

Again, Bipo took his time. At last, he said, "You're right, I made up the story."

Big Brah didn't say anything. Instead, he rocked back in his chair, calm, ready to listen for more. Bipo was taking so much time to say anything. Was it to tell us the truth or make up a new story? I craned forward. I wanted to listen carefully.

Bipo took a deep breath, exhaled shallowly and continued. "Now that Maile has betrayed me, I have nothing more to hide, I'll tell you everything. Yes, I did make up the story about Izor playfully giving me the money. I didn't want Maile to know the whole truth about Izor. She found me at a time in my life when I thought Izor was evil. Maile was my goddess, she helped me get over Izor. I didn't want her to think I was talking to him again."

Maile and Yo had bonded over Yo's hatred for Izor. It would have been awkward for Yo to receive gifts from Izor. Big Brah nodded, understanding.

Bipo said, "But the first day, on the coastal trail, Izor approached me, told me to give him a chance. He knew I hadn't stolen the lumber, he was close to identifying the thief, I'd know as soon as he did.

"I couldn't resist listening to Izor. He gave me the first check and every check afterwards with the same words, please don't say no to this. The day before the murder he told me he knew who the thief was, he'd expose the thief the very next day! He sounded sincere, I believed him, but I didn't want Maile to know.

"I had to protect her. So I made up a story of being pranked. Maile believes everything I tell her, she accepted my story. Then I didn't want to get involved in the murder investigation, so you heard the same story. Sorry!" Bipo paused, remorseful.

Big Brah was sympathetic. "On the morning of the murder, what happened?" he prompted.

Bipo said, "I went out to meet with Izor. I'd given Maile the impression I might run into him, but no meeting was planned, so she wouldn't worry about me. I found him lying on his side, on the ground, behind his truck, he wasn't breathing. There wasn't much blood, only a stain around where the dagger was stuck in his back.

"I bent down, lifted his wrist, checked for his pulse. I couldn't find a pulse. I was convinced he was dead.

I looked around. There wasn't anyone around. What if people thought I killed him out of the old hatred?

"I decided it would be too dangerous for me to be involved with Izor's death, even if it was to call 9-1-1. Izor was beyond help, I was scared, I fled."

I rocked back in my chair. Bipo had been there. He was saying he had found Izor dead, but he could just as easily have killed Izor. On his own admission no one had been around. No witnesses. Perhaps he had asked for more than ten thousand dollars. Izor refused. Bipo killed him. Could be, no? Big Brah didn't say anything.

Bipo said, "I'm not proud of what I did, I did it to protect Maile's happiness, I love her."

Big Brah softened. He reclined in his chair and gazed at Bipo. "Love is precious, you've found it, you keep faith in it. You love each other, you should find it easy to trust each other. Love makes you stronger, you should trust each other's strength."

Unyielding, Bipo rose stiffly. "We can talk philosophies another day. Now that I've told you the whole truth, I've only one request, hope you'll mind it. Going forward, I want you to focus your investigation on me, not Maile. Ask me anything, just leave her alone!"

Big Brah got up slowly. "I'll see what I can do," he said.

Bipo left. It was past dinner time. Swiftly Big Brah made pizza for us. His special deep-dish pizza with fresh mozarella cheese, sautéed onions and mushrooms. We sat down to eat at the kitchen table. Without Kali, Wiliwili and Poli`ahu moped. They weren't at the round table. I missed Kali too. The pizza was delicious. For a while we ate in silence.

"Wish Kali was here," I said.

"Yeah, I miss her too," Big Brah said.

He meant it. But Kali was not to be disturbed. Instead, my mind wandered to Bipo.

I said, "About Bipo, you think he told us everything this time?"

Chewing on his pizza, Big Brah shrugged wordlessly. He was zoned out. But we had only 36 hours left to solve the murder. I pressed on.

I said, "Last time, you told me Bipo was hiding something, he was. You still think he's hiding something?"

Mysteriously Big Brah said, "Umi, only time will tell. Listen, we have a big day tomorrow, we've got a lot of things to do, I want you to get a good night's sleep. After tonight, we may not get much sleep. We'll head out early tomorrow."

We were running out of time. I knew it. But as long as Big Brah was on it, I wasn't going to worry about it. I got into bed, tired. It had been a long day. Starting with the meeting with the chief, so many things had happened. But the murderer still eluded us. Something Big Brah had said in the chief's office bothered me.

The murderer had planted the baseball cap to make it look like Ohia had killed his father. Very manipulative. I shivered. We had to find the elusive murderer before it was too late. I was tired. I gave in to the swaying palm fronds' lullaby and slept soundly.

Refreshed, the following morning, after an early breakfast, Big Brah and I headed out in the big truck. The sky was overcast, the ocean choppy. A drizzle made the surroundings gray. The storm was getting closer.

But I was excited, ready to solve the mystery. I had my hopes high. "Where are we going?" I said.

Big Brah didn't disappoint me. "Someone, somehow

replaced the costly hardwoods with cheaper lumber and the scam had to have happened at the lumber yard. I think I know how it happened, but to be sure, we're going to the lumber yard, talk to Garth."

Clever. Trust Big Brah to have figured out how the lumber was stolen. The scam was an important part of the puzzle. Izor was murdered right after he revealed he knew who the thief was. *If we can figure out the thief, we'll have our killer,* I thought with enthusiasm.

I nodded vigorously. "Great idea, let's do it," I said.

Big Brah maneuvered the big truck onto the exit lane for the lumber yard. I shivered in anticipation. Here we go. With visibility low, we drove in the big truck, surrounded by wilderness. The gray drizzle shrouded the tops of the trees. The tall grass and bushes by the roadside got steadily wetter. The road evened and the high fence started. The truck turned left onto the driveway.

The big truck stopped in front of the closed, metal gate. The large concrete gate posts looked like sentinels, guarding the secret of the lumber yard. The camera on the left post cap swiveled.

Garth spoke through the two-way speaker system installed on the wall. "Welcome to Global Quality Lumber, this is Garth, how may I help you?"

Big Brah stuck his head out of the window. A few days had elapsed since our last visit. Garth still remembered Big Brah.

Garth sounded warm. "Oh, it's you, Big Brah! I should've known, your vehicle looked familiar. Come on in, you know where to find me."

In no time Garth had the metal gate open, and Big Brah drove the big truck in. The misty rain obscured the top of the warehouse and the sign on the pickup shed. Big

Brah parked the truck in front of the log cabin.

Overhead lights brightened the inside of the log cabin. The office smelled of coffee from the coffeemaker in the corner. Garth sat at his desk by the window. The top of the desk was still crowded with the computer and hand-sized blocks of sample lumber.

Behind the desk, on the wall, the same faded printed papers were stuck to the corkboard with colorful push pins. Garth saw us.

Garth got up, all tall and lanky. Like the other day, he was dressed in a shirt, jeans and sneakers. His cropped hair, beaklike nose and beard still made him look like a bird. He gestured for us to sit. I couldn't help notice the tremble in his hands. He was nervous. We sat down on the chairs across from his.

Hospitably he said, "Coffee?"

Island sensibility required for us to politely say no so as not to inconvenience the host, in this case, Garth. Of course, Garth could repeat his offer. Then the same politeness demanded we say yes whether we really wanted the coffee or not. Without waiting for our responses, Garth poured coffee into paper cups, brought the cups over to the crowded desk and sat down. He knew we wanted it.

He sat back in his chair uneasily and sipped coffee. "It's a rainy day, what brings you here so early?" he said.

Big Brah said, "I've been thinking about what you told us last time, I think I know where and how the costly hardwood was replaced with cheaper lumber."

Garth started. Coffee almost spilled from his cup. Garth set the cup down on a block of wood hastily. "Where'd it happen?" he said.

Big Brah tapped the desk lightly with his forefinger.

"Right here," he said.

Garth frowned. "Right here? I'd sure like to hear about it," he said.

Big Brah said, "First, let me see, if I understand the delivery process. You get a copy of the order from the sales office, you enter it on this computer, then give a copy of the order to the crew.

"The crew gets the order ready, loads the lumber in the metal bins in the pickup shed and gives you the bin numbers. You make sure the lumber is the right quality, it's a tricky job, you do it carefully. So far, I don't see a problem.

"You then return from an inspection of the pickup bins to this very desk and enter the pickup bin numbers against each order. You notify the client, I still don't see any problem. But then, the clients don't pick up the lumber immediately, do they?"

Garth shook his head. "No, they don't. Often the order is ready, the bin loaded, but our pickup day is Thursday, so we wait one, two, maybe even six days."

Big Brah nodded. "I thought so, then, isn't it possible, after you leave, for the scammer to come into this room, log into the computer and change the bin numbers against each order?"

Garth's eyes widened. "Wow. I didn't think of that. You're right! If someone changed the bin numbers, I'd not even know. Easy. The trucker comes in on pickup day, I print out the order with the bin number, I give him the right number, he goes to the wrong bin. If the lumber looks similar, the trucker, the crew, they're not lumber experts, no one notices!"

Garth got it. He really warmed up to Big Brah's idea. "Yes, I agree, that's the only way it could've happened."

Big Brah leaned back in his chair. He rested his elbow on the armrest and his chin on the back of his hand. "Now, my question for you is, who has access to this computer?" he said.

Frowning, Garth grew thoughtful. "It's a standalone computer, that means it's not on any network, it can't be operated remotely. Someone has to be physically here, in this room, to operate it.

"During work hours, I'm the only one who works on this computer. Crew members go in and out of here, they know not to mess with the computer. Besides whenever they come in, I'm always here, I even eat lunch right here at my desk. So, it can't be them. I'm also the last to leave.

"After hours, I turn off the camera and audio system. I don't lock this office, I only lock the metal gate. The computer doesn't have a password, we never needed one, so anyone can climb the gate, come in here. I keep the instructions on how to operate the computer and the data entry right there on the wall," he pointed to the printed papers stuck on the corkboard with pushpins, "using those instructions, anyone could've changed the bin numbers, unnoticed!"

Big Brah said, "Unnoticed, yes, and it could have gone on for days."

Garth agreed. "Yes, yes, you're right. The Digalo order, we got the supply over months, it must've happened over many days."

Big Brah said, "In that case, the computer, it must have a record of these after-hours transactions…."

I was following along. "The records will provide evidence the scam happened the way we think it did!" I said.

Garth grew animated. "I'm sure the computer does

have the information."

Big Brah said, "The computer should also have the information about the other client orders during the days of the Digalo order. One of those clients is the scammer. Can you get me the client list?"

I expected Garth to start checking the computer for the information right away. Instead, Garth made an apologetic face. "But you know, I told you my background is in sales, I'm not much of a computer nerd, and today's Tuesday, not a light day. Then we have this storm, I have to get the place secured."

I slumped, disappointed. Big Brah just listened.

Garth must have seen the disappointment on my face. "Why don't you call me around 2 in the afternoon? I can try to dig the information out for you," he said.

We had no time to waste. Big Brah got up. "Mahalo, I'll check in with you then," he said.

In the light rain outside, we headed back to the coastal highway in the big truck. I sat back in the passenger seat. Big Brah had found out how the scam had been done. And we were closer to identifying the scammer. But so little time left. I was balancing on a shaky tightrope of hope. I glanced at him.

Big Brah's strong hands gripped the steering wheel firmly. His sharp eyes were focused on the gray, slippery road ahead, his handsome face determined. "I have to examine the stone daggers in the Gomez living room, we're going to Bomino Court."

Alarmed I sat up. "It's too early, Antonio will be home!"

Big Brah nodded, his face still determined. "This time, I want to see both Antonio and Maria."

But Antonio wasn't home. Good. Maria Gomez opened

the front door. She was dressed in a loose t-shirt and a long skirt. She didn't look happy to see us.

She stood behind the screen door. "It's Antonio's day off, he's gone out to get storm supplies, he'll be back very soon," she said.

Big Brah said, "I'd like to examine the daggers on your living room wall."

"But I haven't even told Antonio you know about his stone daggers."

"It'll only take a few minutes...."

Her voice loaded with misgiving, she said, "Okay, only a few minutes, come in, then."

Maria pushed the screen door open. We entered the large living room. The glossy blinds smothered any light from the large windows. The chandelier's light cast a zigzag pattern around the room. The dining table had a couple of plates, bowls and coffee mugs on it.

The couple had breakfasted together at the table. Maria turned on the lamps in the sitting area and it was almost daylight in there. The windowless wall still had the display of stone daggers in precise rows and columns, each dagger balanced with its blade on a hook and the handle on a wooden block. Big Brah ambled over to the wall.

Obviously worried about Antonio's return, Maria looked toward the door and frowned. I shot a glance at the door. The disturbing prospect of Antonio Gomez storming in anytime worried me as well.

Big Brah went from dagger to dagger, studying each one intently. He looked up, down, right and left. Each dagger on the wall got the same intense scrutiny. I had no idea what he was looking for. He was lost in his own world. Maria Gomez kept on frowning.

She wrung her hands. "Antonio should be back any minute," she said.

His focus intense, Big Brah gazed at one of the daggers. He shook his head. Something was wrong with the dagger. At last, he straightened from gazing at the daggers. We were at the finish line here. I almost cried out in relief.

The growl of a car engine outside put me on high alert. The sound was familiar from last time. It was the sound of Antonio Gomez's silver sedan. Antonio was back. Panic. I looked at Big Brah. *What do we do?*

Chapter 16: Cold Hard Evidence

Big Brah was unperturbed. He had told me he wanted to see both Maria and Antonio. He had anticipated Antonio's return. He had wished for it.

Maria Gomez looked toward the door fearfully. "He's back, there's no use doing anything, did you drive the same truck?" she said.

Big Brah nodded, still not looking worried.

She said, "Then he's recognized the truck, he knows you're here."

Big Brah and I looked at each other.

She took a deep breath and closed her eyes. "Goddess, give me strength," she said.

Silently I repeated, *Goddess, give me strength.*

Maria opened her eyes with a new resolve. "Don't worry, I won't let him behave badly again. You're here on my invitation, it's also my home, he'll respect that."

I didn't share her confidence but Big Brah was calm. I took deep breaths to lower my heartbeat. Crew cut and buff, Antonio Gomez appeared at the door. He yanked the screen door open and strode toward us. He carried no grocery bags. As Maria had predicted, he must have seen our truck. And come rushing in.

I looked past Antonio at the door longingly. The screen door had closed. The front door was still open. I was ready to get out. Silently Big Brah raised a hand, palm outward, signaling for me to stay. He had read my mind.

Maria Gomez confronted her husband before he reached us. "Now, Antonio, Big Brah and Umi are here on my invitation, you'll either join us or go inside and freshen up, which one?" she said.

Antonio Gomez was like the ocean. Last time he had been high tide, big waves roaring. This time he was low tide, hardly any waves, only ripples.

He threw up his hands in the air. "Honey, I'm sorry, I even said you talk too much in front of Big Brah and Umi, I should never have done that. And Big Brah, Umi, will you ever forgive me for turning you out of my house?" he said.

Big Brah had his easy smile on. "For that, you're forgiven already," he said.

Antonio sank into an armchair. Big Brah and I settled down on the couch. Maria sat on an ottoman.

Antonio said, "Please understand, I was stressed out, I didn't want any word of my feud with Izor to spread around the island. If it did, I thought, the police are going to suspect me of the murder."

"The police need more than island gossip to suspect someone," Big Brah said.

"I know, maybe they do need more than island gossip." Antonio Gomez clasped his hands and looked furtively at the stone daggers hanging on the wall.

Big Brah followed his gaze. "Your stone daggers, they're something else," he said, admiringly.

"I sweat making them." Antonio wrung his hands. Clearly something was bothering him. He looked at his wife in a woebegone way.

Big Brah said, "Those daggers may have gotten you into trouble."

Maria was startled. "Antonio! Big Brah, why're you

saying that?" she said.

Antonio gazed gloomily down at his hands. "I make each one of them with my hands the same way, carve them out of the hard stone."

Maria was agitated. She got up, went over to Antonio and knelt on the rug in front of him. "No! It can't be!" she said.

Big Brah got up and strolled over to the wall. "The police won't arrest you for murder based on some idle gossip, but I studied the style, Tutu Pika told me how, the patterns of craftsmanship, of blemishes on the murder weapon. I just finished examining each of your daggers, I'm sure one of them was used for the murder. So, the police may suspect you," he said.

Antonio took both Maria's hands in his and looked into her eyes. "Honey, one of my daggers is missing," he said.

Her voice filled with feeling. "How can that be, Antonio?" she said.

"I don't know, honey, you tell me," he said.

While examining the daggers, Big Brah had shaken his head at a particular dagger.

Big Brah pointed to the stone dagger now. "This dagger doesn't belong to you, I recognize its style, I'm familiar with it, it's one of Tutu Pika's. Available at any gift shop on the island. One of your daggers isn't just missing, it's been replaced by this dagger, hasn't it?"

Antonio hung his head. "It's true, but I didn't replace it," he said.

Big Brah strolled back to the couch. "Even if I believe you didn't replace it, both of you have a lot of explaining to do."

Maria said, "I can explain."

Big Brah sat down. "Tell me, what happened on the morning of the murder?"

Maria settled herself at Antonio's feet. Maria and Antonio were one, undivided. She said, "It was a Tuesday, like today, it was your day off, Antonio, wasn't it?"

Antonio slowly raised his head and gazed down at the back of her head. "Yes, Maria," he said.

She looked at Big Brah and me. "Today is Tuesday, Antonio's yard cleanup day, but it's rainy, there's the big storm tonight. Besides he wasn't feeling up for it, he told me this morning, he was upset, it's not like him at all.

"I knew something was wrong. To get his mind off this awful murder, I sent him to get the storm supplies. I hoped it'd distract him. Anyways, that Tuesday, the day of the murder, it was his day to go out and trim the ohias."

Antonio spoke up. "For some weird reason, Izor liked those ohia trees to grow wild, so I was only going to trim the ones on my side of the fence."

The ohias had been the cause of the feud. Antonio had gone out to trim them. What if it fueled a dormant anger? And Antonio killed Izor. Definitely suspicious. I listened closely.

She said, "Antonio likes to take his icebox, his saws and tools, he likes to start early, as soon as there's sufficient daylight, and he doesn't like being disturbed."

Antonio said, "It's safety. I don't like being disturbed, especially because I have to use the chainsaw for those damn trees. When I use power tools, I like to focus, they can injure you if you're distracted. I use active noise reduction, military grade headsets, these things you can wear to block out the noise while riding an armored vehicle. I see or hear nothing else, helps me work."

She said, "I wasn't complaining. I do the accounting

work for the charity, I'd fallen behind, I had some catching up to do. I had several hours of work ahead of me. I was busy in my study upstairs. From there, with the window open, I can hear any car on Bomino Court.

"I remember, it was sunny that day, and I had the window open. The news at 7 was going to show clips of us cleaning up Waikahe Beach! I was looking forward to see what they'd done. Ten minutes before 7, I heard Izor leave in his truck. I didn't think much about it. Izor leaves early often, usually for a walk at the beach."

That would be Izor leaving for his special meeting with Ohia. No doubt the scenic Waikahe Beach under a new morning sun was a great place to resolve a father-son dispute.

Maria reached for and took Antonio's hand in hers. "Antonio, I could hear you working, the noise you make with your power tools, I couldn't really see you from the window, I wished I could, but knowing you're there is always so reassuring."

He said, "Maria, I heard nothing, I had my headset on, I saw nothing, I was focused on my work, I swear."

She said, "The court was quiet and normal the entire morning, I heard no other cars, no one came or left, I'm sure."

She was sure. That ruled out everyone from the court. Not just Antonio, but even Papa Bomino and big brother Romo. Big Brah listened intently, as he always did.

Maria said, "Wait a minute, I remember something. Around 8, the news wasn't done yet, but they'd finished the beach cleanup segment, so my attention was drifting. I heard a car coming into the court. I couldn't tell who it was. Whoever it was, he or she was in a hurry."

It must be Ohia visiting Romo after meeting with Izor, I

thought. He'd get late for work. Hence the hurry.

Sure enough, she said, "The car drove past our home, went to Romo's. I know it left after a short while, I can't tell you exactly when, but I heard it leave soon enough. I was in the kitchen getting some more coffee. Antonio returned when the sun got high, around noon.

"We ate lunch together in the back lanai. It was a quiet, peaceful day like any other, and neither of us could've imagined Izor was dead, no, murdered at the time."

Big Brah sat up. "Are you sure, you didn't hear any other car enter or leave the court?" he said.

"I'm sure," she said.

Big Brah pointed at the daggers on the wall. "Maria, did you replace the stone dagger?" he said.

"Of course not!" Maria Gomez rose and returned to the ottoman.

Big Brah said, "Maria, I believe you didn't replace the dagger, and, Antonio, you say you didn't, then who did?"

Both Maria and Antonio shook their heads.

Antonio said, "We did have a lot of visitors on the Saturday prior to the murder."

Maria said, "That's right, the prior week, on Saturday, we did a beach cleanup, then we gathered here for refreshments, remember I told you?"

"I remember," Big Brah murmured.

Maria waved toward the dining room and its chandelier. "I told you there was food, people from all over the island, even strangers...any one of those men and women could've replaced the dagger, no one would've noticed."

Big Brah wasn't going to give up so fast. He persevered. "I want both of you to think carefully. Of the people who attended the party, who among them knew the victim really well?" he said.

She said, "Why, the entire Bomino family, Papa Bomino, big brother Romo, Ohia, Lei, they were all here... except Izor...then...."

Antonio showed knowledge about Izor he hadn't before. "The Bipos were here, they came in late as usual, they aren't comfortable with any of the Bominos. They live near the beach, lots of people volunteer for the cleanup from the Waikahe neighborhood. I've heard Yo Bipo worked with Izor, had trouble with Izor," he said.

Not surprised, I glanced at Big Brah. Big Brah didn't bother asking how Antonio had learned about Bipo. It was a small island. Word got around. Big Brah listened attentively. The conversation turned even more interesting.

Antonio said, "Also Bo Digalo."

Big Brah said, "Digalo doesn't live around here, why would he join the Waikahe Beach cleanup?"

I thought Big Brah was on to something.

"I hear Digalo was also having trouble with Izor," Antonio said.

Big Brah said, "How did you learn about Digalo and Izor?"

Maria said, "Oh Digalo, he likes Antonio, he comes to our house, he volunteers for the cleanups. Couple decades now, Antonio's been his physician!"

Darn, nothing there.

Big Brah nodded, satisfied. "Can you think of anyone else who knew the victim?" he said.

Maria said, "The Bomino family has lived on the island for generations, a lot of those present knew Izor Bomino."

Slowly Antonio nodded. "Any one of them could've taken the dagger, replaced it," he said.

Big Brah said, "Have you touched the replaced dagger?"

"No," Antonio said.

Big Brah leaned forward. "Okay, then, the first thing you should do is contact Loni at the PD. Tell him everything you told me, show him the replaced stone dagger, tell him everything we talked about today. Don't touch the dagger, Loni will want to have it examined for fingerprints.

"If the killer was stupid enough to leave fingerprints, you're saved, but from what I've seen so far, we're dealing with someone who is shrewd and doesn't make an amateur mistake like that. Still, your best bet is to come clean with Loni."

Antonio was going to tell Loni the murder weapon was his. Surely that would make Loni reconsider arresting Ohia as the killer. It would also give Loni something to do other than sulk about Ohia. Maybe it would buy us time to gather cold, hard evidence. We were almost at the door.

Unexpectedly, Big Brah turned back to face our hosts. "Can I take a look at the ohia trees?" he said.

Antonio frowned suspiciously at Big Brah. Grudgingly he said, "Be my guest."

I didn't know what kind of evidence the ohia trees would provide, but they had been the cause of the feud. Big Brah wanted to look at them. He was on to something. There was hope yet. As we ambled toward the trees, the light rain pattered gently on my head. I looked ahead at the ohia trees.

The trees near us were shorter. Dull green leaves and

red, spiky flowers. They looked about the same. Antonio hadn't lied. He had trimmed and pruned the ohia trees on his side of the fence. We got closer. The fence here had a gate.

The trees beyond the gate grew wild. There were all kinds of ohia, tall, short and in-between. An immensely tall ohia grew side trunks at the base of the trunk. The side trunks lifted the main trunk above the ground.

Each tree looked different, like individuals, like people. Why had Izor not wanted to trim the trees? Finally, I understood. The trees were perfect, as they were. Big Brah stopped under a tree, out of the drizzle.

He looked around. I rested my back on the tree trunk and let my eyes wander. To my right, far away, the clear fence and beyond it the asphalt road. In the distance the Gomez residence was shrouded by rain. And to my left, beyond the fence and the gate, Izor's ample, two-story house and garage chock full of Jet Skis. The garage door was closed.

I stared at the closed door. There had been fourteen Jet Skis, old and new. What a collection! I imagined them as Lei had described them to us--outside and ready to go. I felt a nudge on my shoulder.

It was Big Brah. He was also staring at the closed garage door. "Are you thinking what I'm thinking?" he said.

Chapter 17: The Goddess Works in Mysterious Ways

Cold excitement washed over me. I got it. Antonio had told us he was working here on the morning of the murder. He had seen or heard nothing. Maria had heard the noise of his power tools. But Maria had the TV on.

She was distracted. If Antonio took a break, Maria wouldn't have noticed. Antonio could easily have had the stone dagger hidden with him. When he saw Izor leave, Antonio, like Maria, knew Izor was going down to Waikahe Beach. Antonio borrowed a Jet Ski. Izor was not there to stop him.

The shortest way to the beach was the river. The fastest ride to the beach was the Jet Ski. The long, windy road and the speed of Izor's white truck was no match for the short river route and the speed of the Jet Ski.

Antonio rode the Jet Ski down the river to the beach. He killed Izor, striking the heart with a surgeon's precision. Then he returned the same way, riding the Jet Ski up the river. In no time, he went back to work on the trees. *Diabolic.*

I shivered. "Maria's window is in the front of the home."

Big Brah nodded, approvingly. "Exactly," he said.

"She wouldn't even hear the Jet Ski!" I said.

Back in the big truck, my mind was in a whirl. The

dashboard clock showed we had less than 24 hours. Big Brah had identified the real killer. A big relief. What was he going to do about it? First, he needed more evidence.

It wasn't enough the murder weapon had been made by Antonio. Antonio had confused the issue by making up the story about its replacement, so pointing the suspicion away from himself. Big Brah would now need something more substantial. Second, Big Brah always visited our heiau, whenever he began and ended work on an investigation.

He would return to the heiau, before he finally caught the killer. I glanced at him. His face wet from the rain but otherwise serene, he started the big truck.

"Where to now?" I asked, expecting he would say the heiau.

To my surprise, he said, mysteriously, "The hospital. I have to see Papa Bomino."

Papa Bomino? It had to be Big Brah's method. He had to see the victim's father. Maybe he hoped to get some proof about Antonio. After all Papa Bomino had been a neighbor and known Antonio a long time. And Big Brah had met everyone else who knew Izor closely.

I knew better than to ask him about it. So close to the deadline, and so close to catching the killer, my questions would only disturb his focus. I must have had a puzzled frown on my face all the way to the Island Hospital's intensive care unit.

The solemn waiting area had its walls decorated with framed paintings of island scenery. A sprinkling of enduring near and dear friends and relatives with careworn faces reposed on chairs, recliners and couches. We headed toward the nurse's desk. From the corner of my eye, I glimpsed a person rise deliberately from one of the leather-upholstered reception chairs.

Silver-haired, Sister Agatha. Surprise. She was dressed in her usual modest long-sleeved shirt, long skirt and flat-soled sandals. She held a phone. Unusual. Big Brah and I must have seen her at the same time. We stopped. She came to us, all smiles, her cheeks flushed.

She held the phone up. "I was about to call you. Papa Bomino has been up, I told him everything about your investigation. Right away, he wanted to see you! The goddess, she works in mysterious ways, she's brought you here," she said.

The goddess does work in mysterious ways, especially for Big Brah. He wanted to see Papa Bomino. Papa Bomino wanted to see Big Brah. Perfect. Sister Agatha led us down a corridor. The walls here were decorated with framed photographs of the volcano, the beaches and the waterfalls. Papa Bomino's room overlooked a courtyard with a bird bath.

A soaked brown mynah perched forlornly on the concrete bird bath. Papa Bomino lay still on a raised bed surrounded by gadgets and screens silently monitoring his vital signs. The thin, wispy hair on his nearly bald head had been combed by a nurse's caring hand. The scraggly, white beard grown during his stay here at the hospital had been left untouched for now. His eyes were open.

Big Brah went to his bedside and bent over him. Papa Bomino blinked. His hand moved weakly. He wanted to touch Big Brah, to make sure Big Brah was for real.

Gently Big Brah took the old man's hand in his. "You wanted to see me," he said.

Papa Bomino's mouth opened. For a moment it looked as if he wouldn't be able to say anything.

He spoke, his voice unsteady. "Koa, I knew your father, your grandfather and your great-grandfather Kahua, their kindness, their generosity was well known all over the island. Look, I was sick, this hospital, your family's gift to the island, its hardworking doctors and nurses, they saved me!"

Big Brah smiled, encouragingly. "You're looking good!" he said.

Papa Bomino tried to smile, but he could only grimace. "Your grandpa and your father, they died together, in a way lucky for your grandpa, he didn't have to bear the pain of living on after his son. I'm not so lucky, I'm having to deal with Izor's death, no, murder." He paused, breathless.

I pulled up a chair for Big Brah. He sat down without letting go Papa Bomino's weak hand. He had eyes only for the frail man. Papa Bomino recovered his breath.

He turned his head slowly on the pillow to look at me, then back at Big Brah. "Here you are, the two of you, upholding the Waialeale honor, the Waialeale pride, you serve the island just as your forefathers did, for that mahalo!"

Big Brah tilted his head modestly.

Papa Bomino said, "Like your father, in my heart, I had two boys. Izor like Umi, younger, adorable, and Romo, like you Koa, big and responsible, I saw them that way. When Izor wanted to start his lumber business, Romo and I helped him. For our furniture business, we order lumber from him. But it's changed forever, and Izor is gone."

"What do you want me to do?" Big Brah said.

Tears leaked from the corners of Papa Bomino's eyes down his temples and onto the pillow. His face grave, Big Brah held Papa Bomino's thin hand comfortingly. Papa

Bomino lay there, wordlessly, as if he was either done or too tired to speak again. Protectively Sister Agatha stepped forward to intervene.

I knew Big Brah's ways better than she did. If Big Brah thought Papa Bomino was truly exhausted, Big Brah would stop immediately. I raised a warning hand signaling for her to stop.

At last, Papa Bomino let out a deep sigh. When he spoke, strangely, his voice though shaky had strength in it. "I want you to bring Izor's killer to justice."

"That I will," Big Brah said, with certainty.

Papa Bomino raised his head from the pillow such was the intensity of his emotions. "Koa, make me a promise," he said.

"A promise?" Big Brah said.

Papa Bomino said, "Koa, you take care of your family honor so well, promise me, in your investigation, you'll protect my family's honor just as well."

Solemnly Big Brah said, "I promise."

"I trust you will." Papa Bomino's head fell back on the pillow. He closed his eyes. He was completely exhausted. Soon his thin chest rose and fell uniformly. He had gotten a great weight off his chest. He slept peacefully.

Carefully Big Brah let go Papa Bomino's frail hand and got up. Sister Agatha joined Big Brah by the bedside and together they gazed down at the sleeping man quietly.

Sister Agatha said, "He's a good man, he cares deeply for his family."

Outside, back in the big truck, I was still feeling sorry for a father who had lost his son. Big Brah was in a somber mood. His face was solemn, his brow furrowed. He didn't hum or tap or anything, as he drove us out of the hospital.

Big Brah took the promises he made seriously. Clearly

the promise he had just made to Papa Bomino was on his mind. He had already promised Lei he would protect the Bomino family honor. We were this close to proving to Loni that Ohia Bomino wasn't the killer. Antonio Gomez was. Big Brah was already protecting the Bomino family honor.

I couldn't tell exactly what else was bothering him. "What next?" I said.

Gloomily he said, "I'm hungry!"

When we had work to do and no one was home to cook, Big Brah did the next best thing. He picked up food from Manny's food truck. Manny was a distant cousin of ours. He was older than I was but younger than Big Brah. For easy access, Manny always parked his food truck across from Keiki Beach. Keiki Beach was on our way home.

Soon we were driving alongside the delightful stretch of golden sand that was Keiki Beach. My mood picked up. The beach was crowded on a sunny day, but the rain hadn't deterred all beachgoers. People were out in the water having fun. We parked near the blue and green painted food truck. The food truck had "Manny's Grindz" written in black cursive on its sides. There was a line of hungry and thirsty beachgoers in front of the food truck.

Manny was at the counter, serving the line. While it was true Manny studied the culinary arts in high school and college, he freely admitted he really learned to cook from Big Brah much earlier. I believed him. I knew firsthand how good a teacher Big Brah was. In any case Manny was always pleased to see us.

He waved to us cheerfully. He had set up canopies next to the truck, so his customers could get out of the rain while they ate. There were plenty tables and chairs.

We seated ourselves at a table. Manny finished with the line, then came over to us. Manny wasn't big or tall.

Manny liked to show off his local pride and mana by growing his hair long. Today he had his hair in a ponytail. He had amazing tattoos covering his neck, chest, arms and legs. He had on a revealing local pride tank top that flaunted his jaw-dropping tattoos: tiki, the mythical first human, sharks, geckos and volcano.

Manny said, "Always good to see you, Big Brah, Umi, I got pork laulau, steamed rice, coconut water and malasadas, will that do?"

"Yes." I nodded vigorously.

"That will do very nicely, mahalo, Manny," Big Brah said.

Manny served us the food, then settled down on a chair to talk story as we ate. He said, "I hear you're investigating the Bomino murder. It's all over the news, I don't believe it, but they're saying tomorrow the chief will announce the cops have the killer...and you don't."

Big Brah forked laulau and chewed moodily. He gazed out at the drenched highway and the beach beyond. He finished chewing and shrugged. "My job is to make sure the police catch the killer, that's all," he said.

Manny grinned. "I know you'll get the killer, you always do. The cops are just lucky to have you on their side, Big Brah," he said.

Strengthened by Manny's food and his faith in Big Brah, we drove home. The rain fell harder. Big Brah listened to the island weather forecast intently. The biggest storm of the season was approaching fast. The wind and rain would intensify throughout the evening.

High surf and flash flood warnings were already in effect. The storm was expected to hit the hardest tonight.

We turned the familiar corner. In the gray rain, I almost didn't see Loni's unmarked, green sedan parked outside our home. More trouble. Big Brah invited Loni into the main office.

We entered the office together. Soothing light filled the office. The blackout curtains kept the storm out. Loni sat himself down in the chair across from Big Brah's gleaming desk. Big Brah and I took our places. Loni looked annoyed.

His thick mustache bristled. "We have the biggest storm of the season on top of us, the chief's deadline's only twenty hours away, I want to know, what's all this about Antonio Gomez? The man calls me, says you told him to contact me," he said.

Big Brah nodded. "I did, I told him to contact you, I wanted you to know what I'd found out about the murder weapon. Did the replacement dagger on the wall have any fingerprints on it?" he said.

Loni shook his head. "No fingerprints," he said.

Big Brah sighed. "The killer didn't make it easy for us," he said.

Loni frowned, annoyed. "I already have the killer, it's Ohia Bomino!" he said.

Big Brah was perturbed. He sat up. "But you didn't have the evidence of the stone dagger when you thought Ohia did it, now that you do, doesn't it change everything?"

"Change everything, how? Nothing's changed. Sure, I should thank you for bringing the murder weapon to my attention. Mahalo! But I interrogated Gomez for 20-30 minutes, and it turns out Ohia Bomino was in the Gomez living room only the Saturday prior to the murder! Ohia knew about his father's feud with Gomez, he knew Gomez made stone daggers.

"So, Ohia bought a stone dagger from a gift store anonymously. When he was in the Gomez living room, Ohia sneakily replaced one of Gomez's daggers with the dagger he'd bought. Ohia then used the stolen dagger for the murder. Clever. Gomez didn't find out one of his daggers was missing until after the murder. Ohia wanted to make it look like Gomez was the killer. Case closed!"

Big Brah shook his head, frustrated. "What are you going to do?" he said.

Loni got up. He looked down at Big Brah. "Tomorrow, storm or not, I'm going to arrest Ohia Bomino for the murder of his father," he said.

Big Brah said nothing.

Loni stormed to the door. "Don't try to stop me!"

Chapter 18: Wind Music and Ocean Chant

Loni left. Big Brah continued to sit at his desk. He held his head. Ever since he had made Papa Bomino the promise, Big Brah had been worried. I got up and paced the floor in front of his desk.

I understood why Big Brah was worried. "You knew Loni would never change his mind about Ohia. Loni will single-mindedly continue to chase after poor Ohia. You anticipated his stubbornness, didn't you?" I said.

Big Brah groaned. "Loni has to get things done, his stubbornness is a strength."

I wasn't going to be as charitable as Big Brah. "Loni blew it!" I said.

Big Brah sat there looking downcast. I paced the room some more. As Loni had pointed out, we had twenty hours left to the deadline. In reality the storm made it so we had four maybe six hours before everything shut down on the island. Mudslides, flash floods, lashing rain, thunder and lightning. We were going to have it all tonight. Big Brah sitting there looking downcast wouldn't do.

Besides I wanted to console him. "It's all right, you gave Loni the opportunity to catch the real killer."

Big Brah gazed at me. He was the sad surfer looking at a tranquil ocean with no waves.

I said, "It was a huge sacrifice, and you did it in your just way."

"I have no idea what I'd do without you, Umi," Big Brah said.

"Loni didn't take the opportunity, now we nab the killer ourselves!" I said.

Big Brah heaved a big sigh. "Sometimes you make me think I'm the younger brother and you my big brah!"

Did he now? Unexpected. I stopped pacing to take in the praise.

Big Brah got up, all alert. "Let's put on our ponchos, Umi, we're going to the heiau!" he said.

The significance of his words hit me. Going to the heiau meant he was getting ready to announce the killer.

Excitement coursed through me. "Do you have a plan?" I said.

He shook his head, despondently. "I need the goddess!" he said.

He meant goddess Pele but the thought crossed my mind he needed Kali. No doubt he was missing her. Also, when he needed a plan fast, Kali was a big help. But we still hadn't heard from her. At the heiau, the wind picked up and scattered the rain.

Rain sprayed down on our ponchos. Facing the heiau, we stood on the wet compact sand. Deep in thought, Big Brah had his brow furrowed. I enjoyed the cool rain on my face. The rain was the storm god's gentle warning for every creature to find a safe place. The storm was coming.

The energetic music of rustling palm fronds and the reverberating chant of the ocean was all around us. The wind jammed with the ocean. The palms swayed in a cosmic trance. The black lava rocks of the heiau were arranged in lines, arcs and stacks, some precise, some not, all familiar. Rocks set in time and place. The familiar rocks remained unchanged in a changing world, a tangible link to our lost ohana.

Big Brah closed his eyes and bowed his head. It was how he prayed. I closed my eyes. I prayed too. I forgot the rain, the wind, the ocean.

Silently I said, again and again, "Goddess, let justice be done."

I opened my eyes. Big Brah stood next to me.

His eyes were open and he had a smile on his face. "Good, you're done, Umi. Let's go, I have a plan!" he said.

I knew better than to ask him what the plan was. We didn't have much time. No time to waste on talk. He always told me everything. Sometimes I had to wait. Before I could say anything, the phone inside his poncho pocket jingled. Big Brah sheltered the phone from the rain as best he could and answered. The wind music and the ocean chant made it impossible for me to hear anything.

Big Brah listened and asked a couple of questions. Then he said, loudly, "Hang on, we'll be right there!"

He put the phone away and turned to me, his face grim. "Umi, quick, that was Keanu, he's in trouble, let's go!"

"What about your plan?" I shouted to be heard.

"The plan will have to wait. Keanu is in real trouble, he needs our help now," Big Brah said.

Big Brah was ready to throw away all the hard work he had put in to build his reputation with the chief and the community to save a single soul. Now, that was my Big Brah. No rules if someone needed our immediate help! Rain or not, we sprinted up the path from the beach to the front of the house. In the garage we jumped into the truck. Big Brah had the truck out and on the coastal highway in minutes.

Grimly Big Brah said, "Keanu's out west side, he's walking the shoulder of the highway, he's hurt, he can't or won't call 9-1-1…he won't say why, that's all I could get out of him, I told him we'd be right over."

His face stern, Big Brah drove fast all the way to the west side. The rain hadn't reached this part of the island, but storm clouds were gathering overhead rapidly. We were driving down a straight and level patch of the deserted coastal highway. If we hadn't been looking for Keanu, I may not have recognized him.

Disheveled, droop-shouldered, his clothes in disarray, Keanu hobbled miserably on the side of the road. Big Brah must have seen him too. The truck slowed down. We got closer. I jumped out of the truck and ran to him. Keanu looked terrible.

His short hair was covered with red dirt. His nose looked like it had taken a blow. Blood had dried below his nostrils. His shirt had dried blood on it, his trousers were torn and he had lost a shoe. How long had he been in this state? He saw me and looked relieved.

He tried to smile. Exhaustion got the better of him. He lurched and fell forward. I caught him just in time. He held on to me, until Big Brah parked the truck and joined us. Both Big Brah and I knew first aid. Together we got Keanu into the backseat of the truck.

Big Brah cleaned up the cut on Keanu's nose. "How did this happen?" he said.

Keanu grimaced. Something else was hurting him badly. "I don't want to worry about that, I just want to go back to Aunty Lena, if she'll have me back," he said.

Reassuring, Big Brah said, "Of course Aunty Lena wants you back. But first, why were you walking, where's your car?"

"It's gone, broken, destroyed."

"How did that happen?"

"I don't want to talk about it."

Perplexed, Big Brah glanced at me. I let my shoulders rise and fall. I had no clue what was going on with Keanu either. Big Brah turned back to Keanu.

He made sure Keanu was all right. Nothing broken. "Okay, fine, I'll take you back to Aunty Lena, but only if you show me your car. She'll want to know why you abandoned the car after working so hard to pay for it," Big Brah said.

Keanu gazed at Big Brah for a long moment. "I screwed up, she'll be mad, won't she?" he said.

"Aunty Lena won't be mad if she knows what happened," Big Brah said.

"I'll take you to my car," Keanu said.

In the big truck, following Keanu's directions, we took an exit from the coastal highway, and soon we were in a residential neighborhood. We crossed a mart then a park. We were driving down a street with homes old, new, big and small, a mixed neighborhood, not uncommon on the island.

Keanu spoke from the backseat. "There, you see the car? The red sedan parked streetside?"

Big Brah parked the big truck behind Keanu's car. Keanu stayed inside the truck. Big Brah and I got out to look at Keanu's car. You could barely tell the car was the same good-looking red sedan we had seen parked outside Global Quality Lumber's downtown sales office.

The sedan was badly dented and damaged. Someone, or more likely some people had beaten it up with iron rods and baseball bats. The front and rear windshields were shattered. The windows were broken. The tires were slashed, deflated. The car was almost totalled. The damaged red sedan was the injured red fish from my strange dream about Keanu!

Ironically the heartwarming red on white "I ♥ my ohana" sticker on the chrome bumper was the only thing intact. The violence suffered by Keanu was appalling.

At the sight of the damaged car, Big Brah clenched his jaws. He strode back to the truck, and I followed him.

Frowning he peered into the cabin. "Keanu, what were you doing here?" he said.

Chapter 19: Second Chances

Beyond the car was the rusty gate to a neglected home with its paint peeling off. Keanu pointed to the neglected home. "I grew up there. My family, my father, his many brothers, his family, their families, all live there. Aunty Lena says everyone deserves a second chance. While I was away from her, I realized how true that is. So I went to my family, told them about Aunty Lena, they-they don't understand, they told me, you think you're better than us, you think you can teach us things, they--" he started to cry.

"They destroyed your car, beat you up, is that why you wouldn't call 9-1-1, so you wouldn't get them into trouble?" Big Brah said.

Softly Keanu cried. "Yes, I don't want to cause anyone any trouble," he said.

Big Brah and I exchanged looks. He said, "Keanu, you sit here, as long as you're inside the truck, no one can harm you. Umi, come with me!"

Big Brah turned and strode away fast. I had to run after him to catch up. As we got close to the neglected home, the stench of rotting trash filled the air. Even the old, corroded wire fence looked nasty. The small front yard had weeds growing around the littered trash. We entered through the rusty gate and stomped up the creaky, slippery steps to the dilapidated lanai.

Big Brah knocked loudly on the decrepit front door. I

could hear feet scurrying and whispers from behind the door. They had to have been watching us. Finally, the front door creaked and a crack opened up.

A man peered out. "What you want?" he said.

Big Brah said, "I want to talk to Keanu's family."

The front door opened some more. The man looked a lot like Keanu but wrinkled, grayed and older. "I'm Keanu's uncle, no one else home, you talk to me," he said.

Big Brah said, "I had something to say to his family, will you give them my message?"

The uncle sneered. "A message? That boy's never been any good," he said.

Big Brah said, "Keanu is a good boy, he has people who care for him. Next time, don't make the mistake of thinking he's alone, you'll have to deal with me first. Tell them the message is from Koa Waialeale."

The man's eyes widened until I feared his eyeballs would pop out. Not that I cared. The people who had treated Keanu so badly deserved much worse.

"You're Big Brah," the man whispered almost to himself.

Back inside the big truck we drove homeward in silence. As we drove east on the coastal highway, the rain started again and the sky turned grayer.

Big Brah said, "Keanu, mind telling me why you left Aunty Lena so suddenly?"

From the backseat, Keanu said, "Out of the blue, Izor died. He'd been kind to me, he was like...like a father. Then the burglary. I was confused, I was nervous, I felt I had to leave, so I left. I didn't mean to cause anyone any trouble.

"I thought, best take myself out of it all. I camped, I fished, I thought some more. Izor, the Bomino family,

Aunty Julie, Aunty Lena, they all trusted me, relied on me, I realized it was wrong of me to run away from them. I decided I'd return and face the consequences."

Big Brah nodded, approvingly. "Good decision."

"But before I did, I also wanted to give my family a second chance."

Big Brah said, "They've used up all their second chances."

"But I always think of them as my family, I thought they'd change if I gave them a second chance," Keanu said.

Big Brah shook his head.

Keanu sighed. "They'll never change."

For a while we drove in silence. Then Keanu groaned.

"You okay, little brah?" Big Brah said, sympathetic.

Keanu groaned, again. "What should I do?"

Big Brah sighed. "You'll have to grow up, Keanu."

"But, how?" Keanu asked, his voice full of angst.

"You are part of Aunty Lena's ohana now. Aunty Lena loves you," Big Brah said.

Keanu's voice filled with remorse. "But I left her with just a goodbye note."

Big Brah chuckled. "She has never stopped loving you," he said.

There was a comfortable silence. We took the exit for Aunty Lena's hostel. The big truck climbed the steep road.

Big Brah said, "Aunty Lena loves her ohana, she will also never change, she'll always be your Aunty Lena."

Big Brah stopped the big truck outside the hostel. Keanu sat on the backseat, unmoving. Big Brah and I waited, sympathetic. I looked back at him and smiled encouragingly.

"It's been quite a ride, huh?" Keanu said.

I nodded, smiling bigger. "All's pono that ends pono," I

said.

Tears filled Keanu's eyes. He blinked them away. "From this moment, Umi, you my little brah." He looked reverentially at Big Brah. "And you my Big Brah."

Keanu left. He would be safe in Aunty Lena's loving care. Back home, Big Brah called one of our cousins who was an auto expert and could make any car new again. The cousin owned the island's best auto shop and several tow trucks. He lived on the west side.

Big Brah instructed the cousin to pick up Keanu's damaged car, repair it and deliver a like-new car to its owner. The cousin didn't bring up money. He knew Big Brah paid generously. By the time Big Brah was done, it was 2 o' clock on my phone.

Big Brah headed to the main office. "Time to call Garth at the lumber yard, my plan depends on what he has to say."

His plan. My pulse quickened. I ran after him. My prayers at the heiau had to be paying off. The investigation was back on track. We were back! In the calm, illuminated war room of the main office, Big Brah settled down behind his gleaming desk. Ready for action, I sat behind the organized clutter on my desk. Swiftly Big Brah placed his phone on the table. He called Garth, using the speakerphone.

Garth sounded apologetic. "Big Brah, I've been learning a lot about computer logs, I did little else today, but I'm still far from extracting the information you wanted. With the storm and all I can't stay here much longer either. Once the storm passes over, I'll be back. I'm confident I can get the information for you tomorrow."

Disappointing though the news was, Big Brah thanked Garth and hung up.

Frowning Big Brah looked at me. "Loni will have to help, let me call him," he said.

Mysterious. What did Big Brah have in mind? He called Loni. Loni answered promptly. Loni had left in a huff. He knew we had to work together. Big Brah asked him to come over. Loni was glad Big Brah had overlooked his dramatic exit. Soon Loni was back in the chair across from Big Brah's gleaming desk. Loni looking sheepish but nonetheless combative.

Big Brah said, "Another aspect of the investigation that's been bothering me is the possible connection between the theft of the hardwoods at Izor's lumber yard and his murder. I've been looking into it, I believe there's evidence hidden in the computer logs at the yard."

Loni frowned. He pulled at the ends of his dark mustache thoughtfully. "I hope the computer records will prove to you once and for all the killer is Ohia!" he said.

Big Brah said nothing.

Loni said, "After all, Ohia is Izor's son, who could've had better access to the lumber yard? But I have to thank you for digging up this new evidence for me, the chief will be pleased." He got up.

Big Brah looked up at Loni. "There is one more thing," he said.

Loni looked pleased. "Just one more thing? I'm glad we're getting to the end of this investigation."

Big Brah said, "I'm going to call Lei, Ohia and Romo Bomino, Bo Digalo, his wife and ex, Moa and Joanna, the Bipos, Antonio and Maria Gomez, Garth and Aunty Julie, invite them for a meeting at 5 o' clock here in my office. I'm going to tell them about the possibility of evidence from the computer at the lumber yard."

Loni shrugged, uneasily. "I don't know if the chief will

like everyone being told about evidence, he doesn't like to stress out the community."

Big Brah said, "I'll take the responsibility for it."

"What do you want of me?" Loni said.

"Watch the lumber yard, be there at 5 p.m. just in case one of them gets the bright idea of destroying the computer log evidence right after the meeting and heads over to the yard. Be prepared to spend the night, I'll join you after the meeting. You arrest anyone who tries to get inside!"

Loni tugged at the ends of his mustache, thinking. Then he nodded. "Your plan will work, your plans always work. I'm going to end up arresting Ohia earlier than I thought. I'll be waiting at the lumber yard," he said.

After Loni left Big Brah got busy calling everyone. I used the time to rearrange the office, so all our guests could sit comfortably. We had a dozen guests. In front of Big Brah's desk, I made three rows with four chairs in each row. The chairs filled the office all the way to the wall. Despite the stormy weather our guests started arriving early.

As they arrived, I escorted them to the main office. Most people were particular about how they seated their guests but not Big Brah. He let the guests decide. Lei arrived first with Ohia and big brother Romo.

Lei had her hair down. The black and white of the sarong-dress she wore matched the salt-and-pepper of her hair. She looked strong, prepared for anything and confident the truth would prevail. Ohia shared her attitude, but he had dressed down for the occasion in board shorts and tank top.

His wind-blown curly hair and jutting chin made him look like a rebel. Big brother Romo was impeccably dressed in shirt, trousers and wing-tips. Smart gold-rimmed glasses and elegant wristwatch with its golden band completed his classy attire. Both Lei's and big brother Romo's concern for Ohia was apparent.

They walked on either side of Ohia. They were his guardians. Lean and smooth-faced but for the goatee, Yo Bipo showed up alone. No Maile. He was aloof and cold. I greeted him at the front door.

He said, "Whatever you guys have to say, I can listen. Maile doesn't need to be involved."

I ushered Yo Bipo in. Lei was sitting in front of Big Brah, next to her Ohia then big brother Romo. Big Brah sat behind his desk and casually discussed the storm with Lei. I told him Maile wouldn't be joining us. He thanked me. He continued the storm discussion. Bipo wasn't on good terms with the Bominos.

Bipo sat in the last row as far away from them as possible. Maria Gomez walked in, holding hands with Antonio. Both of them were in casual shirts, jeans and sandals. Her long-sleeved shirt with the cuffs rolled up covered her arms and his short-sleeved shirt accentuated his muscles. They seemed intent on behaving as if everything was normal.

At the door, she said to me, "Oh, this is so exciting, what will Big Brah tell us? Antonio and I can't wait to find out."

I led them to the main office. They were supposed to be neighbors to the Bominos. But they joined Bipo at the back. *Strange.* Around five o'clock, Garth, tall and lanky, and Aunty Julie, short, brown hair in place and no makeup, the two worker bees, arrived on time one after the other.

Both of them chose to sit behind the Bomino family,

in order to show their solidarity with their employers. Digalo was the only one missing. He arrived a few minutes late but in style. Big and tall, he had a woman hanging on to each of his fleshy arms.

In the foyer, he said, "Sorry I'm late, I was working."

I recognized the plump, brown-haired woman to his right. Moa, his second wife. I greeted her warmly.

He introduced the tall, slim woman to his left. "This is Joanna, my first wife."

I greeted Joanna cordially.

Grandly Digalo said, "Moa and Joanna, they're both here to show they trust me. I'm not a killer!"

As soon as I got the trio into the office, Lei rose to hug Moa and Joanna. Not surprisingly Digalo chose the unoccupied fourth chair next to big brother Romo in the front row. I guess Digalo wanted to be as close to Lei as possible. Moa and Joanna sat in the second row, behind Digalo and big brother Romo. There was only one empty chair left at the back.

The chair meant for Maile next to Yo Bipo's. Big Brah had accepted she wouldn't be joining us. We were ready. I took my place behind the desk. The guests quietened.

Big Brah grew serious. "Mahalo for coming at short notice. I'm going to keep this brief, so you can all get back home safely before the storm hits really hard. As most of you know, Loni has set a deadline to arrest Ohia."

Ohia shrank deeper in his chair. The others didn't move.

Big Brah had their attention. He said, "The deadline expires tomorrow at ten in the morning. This is the last update before the storm and the deadline. I called you here because each of you knew Izor. I got to know him during my investigation. In his last days, Izor was working to solve the lumber yard scam, something that had troubled him ever since it first happened. When it happened again, Izor could see the similarity. I think he was very close to calling out the scammer.

"But there was something holding Izor back. I'm going to finish the work for him. The answer is hidden in the computer logs at the lumber yard. I'd have those computer logs tonight, but I ran into a snag, the storm! Garth, will you raise your hand so everyone can see you?"

Garth was lounging in his chair. He sat up and raised his hand. "Hi, I'm Garth, I'm the supervisor at the lumber yard. I operate the computer there. Big Brah is right, I'd have those computer logs tonight, but I'm on my way home due to the storm. I'll be back in the morning, once the worst of the storm has passed. Then Big Brah, you can have the proof you require to nab the real killer and prove our Ohia is innocent!"

Lei, Ohia and big brother Romo, the entire front row, except for Digalo who was sitting closest to me, gratefully turned in their seats to look back at Garth and acknowledge Garth's words and effort.

Big Brah nodded, approvingly. "When I took on this case, I'd promised you, Lei, I'd take care of the Bomino family honor, I intend to keep my promise. I believe Ohia is innocent. I also believe whoever did the scam also killed Izor."

I surveyed each of their faces. No one flinched. *Well, then. Who would show up at the lumber yard tonight?*

Chapter 20: Windshield Waterfall

Silently our guests left. I escorted them out. The meeting over, Big Brah went away to pack food for our night watch at the lumber yard. I tidied up the main office and returned the chairs to their usual places. Someone else arrived outside.

The sound of the truck was familiar. The old, blue truck. It was Kali. Grinning joyfully, I flung the front door open. Kali stood there, bubbly and lithe, her long, black hair wet. She gazed at me with those big, brown eyes of hers, a fond expression on her beautiful face. She looked happy.

Affectionately she hugged me. "Umi! Where is he? Oh, I've missed the two of you!" she said.

I closed the door behind her. "You're in time for the grand finale, we nab the killer tonight at the lumber yard."

Kali grinned, pleased. "See, I'm always on time!" she said.

I said, "You're a goddess, you probably knew about the grand finale. And your kahuna knows you'll be here, he's waiting for you in the kitchen."

Kali bounced past me toward the kitchen. "Umi, you say the sweetest things!" she said.

It was good to have her back. I followed her. Poli`ahu and Wiliwili bounded down the stairs, meowing. In the kitchen, under the bright lights, Big Brah stood leaning against the counter with a knowing grin. He saw Kali and held his arms out for her. She ran into his arms and lovingly nuzzled his broad chest.

He held her close. "Good to have you back where I can see you," he said, softly.

"Thank you for waiting, Koa." She gazed up at him.

He looked into her eyes. "For eternity and beyond, that's what I signed up for," he said.

Heartwarming. I was thirsty after the big meeting. Casually I walked to the kitchen refrigerator to get myself a drink. "Ahem, won't you guys kiss already?" I said.

They kissed. But they kept looking at each other dreamily.

"We have important work to do, people!" I said.

"Yes, work!" they chorused, snapping back to reality.

Wiliwili and Poli`ahu meowed louder. I shook my head at them. "They've been missing you," I said.

Kali knelt down, picked the cats up one by one and hugged them fondly. "I missed both of you too," she said.

She got back on her feet. Both Big Brah and I looked quizzically at her. She recognized our expressions.

She said, "I know, I know I can explain what happened this time. I opened a few nasty emails from the loveless family on the mainland, they were expecting a gift in exchange for the belated wedding invitation. It made me furious and I was on the verge of getting into the 'why me' mode around the time you left the lilikoi ice cream."

Big Brah and I exchanged knowing looks.

"So it was the lilikoi ice cream that did it?" I said.

Kali smiled. "Lilikoi ice cream with all that sweet, sweet aloha, always works. Made me realize, ever since I came to the island, I've never been alone, I've always had ohana. I've had Aunty, I have all of you, I have everything.

I am the luckiest person on the island, and…I adore you."

Purring enthusiastically, Poli`ahu and Wiliwili agreed. If Big Brah and I were cats, we would have purred too. For a magical out of the body moment, I looked at Big Brah and Kali. Perfect together with Poli`ahu and Wiliwili happy at their feet, and there I was, all giddy. *Ohana, for sure.*

The moment passed. I said, "I'm going to get ponchos, flashlights. Big Brah's packing us food, coffee, then we go to the lumber yard!"

Kali and Big Brah were both still dreamy, as we drove to the lumber yard in the big, black truck. Wide awake and alert for any trouble, I enjoyed the cozy luxury of the backseat. The wind gusted and the truck trembled.

The wind gusted harder, threatening to blow away the truck and us along with it. I was glad our truck was big and sturdy. The rain intensified. It came down in buckets. The windshield wipers wiped water away crazily, providing much needed glimpses of the road ahead. Inside the cab, the atmosphere was one of high romance.

Big Brah and Kali had the vibes of a loving couple reunited after suffering years of separation. It had been only days. They just loved to be together. By the time we neared the driveway to the lumber yard's metal gate, it was dark.

The lights on the sentinel-like concrete gate posts and the light illuminating the "Global Quality Lumber" signboard did little to dispel the darkness. Loni was nowhere in sight. Surprise. The truck's headlights revealed only the rain, the empty road, tall grass and wild bushes, but not Loni or his unmarked, green sedan. Big Brah decided to circle the place, as we had done the first time we had come here.

In the wash of the headlights, the four-foot wall and barbed wire fence looked secure. We were close to the driveway again. We crossed a convenient break in the tall grass and wild bushes to our right. Swiftly Big Brah stopped and backed the truck expertly into the gap.

Once we were invisible to anyone looking our way from the road, he stopped the truck. "This'll work for us nicely," he said.

Big Brah's phone jingled. He answered.

Loni's triumphant voice came over the phone's speaker. "I can see you, you can't see me!" he said.

Big Brah chuckled. "Loni! Brah! Where are you?" he said.

Importantly Loni said, "You can't see us, we're on official business and undercover, we have the place surrounded."

"We?"

"Yeah, I had the chief assign me ten of our best for the job."

Ten of our best? That was what like half the PD! I remembered Big Brah saying how Loni's stubbornness could be a strength at his job. So true. Also, the biggest storm of the season and our law enforcers without a thought for their own comfort were out on a stakeout to apprehend a criminal. The island police. Big on duty. It filled my heart with pride.

Big Brah said, "I'm impressed, mahalo!"

Loni said, "If he's foolhardy enough to try and get inside the lumber yard on a night like this, if he so much as dares to show up, I'm going to arrest Ohia!" He ended the call.

Big Brah sighed. "Loni can be so stubborn," he said.

It took a while to get used to the darkness. The wind whistled through the trees, shrubs and grass. No creature stirred outside. The feral pigs, cats and chicken had all found their safe spots to weather the storm.

The rain splashed down in a torrent from the skies and drummed the cab's roof wildly. The dim light on the signboard and gate posts were a blur. Of Loni and his team there was still no sign. In the event we had to get out of the truck in a hurry, I had a poncho and a flashlight ready by my side. I gave Big Brah and Kali theirs. Somehow, I knew we had a long wait ahead of us. This was where the goodies Big Brah had packed came in handy.

The cheese, mushroom and fresh basil topped pizza and the sweet coconut-y haupia pies he had made earlier. The cooler was loaded with delicious lilikoi icecream and our travel mugs filled with aromatic island coffee. I settled back for a feast. Kali didn't eat much when she was away from Big Brah.

Kali ate hungrily. Big Brah stared out the windshield waterfall, unwavering. He listened for the sound of any approaching vehicle deep into the night. It was only an hour to dawn, the night still totally dark. The storm raged. Lightning split the eastern sky.

Thunder clapped in the distance. At first the rumble of thunder was far away. It got closer and closer. Lightning flashed dangerously close. Earsplitting thunder. The truck shook.

Big Brah stirred in the driver's seat. In the darkness, he used his phone. "Loni, the vehicle is here," he whispered.

Loni sounded sleepy. "I don't see anything," he said.

"You'll hear the vehicle first," Big Brah said.

I heard it then. The faint growl of a car

engine. Approaching. The driver had chosen the most frightening part of the storm to venture out. Everyone was huddled inside. The chances of being seen were negligible. Cunning. Lightning lit up the world outside, the thunder almost over our heads.

The truck shook again as the world reverted to darkness. The car got closer. In a few seconds, the car would pass in front of us. *Goddess, please.* I prayed for lightning to flash again so we could see the driver. The feeble glow of the approaching car's headlights appeared. The feeble glow grew stronger. The black form of a car drove by. But, no lightning.

Big Brah grabbed a flashlight. "Don't turn yours on until I say so," he cautioned.

Big Brah scrambled out of the truck. Kali and I followed him. Our ponchos forgotten we clutched our flashlights. The car turned onto the driveway. Red brake lights glowed. The car skidded to a halt in front of the metal gate. The growl of the car engine died out. The glow of the headlights and brake lights disappeared. Big Brah rushed forward, Kali and I close behind.

At the edge of the asphalt road, Big Brah paused and raised a hand wordlessly. We waited. The rain soaked us. It was raining so hard I couldn't tell what kind of car it was. A car door slammed. Someone had gotten out.

I strained to identify the driver. Nothing. The driver was a blur. The sound of metal hitting asphalt. The driver took out a metal ladder. About a minute passed. Clang of metal on metal. The driver had set up the ladder to climb the gate. Then the lightning I had prayed for finally split the sky.

A series of lightning bolts stabbed the sky, revealing the driveway and the metal gate. My eyes glazed over the parked sports car and focused on the movement at the metal gate. An extended telescopic ladder was propped up against the gate.

A man was halfway up the ladder. The lightning started to subside. In moments, the light show was going to end. We would plunge back into darkness. The man would get away.

Just then the sonic boom of the thunder started. The ground shook. Total darkness. Another flash of lightning. Just enough to see. The ladder tilted, the man on it swayed. Man and ladder crashed down to the ground. I stared in awe. *The goddess always delivers, on time.*

Big Brah turned on his flashlight and bounded forward. "Let's get him," he yelled out.

Kali and I raced after Big Brah. A police siren wailed, then another. We sprinted across the road. Police cruisers, their headlights blazing, chased after us. Big Brah was the first to reach the intruder.

Big Brah stood with his head bowed, glaring down at the fallen man. Kali joined Big Brah and took his hand. I stood by them, the rain, the thunder, the lightning forgotten. The intruder struggled to stand up on the wet asphalt, slipped and fell again. Still defiant, he cursed loudly. Rainboots squelched to a stop next to us.

It was Loni. In the light of our flashlights and the headlights of the police cruisers behind us, Loni stared down at the defiant man. An elegant wristwatch with a gold band peeked from under the sleeve of the man's rain jacket. The hood had slipped off revealing hair plastered on his scalp. Rain lashed his smart gold-rimmed glasses and blinded him.

Astonished, I had no problems recognizing the murderer.

Chapter 21: Time to Talk Story

Bewildered Loni grunted. "But it's Romo Bomino, Ohia's uncle! Is he here to save his nephew?" he said.

Gravely Big Brah shook his head. "Officer Loni, arrest the man who murdered Izor Bomino!" he said.

Romo Bomino groaned. "Yes, yes, I stabbed Izor, I killed the little brat! Dammit! Damn this storm. It won't let me...." Defeated he collapsed in a crumpled heap.

Loni arrested Romo Bomino. The rain, the thunder and the lightning gradually died down. Dawn broke over the eastern horizon. Loni was silent and serious. Competently he wrapped up the investigation. The events of the night would give him fodder to brood for months. The chief was informed.

The chief quickly scheduled a public announcement later in the day. He got busy calming his beloved island community and Loni. Back in the big truck, Big Brah, Kali and I left the lumber yard, our job done. Roosters crowed and songbirds sang in the light of a new day.

We drove surrounded by the wet, lush wilderness. In the distance the ocean rested calm now after thrashing throughout the storm. Kali hugged Big Brah's arm and snuggled. Dreamily she rested her head on his sinewy arm. He was her hero. I lay back in the backseat. *Time to talk story.*

My favorite thing to do in the world. "How did you do it, Big Brah?" I said.

Big Brah drove on in silence, gathering his thoughts. Then he said, "The first time we met Ohia at Lei's, Ohia told us he'd been fighting with Izor over inheritance. There was a conflict over family money."

Big Brah had gone into a trance the first time we saw Ohia in Lei's living room. I remembered.

Big Brah said, "It pointed to a murderer who valued money over human life. A person who was desperate enough to kill for money."

At the end of the trance, Big Brah had shivered. He had seen a bad vision. I said nothing. I was totally into his story.

Big Brah said, "Of course the conflict over family money pointed a finger at Ohia. But Ohia's not a killer. Then it had to be another family member.

"I'd promised Lei I'd take care of the Bomino family honor. It wasn't easy keeping the promise, I had to walk a tightrope, and at some point, I had a decision to make. Then we met Romo Bomino, we were at Lei's again."

"But everyone agreed Romo Bomino was a successful man," I said.

Big Brah said, "Loni will check Romo's finances, it'll show Romo's been living in debt way beyond his means. He was no successful businessman, he was a cheat and a fake."

I said, "Wow! So he killed his little brother just for money?"

"Uh-huh. When Izor first started out, he supplied the lumber to the Bomino furniture business. Romo stole from Izor regularly, making it difficult for Izor to turn a profit. Izor got to know of the scam.

"Bipo got blamed for it. Recently, Romo needed money desperately, so he stole again, this time there was no Bipo to blame. Not just that....

"Romo worked to make Izor's marriage unsuccessful. He separated the couple, Izor moved back to Bomino Court. There, Antonio and Maria Gomez thought the world of Romo, they disliked innocent Izor. Romo must have poisoned the neighbors against his little brother. Then again, Ohia's young and impressionable, easy prey for Romo.

"Romo convinced young Ohia, he, Romo was the cool businessman who knew to get ahead, live in style, and so to be taken as a role model, while his dad was a loser who couldn't get anything right. Romo was giving Ohia bad business advice!"

The big truck slowed, turned and then sped forward on the coastal highway. Big Brah said, "It was Romo's idea Ohia ask for his inheritance, but Izor maturely didn't fall for it, suggesting a business loan instead. And Izor was growing suspicious of Romo.

"Sister Agatha and Brother Rex were both sure Izor was seeing things differently. Moreover, Izor had contacted Bipo and started making amends, so Izor was pretty close to confronting his big brother about the scam.

"I believe he did confront Romo, so Romo killed him. Izor was still trying to work things out, keep things within the ohana. He had love for his big brother, he never thought Romo would kill him.

"Izor was a loving man, he loved his wife, his son, they love him fiercely despite Romo's constant interference. At work, Izor had helped Garth carve out a life for himself, he mentored Keanu to do just so. Aunty Julie who's worked with him for years had only good things to say about him.

"Here was a man who had aloha for his home and work ohana, and his life was snuffed out. He was a victim of his own kindness, taken advantage of by someone he considered close, someone he loved...."

How awful, I thought. To be a victim of your own kindness. To have your wife, son and neighbors alienated from you. To be stolen from. And to be murdered. By someone you loved, someone you naturally trusted, like a big brother. Romo gave all big brothers a bad name. He was no big brother at all.

Big Brah said, "It was time to look for hard evidence, I still had nothing of any substance. I decided to keep up the illusion we were chasing after other suspects. It's a small island, I knew Romo would hear of my actions. Romo got nervous, he stole the files from the office, he knew Izor kept copious notes of everything.

"Romo was afraid the scam would link him to the murder. He wanted to point suspicion away from himself...to Ohia, Bipo, Digalo, Keanu, Gomez, anyone but Romo. Romo had planned the murder shrewdly. First, he stole Antonio's stone dagger.

"So the theft wouldn't be discovered right away, Romo planted the replacement dagger. Then he used Antonio's stone dagger to kill Izor. Next, he stole Ohia's baseball cap and planted it at the crime scene. Loni bought it. I can't blame Loni, we had a cunning opponent."

Cunning, for sure. I said, "But Maria Gomez told us no one left Bomino Court that morning, only Izor did. So how did Romo get to Waikahe Beach, kill Izor and return home without being seen or heard?"

Big Brah said, "Romo was counting on Maria Gomez not hearing him leave or return to the court. She was his first alibi."

"How?" Kali and I chorused.

Big Brah said, "It was simple really, Izor himself drove his killer to the beach."

"What?" we chorused again.

Big Brah nodded. "Romo hitched a ride with Izor to the beach that morning. He must have convinced Izor to leave him out of the conversation with Ohia. While Izor met with Ohia, Romo kept out of sight. Soon as Ohia left to drive to Bomino Court, Romo stabbed Izor."

"But Ohia found Romo home. How did that happen?" Kali asked.

I said, "Yes, Ohia told us he drove from the beach to Bomino Court, took him 15 minutes. Romo was home, Ohia met Romo, how?"

Big Brah chuckled. "Umi, we found sand on the cargo bed of Izor's white truck, remember?"

I remembered. I also remembered Loni's reaction to the find. I mimicked Loni. "Look around you, Big Brah, it's a beach, there's sand everywhere!" I tugged at the ends of an imaginary thick mustache.

Both Big Brah and Kali laughed.

Big Brah said, "The sand on the cargo bed of the truck was there for a reason. Romo's getaway Jet Ski. The Jet Ski had tracked the sand. After murdering Izor, Romo raced Izor's Jet Ski up the river, while Ohia drove the roundabout road there. Romo was back home in Bomino Court easily before Ohia got there. Ohia was Romo's second alibi."

Kali and I were dumbstruck. Then she said, "The deception, it's heinous."

Heinous, for sure. "How about last night, Big Brah?" I said.

Big Brah said, "Romo was close to getting away with

the murder, Loni was unlikely to help us get the court orders necessary to search any home or financial record that wasn't Ohia's! The chief's deadline made it necessary to catch Romo fast. One option was to make Romo insecure enough to do something desperate.

"While Garth was looking for the computer logs at the lumber yard, it was time to see what Romo would do. I figured he'd want to destroy the evidence, the same reason he'd stolen the files from the office. And you know the rest. It worked. We can only thank the goddess."

The big truck took the exit for our home. I said, "I remember Romo from the time we first met him at Lei's. I was impressed, I thought he was pretty cool. He was so calm, so composed."

Big Brah nodded. "That was how I was sure it was him."

I sat stunned. "Sure, how?" I said.

Big Brah had a sudden catch in his voice. "No loving big braddah can be that calm, that composed, after the demise of his...li'l brah," he said.

I felt blessed. "I'm glad you my Big Brah!" I said.

Kali turned in her seat and squeezed my hand. "Aw, Umi, you're the sweetest," she said.

"I feel lucky," I said.

"Then it's time to make a wish!" she said.

Contented, I gazed out at the clouds rolling away restoring the blue sky. I silently wished for Big Brah and Kali to get married.

I couldn't help smiling. "I wish for the biggest party, a luau for everyone."

Of course, both my wishes would come true. They always did whenever Kali told me it was time to make a wish. *There will be a grand luau, and one day, Big Brah and*

Kali will get married. When we got home that morning, Big Brah and Kali were inseparable catching up. While they conjured up a grand breakfast, I sat at the round table.

Sighing blissfully, I used my phone to check island news. The Island Times page was full of news about the investigation. A breaking news story about the arrest was out. Loni was quoted several times and his courage and sacrifice applauded.

Our respected mayor and the chief had promptly made glowing statements praising Big Brah, Loni and their teams. We all knew Big Brah hid from the news like the island crab hid from us.

The editor of the Island Times was Big Brah's friend. Knowing how Big Brah hid from the news, the editor already maintained a collection of Big Brah's pictures for such occasions. If you looked closely, Big Brah was there in every picture but in the background. In line with the editor's island humor, Big Brah and I were seen eating or drinking. I laughed out loud.

Everyone loved my Big Brah. In the weeks that followed, Garth unearthed a heap of evidence from the lumber yard computer. After-hours transactions showed the bin number swaps between Digalo's and Romo's orders. Things settled down to the daily aloha on our small island. Having provided the salve, Big Brah waited for the wounds to heal. Three months passed.

In the three months, I got time to think, and a question grew in my mind. Big Brah had promised to protect the Bomino family honor. He saved Ohia Bomino, but he identified Romo, another Bomino, as the murderer. How had he fulfilled his promise to protect the Bomino family honor?

It was summer. It was time to blow away the remnants of any ill will, anything that took away from our shared aloha. Big Brah invited everyone touched by the investigation. A grand luau, our place. *He's generous, my Big Brah.* On the day of the luau, the sun was out, the sky blue.

The ocean sparkled silver. The entire day Big Brah, Kali and I cooked and made preparations. We had lots of help: Manny, Mohua from the Tavern and our sizable contingent of cousins. Evening arrived.

A pleasant ocean breeze caressed the island. The luau was at the beach by our much-loved heiau. The goddess watched over us. The sun was setting on the other side of the island. Guest parking was in the front of the house. Signs directed guests down the gently-sloping path to the beach. At the end of the path, to welcome our guests as they arrived, Big Brah, Kali and I waited. Big Brah's Waialeale pride was on display.

He was dressed in traditional helmet, cape and kapa malo. Kali had on a red sarong-dress. The color of her dress matched the color of the feathers on his helmet. Red was the color of the moment. The sky was also many shades of red. Celestial together, Big Brah and Kali looked strong and powerful. I had dressed for the occasion in my black party shirt and jeans.

A band of happy musicians, all cousins, played on the beach. Big Brah was going to perform once it was fully dark. Around the band playing party music, there were tables with chairs to seat everyone. Ready to serve our guests, Manny, Mohua and a few more of our cousins were standing by with bright, welcoming smiles. There was a big, white tent for food and drinks.

The aroma of food was everywhere. Yummy fried

chicken, fried rice, pork laulau, steamed rice, spicy ahi poke, adobo, barbecued beef and stir-fried fresh-from-the-garden vegetables. Salad with lettuce, baby spinach, cucumbers, mushrooms and sweet onions. A dressing for the salad with olive oil, vinegar, basil and cilantro. Very refreshing.

Lots of homemade pizza pockets for the kids. For dessert, malasadas, mochi, lilikoi icecream and rice pudding. All mouthwatering! Soon the flickering flames of tiki torches lit up the beach and cast a magical glow around us. First to arrive was Tutu Pika.

Chapter 22: Luau, Karaoke and Fire Dance

Tutu Pika had his children, grandchildren, Akamai and the rest of his huge ohana with him. Tutu Pika had brushed his few remaining gray hairs neatly for the occasion. He looked surprisingly strong and walked straighter than I'd seen him do in a long time.

He was proud of Big Brah. "Koa, I've started a new sculpture symbolizing peace on the island to celebrate your accomplishment in finding the killer," he said.

Such an honor. Big Brah melted with pleasure like lilikoi icecream outside the cooler. "Mahalo for all your expert help, Tutu Pika, couldn't have done it without you!"

Tanned and fierce, young Akamai stood next to Tutu Pika. He was focused on Big Brah.

Tutu Pika placed a hand on Akamai's shoulder. "My new sculpture is coming along very well. I have an able apprentice now."

Akamai straightened and puffed out his chest importantly.

Tutu Pika grinned. "I feel I'm seventy again!"

Akamai also grinned and hugged us all. Very mature. Next to arrive were Yo and Maile Bipo. They held hands. Yo had his goatee specially braided. Most likely Maile had helped. His shaven head gleamed. Maile wore a body-hugging sarong-dress happily showing her baby bump. Both looked radiant. They hugged us warmly.

Yo said, "Mahalo, Big Brah, for making my life better than ever. I harbored no ill feeling, but the Bomino family has been very generous. Izor had already paid me. Over and beyond, Papa Bomino has compensated me. I'm putting in all of the money to grow my family business."

Yo put an arm around Maile and drew her close. He looked far away and had an emotional moment. "My family's growing, we're going to be parents. This was the only thing holding us back, now my baby can have a father. A father who isn't labeled a cheater!"

Maile smiled shyly and self-consciously brushed her bangs. "I'm sorry, I tried to steal the file," she said.

Yo said, "Why did you do it, Maile?"

"I didn't want you to suffer again," she said.

"With you beside me, baby, I can take on anything," he said.

I grinned. Big Brah chuckled.

Kali clapped. "It was a valiant effort for the cause of love, so all's forgiven. Congratulations, the two of you'll make great parents!" she said.

Yo's smooth face creased into lines I hadn't seen before. Yes, the man could grin. Maile also grinned, her nose crinkling sweetly. Aunty Lena, Aunty Julie, Keanu and Garth arrived together. Aunty Lena had gladly taken Keanu back, as Big Brah had predicted. We hugged.

Happily, Aunty Lena looked up at Big Brah through her thick, round glasses. "You've made us all proud, Koa! Mahalo for getting Keanu back safely, he's a good boy."

I almost hadn't recognized Aunty Julie. She had blue highlights in her short hair and even some makeup. No formal office attire. She wore a frilly party dress.

Smiling, she patted Keanu on the back. "Lei and I've decided to call his absence a bereavement leave, he's already back at work with more responsibilities."

"Work is good," Big Brah said.

Kali, Aunty Lena and Aunty Julie got into a lively chat. Keanu had combed his short hair to make it look neat, ironed his clothes and polished his shoes.

He shook hands with Big Brah and me, teary-eyed. "Mahalo for giving me and my car a second chance," he said.

Both Big Brah and I hugged him fondly.

Remorsefully, Keanu said, "I've grown up, I learned my lesson. Next time, I won't quit!"

Big Brah nodded approvingly. Instinctively all three of us turned to look at Garth. Slim and tall, the bearded Garth gazed down at us, awe written all over his face. He wore his usual jeans, shirt and sneakers. Specially for the occasion, all three items had come out fresh from a washing machine.

Eagerly, Garth said, "The old computer has been replaced. Ms. Bomino wanted the upgrade. Julie and I have been attending computer classes together. We've already secured the new computer with a password, the camera at the gate is always on. No one's going to hack into the computer again."

"Good," Big Brah murmured.

Garth's bird-like face broke into a happy grin. "Next, Julie and I, we're in the process of digitizing all the customer and employee records. Izor was always on the right path, he'd created good practices. Julie and I didn't change anything, and business has taken off," he said.

"Good, good," Big Brah said.

At Garth's mention of her name, Aunty Julie broke

away from Kali and Aunty Lena. She gripped Garth's slim arm fondly. She smiled up at him and then at us. "You know what else has taken off? Love."

Love. I knew it. Aunty Julie's new blue hair, new makeup and new frilly party dress. Garth and Aunty Julie attending computer classes together. All explained. Aunty Lena and Kali joined us. They must have heard the word love. They were interested. We waited for the announcement. Aunty Julie was in love with Garth.

But Aunty Julie, no-nonsense as she was otherwise, proved shy about matters of the heart. "My dog Ami, she's in love with Garth."

Garth blushed. "I love Ami," he said.

"Garth now visits Ami all the time, we go for walks together," Aunty Julie said.

Garth blushed deeper. "We're f-Ami-ly, right Julie?" he said.

All of us smiled at Garth's wordplay. No doubt Garth was also in love with Aunty Julie.

Aunty Julie laughed. "Right, Garth-y," she said.

Big Brah chuckled, pleased. He saw a new ohana forming. "Good, good, good," he said.

Antonio and Maria Gomez arrived next. Maria had her long hair down and she had dressed prettily. His crew cut hair made brawny Antonio look young.

Maria held Antonio's arm and leaned against him affectionately. "We both feel so badly about misjudging Izor. We've been praying, God forgive us! You know, to make amends. For these things, they live on long after you're gone. Antonio now takes care of the ohia trees on both sides of the fence. He doesn't trim the trees anymore, he makes sure they grow wild, as they would in nature."

Antonio looked sincere. He nodded. "I'm learning a lot more about the trees."

"Izor had a fascination for trees both at work and home. He'd have liked you learning more about the trees," Big Brah said.

Maria said, "We also finished the first beach cleanup of the summer, we dedicated it to the memory of Izor Bomino. We're going to rename our charity in his name, we hope Izor will forgive us for our mistake, may he rest in peace!"

"Wonderful. Amends can right many wrongs," Big Brah said.

Maria and Antonio Gomez made their way past us to the beach. Up near the top of the garden path, a small, white bus pulled up. The bus had "Pono Church" painted in black on its side. The door opened.

Sister Agatha hopped out, smiling and waving. "I've got Brother Rex," she shouted.

Big Brah, Kali and I ran to help. Soon we had Brother Rex out of the bus.

Sister Agatha said, "Brother Rex never leaves the church, but he wouldn't hear of missing the luau."

Brother Rex radiated joy. He gripped the armrests of his powered wheelchair spiritedly. "Justice brings us all together. I'm sure glad to be here!" he said.

Big Brah smiled. "Mahalo for all your help, Brother Rex," he said.

As we took Brother Rex and Sister Agatha down the path to the beach, Sister Agatha smiled beatifically. "I'm not giving up on Romo, I visit him every week. Papa Bomino has settled Romo's sizable debt."

Big Brah grew solemn. "The pain Romo inflicted is deep."

Sister Agatha said, "Romo is remorseful, he realizes he cheated Ohia of a father. This wrong can never be undone. But Romo is taking steps, he has relinquished his house and his share of the family business to Ohia," she said.

"That's a start," Big Brah said.

At the beach, Brother Rex was delighted to see Tutu Pika. He wheeled forward energetically to join Tutu Pika. Sister Agatha smiled fondly as she watched him go. She left us to mingle, starting with "the adorable couple over there," meaning the Bipos! We returned to our guest watch.

Smiling and laughing, engrossed in conversation, Moa and Joanna strolled down the garden path. Moa had her brown hair done in curls for the occasion. Joanna looked sleek in a colorful summer dress.

They stopped by to thank us for restoring aloha to the island. Big Brah thanked them for joining the luau. Ohia and his girlfriend Kela arrived next. With his curly hair tamed into a ponytail, Ohia looked good and relaxed. Kela turned out to be quiet and gentle. They looked lovely together.

After we all hugged, Ohia said, "Mahalo nui loa, Big Brah, many thanks for saving me. Kela and I are getting married next summer, I'm learning to run the family furniture business, I'm working hard to make Dad proud!"

"You make us all proud!" Big Brah said.

Behind Ohia and Kela, Loni arrived with his sweet wife and cute daughters. Loni must have heard Ohia's last words, but at first, he didn't say anything. Instead, he tugged at the ends of his thick mustache thoughtfully. Loni's wife and daughters also knew Kali very well. The four of them struck up an animated conversation. Kela joined them.

Loni approached Ohia remorsefully. "I'm sorry I suspected you," he said.

Ohia said, "No worries, all's forgiven!"

Awkwardly, they shook hands, hugged and did a shaka over their hearts, in the way islanders did to share aloha. Big Brah nodded, approvingly. I was happy to see Lei and Papa Bomino next.

Lei assisted Papa Bomino slowly down the garden path. It had been really rough for them. They had suffered through the anguish of losing Izor, then Romo, Papa Bomino's ill health and having Ohia under suspicion. We hugged warmly. In the surreal glow of the tiki torches, Papa Bomino looked rejuvenated.

The scraggly beard was gone and he had combed the thin, wispy hair on his bald head neatly himself! He held a white envelope. Lei had on a simple summer dress. Her silver and black hair was done in her trademark top knot.

A new tattoo adorned her left forearm. A stylized lehua flower. A beautiful pua lehua. For her Izor.

Tearfully Lei said, "I'm moving back to Bomino Court, so I can be nearer Papa Bomino, mahalo for everything!"

Papa Bomino said, "Lei's been a rock for the family. She has kept us together through these dark times. Most of all she had the good sense to get the Waialeale detectives in our hour of need."

Papa Bomino handed the white envelope to Big Brah. "Mahalo for keeping your promise to both Lei and me, you protected our family honor!" he said.

Of course, I also believed Big Brah had protected the Bomino family honor. I just had to figure out how.

On the beach, Tutu Pika and Brother Rex had taken up a table together. Papa Bomino wanted to join them. Big Brah helped Lei by taking Papa Bomino over to his friends. Moa and Joanna vigorously waved, summoning Lei to their table. Lei joined her best friends. Coincidentally, Bo Digalo and Iggy arrived next.

Big and tall, Digalo came in a black suit ready to impress. "Now that I know the real reason behind the bad lumber Global Quality Lumber supplied me, I'm not going to pull my business from them. I always liked Izor. Now, I'm working with Lei. We're doing business, by the way," his gaze wandered away from us, "that's her, over there, look!" he said.

I looked. Lei, Moa and Joanna sat at a table, engrossed in conversation.

Digalo started toward the women's table. "I'll go say hi to them, I know them from high school," he said.

Some high school friendships last forever. Both Big Brah and Kali smiled and nodded. Iggy was relaxed as usual in his favorite yellow-and-black checkered pattern shirt.

Iggy grinned. "Me driver also this evening!" he said.

Iggy headed toward the happy musicians on the beach. I gazed after him in wonder. I wouldn't be surprised if Iggy came out as a musician too! He was awesome. I turned back toward the garden path. Small and dapper, the chief walked briskly toward us, his abundant silver hair crimped into five precise waves.

The chief was dressed in his usual blue shirt with a flower print, black trousers and oxfords. Dramatically he stopped near us and smiled winningly. Leaning back a little he flung open his arms albatross wide. He wished to hug us all at once. Then he ran forward. He couldn't wait any longer. He hugged us one by one anyways.

The chief started a profuse mahalo. Big Brah glanced

at me meaningfully. Had I arranged for the karaoke? With a micro nod, I assured him. The chief finished his profuse mahalo. He cared deeply for the community.

In anticipation of meeting and entertaining the community at the luau, the chief smiled and rubbed his hands happily. "Will there be a karaoke jam tonight?" he said.

Big Brah threw me a grateful smile. "Of course," he said.

All our guests were here. It was time for Big Brah, Kali and me to join the luau. Behind us the karaoke started. The chief dedicated the evening to the Waialeale Detective Agency. Loud cheers followed. We were about to turn away, when I thought I saw a movement behind a nearby bush. I looked again. The bush wasn't big enough to hide the giant shadow lurking behind it.

I stepped forward to greet the giant hiding behind the bush. "Come on out, Poha," I said.

The shadow straightened. Poha emerged. He looked about the same. Shaggy eyebrows, flat nose. He had a sheepish grin on his innocent-looking face. He held a stack of books under each arm. Delighted I sprang forward.

He saw me. He knew what I was going to do. "No, Umi!" he cried, warning.

I didn't listen to him. I punched him as hard as I could right in the center of his belly. He dropped the books. The tomes cascaded to the ground. They were all mystery novels, his collection. A gift for me. Too late. The books were on the ground.

Poha heaved me into the air. He giggled. "Fly, fly," he said.

Trying to sound as dignified as I could while I flew, I

said, "Welcome to the luau, Poha."

After Poha joined the others, Big Brah, Kali and I stood together a bit longer. Big Brah looked intense, as he did before a performance.

With a flourish, Big Brah handed me the white envelope he'd received from Papa Bomino. "Assistant, take care of this," he said.

I looked inside. The envelope had a generous check made out to the Waialeale Detective Agency. Papa Bomino had thanked Big Brah for protecting the Bomino family honor. I was ready to ask my question.

In preparation for his performance, Big Brah handed me his cape and helmet. "Any last questions, Umi?" he said.

He got me. It had to be his sixth sense. "I've had this question for a while now," I said.

Big Brah and Kali held hands. "Ask away," he said.

I said, "You had a dilemma, you had to protect the Bomino family honor. Sure, you saved Ohia, but you caught Romo, another Bomino. How was that protecting the family honor?"

Big Brah smiled, satisfied. "I knew you'd get to it, Umi, it's a good question, and it deserves an answer," he said.

My chest swelled with pride. Kali gazed at Big Brah, admiringly. These were the moments she loved him the most.

Big Brah's good-looking face turned solemn. "On the island, we value aloha for a very good reason. It's the only way to secure the future. Look at us, you, me and Kali, we're an ohana. We live with aloha.

"We know aloha works. Waialeales have lived with aloha for generations. When Lei first showed up, I could see she loved her husband and her son. I had to accept the case."

I said, "The Bomino family honor was in danger. Izor was accused of the lumber yard scam. A thief. Ohia was accused of murdering his father. A murderer. If the accusations were true, the family honor was ruined forever."

Big Brah said, "By exposing the scam, we restored Izor's reputation permanently. By identifying the murderer, we saved Ohia. But the culprit was another Bomino. I was still thinking about it, when we visited the heiau a second time.

"At the heiau it struck me, protecting the family honor meant restoring the aloha in the ohana. There's no honor in harboring a criminal. An ohana sheltering a thief and a murderer will have no aloha. There was only one way to restore the aloha in the Bomino ohana. Catch Romo Bomino!"

Kali nodded. "A family must have love, or it's not a family at all."

Wise, beyond wise. The stars shimmered. The tiki torches cast an enchanting glow. Big Brah performed the dance of our ancestors. The Fire Dance. Everyone sat around eating, drinking and watching cheerfully. I sat at a table with Poli`ahu and Wiliwili. The cats basked in chairs on either side of me. The powerful beat of the drums resonated in the air.

Big Brah picked up the fire batons. The drumbeat intensified. Big Brah juggled the fire batons nimbly. The flames at the ends of the fire batons danced in the air. The drums took on an exuberant beat. Big Brah twirled and spun the fire batons to the throb of the drums. The perpetual motion of the leaping and whirling flames created a fiery painting against the dark backdrop of the night. Mesmerizing.

Watching Big Brah, Kali stood in the front enthralled. The golden light of the moving flames flickered on her skin. He danced for her, and she had eyes only for him. Every soul present watched his spectacular performance, hypnotized. Big Brah had helped everyone.

Under Big Brah's spell, the trauma of the murder melted away. In time, the wounds would heal. Our collective inner strength had helped us overcome the tragedy. I looked up at the stars.

The stars shone like jewels in the sky, our ancestors, our kupuna smiling down on us. Izor would be up there, finding his place. Proudly, I looked around at all the happy faces. *My paradise of aloha. My island ohana.*

Umi's island speak

Adobo: Fish or meat dish cooked with vinegar and garlic
Ahi: Tuna
Ahuula: Cape made of feathers
Akamai: Intelligent, supersmart
Aloalo: Hibiscus
Aloha: Love
Anole: Garden lizard
Arare: Crispy rice cracker
Aunty: Address to show love and respect

Big Brah: Big brother
Braddah: Brother
Brah: Brother
Buggah: Bugger, person

Chicken skin: Goose bumps

Fire Dance: A performer dances with fire batons
Fly, fly: A game played with whomever you can lift up, swing around and make "fly, fly!"

Goddess: Island Goddess, Goddess Pele
Grinds: Food

Hale: Home

Haupia pie: Sweet coconut-y pie
Heiau: Temple
Honu: Sea turtle

Kahuna: Traditional spiritual leader
Kakau: Traditional method of tattoos inked by hand-tapping
Kapa malo: Traditional garment
Karaoke: Karaoke
Keiki: Child(ren)
Kupuna: Ancestors

Lanai: Porch
Laulau: Meat, salted fish and taro leaves cooked in a ti-leaf wrapper
Lei: Garland
Lilikoi: Passion fruit
Li'l brah: younger brother
Luau: Party

Mahalo: Thank you
Mahalo nui loa: Thank you very much
Mahiole: Traditional helmet
Mainland: Continent
Malasada: Sweet, fried dough treat
Mana: Life energy
Mochi: Sweet rice flour treat
Musubi: Layers of meat and rice in a seaweed wrapper
Muumuu: Comfy dress
Mynahs: Beautiful brown birds

Nani: Beautiful

Ohana: Family
Ohia: First tree to appear on new land created by lava
Ono: Fish found in the waters around the island

Pau: Done
Papa: Patriarch
Pohaku: Lava rock
Poli`ahu: Goddess of snow
Pono: Righteously good
Pua lehua: Lehua flower
Pua`a: Feral pig

Sarong: Wraparound dress
Shaka: Hand gesture islanders use to show love for each other
Spicy ahi poke: Fresh tuna with mustard
Stuffs: Things

Talk story: Exchange stories
Ti: Island plant with big leaves
Ti-leaf: Leaf of the Ti plant
Tutu: Grandparent
Tutu kane: Grandfather

Uncle: Address to show love and respect

Wiliwili: Flowering island tree

Umi's island poetry

Spread aloha

Spread aloha and you will feel better.
It's easy and found everywhere.
Share aloha; double it together.

Love your surroundings and each critter.
Aloha thrives when you take time to care.
Spread aloha and you will feel better.

Honesty and truth will always matter.
Believe in character, goodness and be fair.
Share aloha; double it together.

If you are sad now or maybe later,
Count your blessings and breathe in the fresh air.
Spread aloha and you will feel better.

Make the one you love your lifelong costar.
That will make each burden easy to bear.

Share aloha; double it together.

So, make a home filled with fun and laughter.
It's the most exciting of any dare.
Spread aloha and you will feel better.
Share aloha; double it together.

***

About The Author

Ishwar Chandra Sen

Ishwar Chandra Sen is a poet, storyteller and novelist. A lifelong learner of human nature, he sees the goodness in human hearts. Ishwar and his fictional heroes are inspired by the same goodness. Ishwar lives with his family in Hawaii.

Acknowledgement

I have many people to thank and
reasons to be thankful for:

Rita and Mele, my awesome publishing team.
My island ohana, full of aloha.
My favorite fiction writers, you are a part of me.
My kind readers, this is all for you.
My dear reviewers, your encouragement is the best.
The goodness I see in human hearts keeps me grateful
and hopeful.

Mahalo.

--Ishwar

Books By This Author

Alone But Not Single

Sen Fiction Romance Short Read.
Welcome to the delightful island of natural beauty and aloha. Discover the legend of the love heiau! Be whisked away to a colorful island paradise each time you read this sweet love story.

Brahma's Dilemma

Sen Fiction Romance Short Read.
When a novelist falls in love with a musician....

Sen Fiction

Kind reader,

Sen Fiction is looking for a few, good fans. Join our reader list at https://www.senfiction.com for the latest news about the detective trio.

BIG BRAH, KALI and UMI will return.

If you enjoyed your visit to the island of natural beauty and aloha, please tell your friends and family. Add your voice to book reviews everywhere. Your comments are welcome at https://www.senfiction.com.

Spread aloha!

Sen Fiction, Hawaii is a publisher of fiction eBooks, print books and audiobooks. Contact us at:
https://www.senfiction.com/contact-us.

www.ingramcontent.com/pod-product-compliance
Lightning Source LLC
Chambersburg PA
CBHW031936240626
47153CB00015B/1979

9 781957 022017